A Maid of the Silver Sea by John Oxenham

John Oxenham was the pseudonym used by William Arthur Dunkerley for most of his fiction works including poetry. For journalism he went by the name of Julian Ross.

Dunkerley was born on November 12th 1852 in Manchester. He attended Old Trafford School and Victoria University, both in Manchester.

He married in America and lived they for a short time before returning to these shores, this time to Ealing in West London becoming both the Deacon and teacher at Ealing Congregational Church in the 1880's.

In 1913 he wrote a bestselling book of poems entitled 'Bees In Amber' followed by 'All's Well" in 1916. As a journalist he was a major contributor to Jerome K Jerome's Idler magazine.

In 1922 he moved to Worthing in Sussex and became the town's Mayor.

He died in Worthing on January 23rd, 1941.

Index of Contents

CHAPTER I

HOW TWO LAY IN A CLEFT

A girl and a boy lay in a cubby-hole in the north side of the cliff overlooking Port Gorey, and watched the goings-on down below.

The sun was tending towards Guernsey and the gulf was filled witn golden light. A small brig, unkempt and dirty, was nosing towards the rough wooden landing-stage clamped to the opposite rocks, as though doubtful of the advisability of attempting its closer acquaintance.

"Mon Gyu, Bern, how I wish they were all at the bottom of the sea!" said the girl vehemently.

"Whe—e—e—w!" whistled the boy, and then with a twinkle in his eye,—"Who's got a new parasol now?"

"Everybody!—but it's not that. It's the bustle—and the dirt—and the noise—and oh—everything! You can't remember what it was like before these wretched mines came—no dust, no noise, no bustle, no dirty men, no silly women, no nothing as it is now. Just Sark as it used to be. And now—! Mon Gyu, yes I wish the sea would break in through their nasty tunnels and wash them all away—pumps and engines and houses—everything!"

And up on the hillside at the head of the gulf the great pumping-engine clacked monotonously "Never! Never! Never!"

"You've got it bad to-day, Nan," said the boy.

"I've always got it bad. It makes me sick. It has changed everything and everybody—everybody except mother and you," she added quickly. "Get—get—get! Why we hardly used to know what money was, and now no one thinks of anything but getting all they can. It is sickening."

"S—s—s—s—t!" signalled the boy suddenly, at the sound of steps and voices on the cliff outside and close at hand.

"Tom," muttered the boy.

"And Peter Mauger," murmured the girl, and they both shrank lower into their hiding-place.

It was a tiny natural chamber in the sharp slope of the hill. Ages ago the massive granite boulders of the headland, loosened and undercut by the ceaseless assaults of wind and weather and the deadly quiet fingers of the frost, had come rolling down the slope till they settled afresh on new foundations, forming holes and crannies and little angular chambers where the splintered shoulders met. In time, the soil silted down and covered their asperities, and—like a good colonist—carrying in itself the means of increase, it presently brought forth and blossomed, and the erstwhile shattered rocks were royally robed in russet and purple, and green and gold.

Among these fantastic little chambers Nance had played as a child, and had found refuge in them from the persecutions of her big half-brother, Tom Hamon. Tom was six when she was born—fourteen accordingly when she was at the teasable age of eight, and unusually tempting as a victim by reason of her passionate resentment of his unwelcome attentions.

She hated Tom, and Tom had always resented her and her mother's intrusion into the family, and Bernel's, when he came, four years after Nance.

What his father wanted to marry again for, Tom never could make out. His lack of training and limited powers of expression did not indeed permit him any distinct reasoning on the matter, but the feeling was there—a dull resentment which found its only vent and satisfaction in stolid rudeness to his stepmother and the persecution of Nance and Bernel whenever occasion offered.

The household was not therefore on too happy a footing.

It consisted, at the time when our story opens, of—Old Mrs. Hamon—Grannie—half of whose life had been lived in the nineteenth century and half in the eighteenth. She had seen all the wild doings of the privateering and free-trading days, and recalled as a comparatively recent event the raiding of the Island by the men of Herm, though that happened forty years before.

She was for the most part a very reserved and silent old lady, but her tongue could bite like a whip when the need arose.

She occupied her own dower-rooms in the house, and rarely went outside them. All day long she sat in her great arm-chair by the window in her sitting-room, with the door wide open, so that she could see all that went on in the house and outside it; and in the sombre depths of her great black silk sun-bonnet—long since turned by age and weather to dusky green—her watchful eyes had in them something of the inscrutable and menacing.

Her wants were very few, and as her income from her one-third of the farm had far exceeded her expenses for more than twenty years, she was reputed as rich in material matters as she undoubtedly was in common-sense and worldly wisdom. Even young Tom was sulkily silent before her on the rare occasions when they came into contact.

Next in the family came the nominal head of it, "Old Tom" Hamon, to distinguish him from young Tom, his son; a rough, not ill-natured man, until the money-getting fever seized him, since which time his home-folks had found in him changes that did not make for their comfort.

The discovery of silver in Sark, the opening of the mines, and the coming of the English miners—with all the very problematical benefits of a vastly increased currency of money, and the sudden introduction of new ideas and standards of life and living into a community which had hitherto been contented with the order of things known to its forefathers—these things had told upon many, but on none more than old Tom Hamon.

Suspicious at first of the meaning and doings of these strangers, he very soon found them advantageous. He got excellent prices for his farm produce, and when his horses and carts were not otherwise engaged he could always turn them to account hauling for the mines.

As the silver-fever grew in him he became closer in his dealings both abroad and at home. With every pound he could scrimp and save he bought shares in the mines and believed in them absolutely. And he went on scrimping and saving and buying shares so as to have as large a stake in the silver future as possible.

He got no return as yet from his investment, indeed. But that would come all right in time, and the more shares he could get hold of the larger the ultimate return would be. And so he stinted himself and his family, and mortgaged his future, in hopes of wealth which he would not have known how to enjoy if he had succeeded in getting it.

So possessed was he with the desire for gain that when young Tom came home from sea he left the farming to him, and took to the mining himself, and worked harder than he had ever worked in his life before.

He was a sturdy, middle-sized man, with a grizzled bullet head and rounded beard, of a dogged and pertinacious disposition, but capable, when stirred out of his usual phlegm, of fiery outbursts which overbore all argument and opposition. His wife died when his boy Tom was three, and after two years of lonely discomfort he married Nancy Poidestre of Petit Dixcart, whose people looked upon it as something of a mésalliance that she should marry out of her own country into Little Sark.

Nancy was eminently good-looking and a notable housewife, and she went into Tom Hamon's house of La Closerie with every hope and intention of making him happy.

But, from the very first, little Tom set his face against her.

It would be hard to say why. Nancy racked her brain for reasons, and could find none, and was miserable over it.

His father thrashed him for his rudeness and insolence, which only made matters worse.

His own mother had given way to him in everything, and spoiled him completely. After her death his father out of pity for his forlorn estate, had equally given way to him, and only realised, too late, when he tried to bring him to with a round turn, how thoroughly out of hand he had got.

When little Tom found, as one consequence of the new mother's arrival, that his father thrashed instead of humouring him, he put it all down to the new-comer's account, and set himself to her discomfiture in every way his barbarous little wits could devise.

He never forgot one awful week he passed in his grandmother's care—a week that terminated in the arrival of still another new-comer, who, in course of time, developed into little Nance. It is not impossible that the remembrance of that black week tended to colour his after-treatment of his little half-sister. In spite of her winsomeness he hated her always, and did his very best to make life a burden to her.

When, on that memorable occasion, he was hastily flung by his father into his grandmother's room, as the result of some wickedness which had sorely upset his stepmother, and the door was, most unusually, closed behind him, his first natural impulse was to escape as quickly as possible.

But he became aware of something unusual and discomforting in the atmosphere, and when his grandmother said sternly, "Sit down!" and he turned on her to offer his own opinion on the matter, he found the keen dark eyes gazing out at him from under the shadowy penthouse of the great black sun-bonnet, with so intent and compelling a stare that his mouth closed without saying a word. He climbed up on to a chair and twisted his feet round the legs by way of anchorage.

Then he sat up and stared back at Grannie, and as an exhibition of nonchalance and high spirit, put out his tongue at her.

Grannie only looked at him.

And, bit by bit, the tongue withdrew, and only the gaping mouth was left, and above it a pair of frightened green eyes, transmitting to the perverse little soul within new impressions and vague terrors.

Before long his left arm went up over his face to shut out the sight of Grannie's dreadful staring eyes, and when, after a sufficient interval, he ventured a peep at her and found her eyes still fixed on him, he howled, "Take it off! Take it off!" and slipped his anchors and slid to the floor, hunching his back at this tormentor who could beat him on his own ground.

For that week he gave no trouble to any one. But after it he never went near Grannie's room, and for years he never spoke to her. When he passed her open door, or in front of her window, he hunched his shoulder protectively and averted his eyes.

Resenting control in any shape or form, Tom naturally objected to school.

His stepmother would have had him go—for his own sake as well as hers. But his father took a not unusual Sark view of the matter.

"What's the odds?" said he. "He'll have the farm. Book-learning will be no use to him," and in spite of Nancy's protests—which Tom regarded as simply the natural outcrop of her ill-will towards him—the boy grew up untaught and uncontrolled, and knowing none but the worst of all masters—himself.

On occasion, when the tale of provocation reached its limit, his father thrashed him, until there came a day when Tom upset the usual course of proceedings by snatching the stick out of his father's hands, and would have belaboured him in turn if he had not been promptly knocked down.

After that his father judged it best for all concerned that he should flight his troublesome wings outside for a while. So he sent him off in a trading-ship, in the somewhat forlorn hope that a knowledge of the world would knock some of the devil out of him—a hope which, like many another, fell short of accomplishment.

The world knocks a good deal out of a man, but it also knocks a good deal in. Tom came back from his voyaging knowing a good many things that he had not known when he started—a little English among others—and most of the others things which had been more profitably left unlearnt.

CHAPTER II

HOW NANCE CAME TO BE HERSELF

And little Nance?

The most persistent memories of Nance's childhood were her fear and hatred of Tom, and her passionate love for her mother,—and Bernel when he came.

"My own," she called these two, and regarded even her father as somewhat outside that special pale; esteemed Grannie as an Olympian, benevolently inclined, but dwelling on a remote and loftier plane; and feared and detested Tom as an open enemy.

And she had reasons.

She was a high-strung child, too strong and healthy to be actually nervous, but with every faculty always at its fullest—not only in active working order but always actively at work—an admirable subject therefore for the malevolence of an enemy whose constant proximity offered him endless opportunity.

Much of his boyish persecution never reached the ears of the higher powers. Nance very soon came to accept Tom's rough treatment as natural from a big fellow of fourteen to a small girl of eight, and she bore it stoically and hated him the harder.

Her mother taught her carefully to say her prayers, which included petitions for the welfare of Grannie and father and brother Tom, and for a time, with the perfunctoriness of childhood, which attaches more weight to the act than to the meaning of it, she allowed that to pass with a stickle and a slur. But very soon brother Tom was ruthlessly dropped out of the ritual, and neither threats nor persuasion could induce her to re-establish him.

Later on, and in private, she added to her acknowledged petitions an appendix, unmistakably brief and to the point—"And, O God, please kill brother Tom!"—and lived in hope.

She was an unusually pretty child, though her prettiness developed afterwards—as childish prettiness does not always—into something finer and more lasting.

She had, as a child, large dark blue eyes, which wore as a rule a look of watchful anxiety—put there by brother Tom. To the end of her life she carried the mark of a cut over her right eyebrow, which came within an ace of losing her the sight of that eye. It was brother Tom did that.

She had an abundance of flowing brown hair, by which Tom delighted to lift her clear off the ground, under threat of additional boxed ears if she opened her mouth. The wide, firm little mouth always remained closed, but the blue eyes burned fiercely, and the outraged little heart, thumping furiously at its impotence, did its best to salve its wounds with ceaseless repetition of its own private addition to the prescribed form of morning and evening prayer.

Once, even Tom's dull wit caught something of meaning in the blaze of the blue eyes.

"What are you saying, you little devil?" he growled, and released her so suddenly that she fell on her knees in the mud.

And she put her hands together, as she was in the habit of doing, and prayed, "O God, please kill brother Tom!"

"Little devil!" said brother Tom, with a startled red face, and made a dash at her; but she had foreseen that and was gone like a flash.

One might have expected her childish comeliness to exercise something of a mollifying effect on his brutality. On the contrary, it seemed but to increase it. She was so sweet; he was so coarse. She was so small and fragile; he was so big and strong. Her prettiness might work on others. He would let her see and feel that he was not the kind to be fooled by such things.

He had the elemental heartlessness of the savage, which recognises no sufferings but its own, and refuses to be affected even by them.

When Nance's kitten, presented to her by their neighbour, Mrs. Helier Baker, solved much speculation as to its sex by becoming a mother, Tom gladly undertook the task of drowning the superfluous offspring. He got so much amusement out of it that, for weeks, Nance's horrified inner vision saw little blind heads, half-drowned and mewing piteously, striving with feeble pink claws to climb out of the death-tub and being ruthlessly set swimming again till they sank.

She hurled herself at Tom as he gloated over his enjoyment, and would have asked nothing better than to treat him as he was treating the kittens—righteous retribution in her case, not enjoyment!—but he was too strong for her. He simply kicked out behind, and before she could get up had thrust one of his half-drowned victims into the neck of her frock, and the clammy-dead feel of it and its pitiful screaming set her shuddering for months whenever she thought of it.

But now and again her tormentor overpassed the bounds and got his reward—to Nance's immediate satisfaction but subsequent increased tribulation. For whenever he got a thrashing on her account he never failed to pay her out in the smaller change of persecution which never came to light.

On a pitch-dark, starless night, the high-hedged—and in places deep-sunk—lanes of Little Sark are as black as the inside of an ebony ruler.

When the moon bathes sea and land in a flood of shimmering silver, or on a clear night of stars—and the stars in Sark, you must know, shine infinitely larger and closer and brighter than in most other places—the darkness below is lifted somewhat by reason of the majestic width and height of the glittering dome above. But when moon and stars alike are wanting, then the darkness of a Sark lane is a thing to be felt, and—if you should happen to be a little girl of eight, with a large imagination and sharp ears that have picked up fearsome stories of witches and ghosts and evil spirits—to be mortally feared.

Tom had a wholesome dread of such things himself. But the fear of fourteen, in a great strong body and no heavenly spark of imagination, is not to be compared with the fear of eight and a mind that could quiver like a harp even at its own imaginings. And, to compass his ends, he would blunt his already dull feelings and turn the darkness to his account.

When he knew Nance was out on such a night—on some errand, or in at a neighbour's—to crouch in the hedge and leap silently out upon her was huge delight; and it was well worth braving the grim possibilities of the hedges in order to extort from her the anger in the bleat of terror which, as a rule, was all that her paralysed heart permitted, as she turned and fled.

Almost more amusing—as considerably extending the enjoyment—was it to follow her quietly on such occasions, yet not so quietly but that she was perfectly aware of footsteps behind, which stopped when she stopped and went on again when she went on, and so kept her nerves on the quiver the whole time.

Creeping fearfully along in the blackness, with eyes and ears on the strain, and both little shoulders humped against the expected apparition of Tom—or worse, she would become aware of the footsteps behind her.

Then she would stop suddenly to make sure, and stand listening painfully, and hear nothing but the low hoarse growl of the sea that rarely ceases, day or night, among the rocks of Little Sark.

Then she would take a tentative step or two and stop again, and then dash on. And always there behind her were the footsteps that followed in the dark.

Then she would fumble with her foot for a stone and stoop hastily—for you are at a disadvantage with ghosts and with Toms when you stoop—and pick it up and hurl it promiscuously in the direction of the footsteps, and quaver, in a voice that belied its message, "Go away, Tom Hamon! I can see you,"—which was a little white fib born of the black urgency of the situation;—"and I'm not the least bit afraid,"—which was most decidedly another.

And so the journey would progress fitfully and in spasms, and leave nightmare recollections for the disturbance of one's sleep.

But there were variations in the procedure at times.

As when, on one occasion, Nance's undiscriminating projectile elicited from the darkness a plaintive "Mool" which came, she knew, from her favourite calf Jeanetton, who had broken her tether in the field and sought companionship in the road, and had followed her doubtfully, stopping whenever she stopped, and so received the punishment intended for another.

Nance kissed the bruise on Jeanetton's ample forehead next day very many times, and explained the whole matter to her at considerable length, and Jeanetton accepted it all very placidly and bore no ill-will.

Another time, when Nance had taken a very specially compounded cake over to her old friend, Mrs. Baker, as a present from her mother, and had been kept much longer than she wished—for the old lady's enjoyment of her pretty ways and entertaining prattle—she set out for home in fear and trembling.

It was one of the pitch-black nights, and she went along on tiptoes, hugging the empty plate to her breast, and glancing fearfully over first one shoulder, then the other, then over both and back and front all at once.

She was almost home, and very grateful for it, when the dreaded black figure leaped silently out at her from its crouching place, and she tore down the lane to the house, Tom's hoarse guffaws chasing her mockingly.

The open door cleft a solid yellow wedge in the darkness. She was almost into it, when her foot caught, and she flung head foremost into the light with a scream, and lay there with the blood pouring down her face from the broken plate.

A finger's-breadth lower and she would have gone through life one-eyed, which would have been a grievous loss to humanity at large, for sweeter windows to a large sweet soul never shone than those out of which little Nance Hamon's looked.

Most houses may be judged by their windows, but these material windows are not always true gauge of what is within. They may be decked to deceive, but the clear windows of the soul admit of no disguise. That little life tenant is always looking out and showing himself in his true colours—whether he knows it or not.

Nance's terrified scream took old Tom out at a bound. He had heard the quick rush of her feet and Tom's mocking laughter in the distance. He carried Nance in to her mother, snatched up a stick, and went after the culprit who had promptly disappeared.

It was two days before Tom sneaked in again and took his thrashing dourly. Little Nance had shut her lips tight when her father questioned her, and refused to say a word. But he was satisfied as to where the blame lay and administered justice with a heavy hand.

Bernel—as soon as he grew to persecutable age—provided Tom with another victim. But time was on the victims' side, and when Nance got to be twelve—Bernel being then eight and Tom eighteen—their combined energies and furies of revolt against his oppressions put matters more on a level.

Many a pitched battle they had, and sometimes almost won. But, win or lose, the fact that they had no longer to suffer without lifting a hand was great gain to them, and the very fact that they had to go about together for mutual protection knitted still stronger the ties that bound them one to the other.

But, though little Nance's earlier years suffered much from the black shadow of brother Tom, they were very far from being years of darkness.

She was of an unusually bright and enquiring disposition, always wanting to see and know and understand, interested in everything about her, and never satisfied till she had got to the bottom of things, or at all events as far down as it was possible for a small girl to get.

Her lively chatter and ceaseless questions left her mother and Grannie small chance of stagnation. But, if she asked many questions—and some of them posers—it was not simply for the sake of asking, but because she truly wanted to know; and even Grannie, who was not naturally talkative, never resented her pertinent enquiries, but gave freely of her accumulated wisdom and enjoyed herself in the giving.

When she got beyond their depth at times, or outside their limits, she would boldly carry her queries—and strange ones they were at times—to old Mr. Cachemaille, the Vicar up in Sark, making nothing of the journey and the Coupée in order to solve some, to her, important problem. And he not only never refused her but delighted to open to her the stores of a well-stocked mind and of the kindest and gentlest of hearts.

Often and often the people of Vauroque and Plaisance would see them pass, hand in hand and full of talk, when the Vicar had wished to see with his own eyes one or other of Nance's wonderful discoveries, in the shape of cave or rock-pool, or deposit of sparkling crystal fingers—amethyst and topaz—or what not.

For she was ever lighting on odd and beautiful bits of Nature's craftsmanship. Books were hardly to be had in those days, and in place of them she climbed fearlessly about the rough cliff-sides and tumbled headlands, and looked close at Nature with eyes that missed nothing and craved everything.

To the neighbours the headlands were places where rabbits were to be shot for dinner, the lower rocks places where ormers and limpets and vraie might be found. But to little Nance the rabbits were playfellows whose sudden deaths she lamented and resented; the cliff-sides were glorious gardens thick with sweet-scented yellow gorse and honeysuckle and wild roses, carpeted with primroses and bluebells; and, in their season, rich and juicy with blackberries beyond the possibilities of picking.

She was on closest visiting terms with innumerable broods of newly-hatched birdlings—knew them, indeed, while they were still but eggs—delighted in them when they were as yet but skin and mouth—rejoiced in their featherings and flyings. Even baby cuckoos were a joy to her, though, on their foster-mothers' accounts she resented the thriftlessness of their parents, and grew tired each year of their monotonous call which ceased not day or night. But of the larks never, for their songs seemed to her of heaven, while the cuckoos were of earth. The gulls, too, were somewhat difficult from the friendly point of view, but she lay for hours overlooking their domestic arrangements and envying the wonders of their matchless flight.

And down below the cliffs what marvels she discovered!—marvels which in many cases the Vicar was fain to content himself with at second hand, since closer acquaintance seemed to him to involve undoubted risk to limb if not to life. Little Nance, indeed, hopped down the seamed cliffs like a rock pipit, with never a thought of the dangers of the passage, and he would stand and watch her with his heart in his mouth, and only shake his grey head at her encouraging assertions that it was truly truly as easy as easy. For he felt certain that even if he got down he would never get up again. And so, when the triumphant shout from below told him she was safely landed, he would wave a grateful hand and get back from the edge and seat himself securely on a rock, till the rosy face came laughing up between him and the shimmering sea, with trophy of weed or shell or crystal quartz, and he would tell her all he knew about them, and she would try to tell him of all he had missed by not coming down.

There were wonderful great basins down there, all lined with pink and green corallines, and full of the loveliest weeds and anemones and other sea-flowers, and the rivulets that flowed from them to the sea were lined pink and green, too. And this that she had brought him was the flaming sea-weed, though truly it did not look it now, but in the water it was, she assured him, of the loveliest, and there were great bunches there so that the dark holes under the rocks were all alight with it.

She coaxed him doubtfully to the descent of the rounded headland facing L'Etat, picking out an easy circuitous way for him, and so got him safely down to her own special pool, hollowed out of the solid granite by centuries of patient grinding on the part of the great boulders within.

It was there, peering down at the fishes below, that she expressed a wish to imitate them; and he agreeing, she ran up to the farm for a bit of rope and was back before he had half comprehended all the beauties of the pool. And he had no sooner explained the necessary movements to her and she had tried them, than she cast off the rope, shouting, "I can swim! I can swim!" and to his amazement swam across the pool and back—a good fifty feet each way—chirping with delight in this new-found faculty and the tonic kiss of the finest water in the world. But after all it was not so very amazing, for she was absolutely without fear, and in that water it is difficult to sink.

They were often down there together after that, for close alongside were wonderful channels and basins whorled out of the rock in the most fantastic ways, and to sit and watch the tide rush up them was a never-failing entertainment.

And not far away was a blow-hole of the most extraordinary which shot its spray a hundred feet into the air, and if you didn't mind getting wet you could sit quite alongside it, so close that you could put your hand into it as it came rocketing out of the hole, and then, if the sun was right, you sat in the midst of rainbows—a thing Nance had always longed to do since she clapped her baby hands at her first one. But the Vicar never did that.

And once, in quest of the how and the why, Nance swam into the blow-hole's cave at a very low tide, and its size and the dome of its roof, compared with the narrowness of its entrance, amazed her, but she did not stay long for it gave her the creeps.

These were some of the ways by which little Nance grew to a larger estate than most of her fellows, and all these things helped to make her what she came to be.

When she grew old enough to assist in the farm, new realms of delight opened to her. Chickens, calves, lambs, piglets—she foster-mothered them all and knew no weariness in all such duties which were rather pleasures.

It was a wounded rabbit, limping into cover under a tangle of gorse and blackberry bashes, that discovered to her the entrance to the series of little chambers and passages that led right through the headland to the side looking into Port Gorey. Which most satisfactory hiding-place she and Bernel turned to good account on many an occasion when brother Tom's oppression passed endurance.

It had taken time, and much screwing up of childish courage, to explore the whole of that extraordinary little burrow, and it was not the work of a day.

When Nance crept along the little run made by many generations of rabbits, she found that it led finally into a dark crack in the rock, and, squeezing through that, she was in a small dark chamber which smelt strongly of her friends.

As soon as her eyes recovered from the sudden change from blazing sunlight to almost pitch darkness, she perceived a small black opening at the far end, and looking through it she saw a lightening of the darkness still farther in which tempted her on.

It was a tough scramble even for her, and the closeness of the rocks and the loneliness weighed upon her somewhat. But there was that glimmer of light ahead and she must know what it was, and so she climbed and wriggled over and under the huge splintered rocks till she came to the light, like a tiny slit of a window far above her head, and still there were passages leading on.

Next day, with Bernel and a tiny crasset lamp for company, she explored the burrow to its utmost limits and adopted it at once as their refuge and stronghold. And thereafter they spent much time there, especially in the end chamber where a tiny slit gave on to Port Gorey, and they could lie and watch all that went on down below.

There they solemnly concocted plans for brother Tom's discomfiture, and thither they retreated after defeat or victory, while he hunted high and low for them and never could make out where they had got to.

Then Tom went off to sea, and life, for those at home, became a joy without a flaw—except the thought that he would sometime come back—unless he got drowned.

When he returned he was past the boyish bullying and teasing stage, and his stunts and twists developed themselves along other lines. Moreover, sailor-fashion, he wore a knife in a sheath at the back of his belt.

He found Nance a tall slim girl of sixteen, her childish prettiness just beginning to fashion itself into the strength and comeliness of form and feature which distinguished her later on.

He swore, with strange oaths, that she was the prettiest bit of goods he'd set eyes on since he left home, and he'd seen a many. And he wondered to himself if this could really be the Nance he used to hate and persecute.

But Nance detested him and all his ways as of old.

CHAPTER III

Tom Hamon and Peter Mauger seated themselves on a rock within a few feet of the narrow slit out of which Nance and Bernel had been looking.

"Ouaie," said Tom, taking up his parable—"wanted me to join him in getting a loan on farm, he did."

"Aw, now!"

"Ouaie—a loan on farm, and me to join him, 'cause he couldn' do it without. 'And why?' I asked him."

"Ah!"

"An' he told me he was goin' to make a fortune out them silver mines."

"Aw!"

"Ouaie! He'd put in every pound he had and every shilling he earned. An' the more he could put in the more he would get out."

"Aw!"

"'But,' I said, 'suppos'n it all goes into them big holes and never comes out—'"

"Aw!"

"But he's just crazy 'bout them mines. Says there's silver an' lead, and guyabble-knows-what-all in 'em, and when they get it out he'll be a rich man."

"Aw!" said Peter, nodding his head portentously, as one who had gauged the futility of earthly riches.

He was a young man of large possessions but very few words. When he did allow his thoughts out they came slowly and in jerks, with lapses at times which the hearer had to fill in as best he could.

His father had been an enterprising free-trader, and had made money before the family farm came to him on the death of his father. He had married another farm and the heiress attached to it, and Peter was the result. An only son, both parents dead, two farms and a good round sum in the Guernsey Bank, such were Peter's circumstances.

And himself—good-tempered; lazy, since he had no need to work; not naturally gifted mentally, and the little he had, barely stirred by the short course of schooling which had been deemed sufficient for so worldly-well-endowed a boy; tall, loose-limbed, easy going and easily led, Peter was the object of much speculation among marriageably inclined maiden hearts, and had set his own where it was not wanted.

"Ouaie," continued Tom, "an' if I'd join him in the loan the money'd all come to me when he'd done with it."

"Aw!... Money isn't everything.... Can't get all you want sometimes when you've got all money you want."

"G'zammin, Peter! You're as crazy 'bout that lass as th' old un is 'bout his mines. Why don't ye ask her and ha' done with it?"

"Aw—yes. Well.... You see.... I'm makin' up to her gradual like, and in time—"

And Bernel in the hole dug his elbow facetiously into Nance's side.

"Mon Gyu! To think of a slip of a thing like our Nance making a great big fellow like you as fool-soft as a bit of tallow!" and Tom stared at him in amazement. "Why, I've licked her scores of times, and I used to lift her up by the hair of her head."

"I'd ha' knocked your head right off, Tom Hamon, if I'd been there. Right off—yes, an' bumped it on the ground."

"No, you wouldn't. 'Cause, in the first place, you couldn't, and in the second place you wouldn't have looked at her then. She was no more to look at than a bit of a rabbit, slipping about, scared-like, with her big eyes all round her."

"Great rough bull of a chap you was, Tom. Ought to had more lickings when you was young."

"Aw!" said Tom.

"Join him?" asked Peter after a pause.

"No, I won't, an' he's no right to ask it, an' he knows it. Them dirty mines may pay an' they may not, but the farm's a safe thing an' I'll stick to it."

"Maybe new capt'n'll make things go better. That's him, I'm thinking, just got ashore from brig without breaking his legs," nodding towards the wooden landing-stage on the other side of the gulf. For landing at Port Gorey was at times a matter requiring both nerve and muscle.

A man, however, had just leaped ashore from the brig, and was now standing looking somewhat anxiously after the landing of his baggage, which consisted of a wooden chest and an old carpet-bag.

When at last it stood safely on the platform, he cast a comprehensive look at his surroundings and then turned to the group of men who had come down to watch the boat come in, and four pairs of eyes on the opposite side of the gulf watched him curiously, with little thought of the tremendous part he was to play in all their lives.

"Where's he stop?" asked Peter.

"Our house."

"Nay!"

"Ouaie, I tell you. He's to stop at our house."

"Why doesn't he go to Barracks?"

"Old Captain's there and they might not agree. Oh ouaie, he'll have his hands full, I'm thinking. And if he's not careful it's a crack on the head and a drop over the Coupée he'll be getting."

"Ah!" said Peter Mauger.

"Come you along and see what kind of chap he is."

"Aw well, I don't mind," and they strolled away to inspect the new Mine Captain, who was to brace up the slackened ropes and bring the enterprise to a successful issue.

"Did you know he was going to stop with us, Nance?" asked Bernel, as they groped their way out after due interval.

"I heard father tell mother this morning."

"Where's he to sleep?"

"He's to have my room and I'm coming up into the loft. I shall take the dark end, and I've put up a curtain across."

"Shoo! We'll hear enough about the mines now," and they crept out behind a gorse bush, and went off across the common towards the clump of wind-whipped trees inside which the houses of Little Sark clustered for companionship and shelter from the south-west gales.

CHAPTER IV

HOW GARD MADE NEW ACQUAINTANCES

Old Tom Hamon gave the new arrival warm greeting, and pointed out such matters as might interest him as they climbed the steep road which led up to the plateau and the houses.

"Assay Office, Mr. Gard.... Captain's Office.... Forge.... Sark's Hope shaft.... Le Pelley shaft—ninety fathoms below sea-level.... Pump shaft ... and yon to east'ard is Prince's shaft.... We go round here behind engine-house.... Yon's my house 'mong the trees."

"That's a fine animal," said Gard, stopping suddenly to look at a great white horse, which stood nibbling the gorse on the edge of the cliff right in the eye of the sun, as it drooped towards Guernsey in a holocaust of purple and amber and crimson clouds. The glow of the threatening sky threw the great white figure into unusual prominence.

"Yours, Mr. Hamon?" asked Gard—and the white horse flung up its head and pealed out a trumpet-like neigh as though resenting the imputation.

"No," said old Tom, staring at the white horse under his shading hand. "Seigneur's. What's he doing down here? He's generally kept up at Eperquerie, and that's the best place for him. He's an awkward beast at times. I must send and tell Mr. Le Pelley where he is."

The little cluster of white, thatched houses stood close together for company, but discreetly turned their faces away from one another so that no man overlooked or interfered with his neighbour.

Gard found himself in a large room which occupied the whole middle portion of the house and served as kitchen and common room for the family.

The floor was of trodden earth—hard and dry as cement, with a strip of boarding round the sides and in front of the fire-place. Heavy oaken beams ran across the roof from which depended a great hanging rack littered with all kinds of household odds and ends. Along the beams of the roof on hooks hung two long guns. One end of the room was occupied by a huge fire-place, in one corner of which stood a new iron cooking range, and alongside it a heap of white ashes and some smouldering sticks of gorse under a big black iron pot filled the room with the fragrance of wood smoke. In the opposite side of the fire-place was an iron door closing the great baking oven, and above it ran a wide mantel-shelf on which stood china dogs and glass rolling-pins and a couple of lamps.

A well-scrubbed white wooden table was set ready for supper. On a very ancient-looking black oak stand—cupboard below and shelves above—was ranged a vast assortment of crockery ware, and on the walls hung potbellied metal jugs and cans which shone like silver.

Two doors led to the other rooms of the house, one of them wide open.

One corner of the room was occupied by a great wooden bin eight feet square, filled with dried bracken. On the wide flat side, which looked like a form, a woman and a girl were sitting when the two men entered.

Hamon introduced them briefly as his wife and daughter, and, comely women as Gard had been accustomed to in his own country of Cornwall, there was something about these two, and especially about the younger of the two, which made him of a sudden more than satisfied with the somewhat doubtful venture to which he had bound himself—set a sudden homely warmth in his heart, and made him feel the richer for being there—made him, in fact, glad that he had come.

And yet there was nothing in their reception of him that justified the feeling.

They nodded, indeed, in answer to his bow, but neither their faces nor their manner showed any special joy at his coming.

But that made no difference to him. They were there, and the mere sight of the girl's fine mobile face and large dark blue eyes was a thing to be grateful for.

"You'll be wanting your supper," said Hamon.

"At your own time, please," said the young man, looking towards Mrs. Hamon. "I am really not very hungry"—though truth to tell he well might have been, for the food on the brig had left much to be desired even to one who had been a sailorman himself.

"It is our usual time," said Mrs. Hamon, "and it is all ready. Will you please to sit there."

At the sound of the chairs a boy of fourteen came quietly in and slipped into his seat.

His sister had gone off with a portion on a plate through the open door.

Gard was surprised to find himself hoping it was not her custom to take her meals in private, and was relieved when she came back presently without the plate and sat down by her brother.

"Ah, you, Bernel, as soon as you've done your supper run over and tell Mr. Le Pelley that his white stallion is on our common, and he'd better send for him."

"I'll ride him home," said the boy exultingly.

"No you won't, Bern," said his sister quickly. "He's not safe. You know what an awkward beast he is at times, and you could never get him across the Coupée."

"Pooh! I'd ride him across any day."

"Promise me you won't," she said, with a hand on his arm.

"Oh, well, if you say so," he grumbled. "I could manage him all right though."

Just then the doorway darkened and two young men entered, and threw their caps on the green bed, and sat down with an awkward nod of greeting to the company in general.

"My son Tom," said Mr. Hamon, and Tom jerked another awkward nod towards the stranger. "And Peter Mauger"—Peter repeated the performance, more shyly and awkwardly even than Tom, from a variety of reasons.

Tom was at home, and he had not even been invited—except by Tom. And strangers always made him shy. And then there was Nance, with her great eyes fixed on him, he knew, though he had not dared to look straight at her.

And then the stranger had an air about him—it was hard to say of what, but it made Peter Mauger and Tom conscious of personal uncouthness, and of a desire to get up and go out and wash their hands and have a shave.

Gard, they knew, was the new captain of the mine, chosen by the managers of the company for his experience with men, and he looked as if he had been accustomed to order them about.

His eyes were dark and keen, his face full of energy. Being clean-shaven his age was doubtful. He might be twenty-five or forty. Nance, in her first quick comprehensive glance, had wondered which.

He stood close upon six feet and was broad-chested and square-shouldered. A good figure of a man, clean and upstanding, and with no nonsense about him. A capable-looking man in every respect, and if his manner was quiet and retiring, there was that about him which suggested the possibility of explosion if occasion arose.

Not that the Hamon family as a whole, or any member of it, would have put the matter quite in that way to itself, or herself. But that, vaguely, was the impression produced upon them—an impression of uprightness, intelligence, and reserved strength—and the more strongly, perhaps, because of late these characteristics had been somewhat overshadowed in the Island by the greed of gain and love of display engendered by the opening of the mines.

To old Tom Hamon his coming was wholly welcome. It foreshadowed a strong and more energetic development of the mines and the speedier realization of his most earnest desires.

To Mrs. Hamon it meant some extra household work, which she would gladly undertake since it was her husband's wish to have the stranger live with them, though in his absorption by the mines she had no sympathy whatever.

Nance looked upon him merely as a part of the mines, and therefore to be detested along with the noisy engine-house, the pumps, the damp and dirty miners, and all the rest of it—the coming of which had so completely spoiled her much-loved Sark.

Tom disliked him because he made him feel small and boorish, and of a commoner make. And feelings such as that inevitably try to disprove themselves by noisy self-assertion.

Accordingly Tom—after various jocular remarks in patois to Peter, who would have laughed at them had he dared, but, knowing Nance's feelings towards her brother was not sure how she would take it—loudly and provocatively to Gard—

"Expect to make them mines pay, monsieur?"

"Well, I hope so. But it's too soon to express an opinion till I've seen them."

"They put a lot of money in, and they get a lot of dirt out, but one does not hear much of any silver."

"Sometimes the deepest mines prove the best in the end."

"And as long as there's anybody to pay for it I suppose you go on digging."

"If I thought the mines had petered out—"

"Eh?" said Peter, and then coughed to hide his confusion when they all looked at him.

"I should of course advise the owners to stop work and sink no more money."

"It'll be a bad day for Sark when that happens," said old Tom. "But it's not going to happen. The silver's there all right. It only wants getting out."

"If it's there we'll certainly get it out," said Gard, and although he said it quietly enough, old Tom felt much better about things in general.

"You're the man for us," he said heartily. "We'll all be rich before we die yet."

"Depends when we die," growled Tom—in which observation—obvious as it was—there was undoubtedly much truth. And then, his little suggestion of provocation having broken like ripples on Gard's imperturbability, he turned on Peter and tried to stir him up.

"You don't get on any too fast with your making up to la garche, mon gars," he said in the patois again.

"Aw—Tom!" remonstrated Peter, very red in the face at this ruthless laying bare of his approaches.

"Get ahead, man! Put your arm round her neck and give her a kiss. That's the way to fetch 'em."

At which Nance jumped up with fiery face and sparks in her eyes and left the room, and Gard, who understood no word of what had passed, yet understood without possibility of doubt that Tom's speech had been mortally offensive to his sister, and set him down in his own mind as of low esteem and boorish disposition.

As for Peter, to whom such advice was as useless as the act would have been impossible at that stage of the proceedings, he was almost as much upset as Nance herself. He got up with a shamefaced—

"Aw, Tom, boy, that was not good of you," and made for his hat, while Tom sat with a broad grin at the result of his delicate diplomacy, and Gard's great regret was that it was not possible for him to take the hulking fellow by the neck and bundle him out of doors.

Old Tom made some sharp remark to his son, who replied in kind; Mrs. Hamon sat quietly aloof, as she always did when Tom and his father got to words, and Bernel made play with his supper, as though such matters were of too common occurrence to call for any special attention on his part.

Then Nance's face framed in a black sun-bonnet gleamed in at the outer door.

"Come along, Bern, and we'll go and tell the Seigneur where his white horse is," and she disappeared, and Bernel, having polished off everything within reach, got up and followed her.

"Will you please to take a look at the mines to-night?" asked old Tom of his guest, anxious to interest him in the work as speedily as possible.

"We might take a bit of a walk, and you can tell me all you will about things. But I don't take hold till the first of the month, and I don't want to interfere until I have a right to. I suppose my baggage will be coming up?"

"Ach, yes! Tom, you take the cart and bring Mr. Gard's things up. They are lying on the quay down there. Then we will go along, if you please!"

Old Tom marched him through the wonderful amber twilight to the summit of the bluff behind the engine-house—whence Gard could just make out his box and carpet-bag still lying on the quay below.

And all the way the old man was volubly explaining the many changes necessary, in his opinion, to bring the business to a paying basis. All which information Gard accepted for testing purposes, but gathered from the total the fact that through ill health on the part of the departing captain, the ropes all round had got slack and that the tightening of them would be a matter of no little delicacy and difficulty.

Sark men, Mr. Hamon explained, were very free and independent, and hated to be driven. They did piecework—so much per fathom, and were constitutionally, he admitted, a bit more particular as to the so much than as to the fathom. While the Cornish and Welsh men, receiving weekly wages, had also grown slack and did far less work than they did at first and than they might, could, and should do.

"But," said old Tom frankly, scratching his head, "I don't know's I'd like the job myself. Your men are quiet enough to look at, but they can boil over when they're put to it. And our men—well, they're Sark, and there's more'n a bit of the devil in them."

"I must get things round bit by bit," said Gard quietly. "It never pays to make a fuss and bustle men. Softly does it."

"I'm thinking you can do it if any man can."

"I'll have a good try any way."

"Whereabouts does the Seigneur live?" he asked presently, and inconsequently as it seemed, but following out a train of thought of his own which needed no guessing at.

"The Seigneur? Over there in Sark—across the Coupée."

"What's the Coupée?"

"The Coupée?—Mon Gyu!"—at such colossal ignorance—"Why, ...the Coupée's the Coupée.... Come along, then. Maybe you can get a look at it before it's too dark."

They had got quite out of sound of the clanking engine, and were travelling a well-made road, when their attention was drawn to a lively struggle proceeding on the common between the road and the cliff.

Tom, setting out after the troubled Peter, had caught sight of the Seigneur's white horse and had forthwith decided to take him home. Peter, agreeing that it was a piece of neighbourliness which the Seigneur would appreciate, had turned back to give his assistance.

By some cajolery they had managed to slip a halter with a special length of rope over the wary white head, and there for the moment matters hung. For the white horse, with his forelegs firmly planted, dragged at one end of the rope and the two men at the other, and the issue remained in doubt.

The doubt, however, was suddenly solved by the white horse deciding on more active measures. He swung his great head to one side, dragged the men off their feet and started off at a gallop, they hanging on as best they could.

Old Tom and Gard set off after them to see the end of the matter, and suddenly, as the roadway dipped between high banks and became a hollow way, the white beast gave a shrill squeal, flung up his heels, jerked himself free, and vanished like a streak of light into the darkness of the lofty bank in front.

"Mon Gyu!" cried old Tom, and sped up the bank to see the end.

But the white horse knew his way and had no fear. They were just in time to hear the rattle of his hoofs, as he disappeared with a final shrill defiance into the outer darkness on the further side of a mighty gulf, while a stone dislodged by his flying feet went clattering down into invisible depths.

"He's done it," panted old Tom, while Gard gazed with something like awe at the narrow pathway, wavering across from side to side of the great abyss, out of which rose the growl of the sea.

"What's this?" he asked.

"Coupée. It's a wonder he managed it. The path slipped in the winter and it's narrow in places."

"And do people cross it in the dark?" asked Gard, thinking of the girl and boy who had gone to see the Seigneur.

"Och yes! It is not bad when you're used to it. Come and see!" and he led the way back across the common to the road.

Gard walked cautiously behind him as he went across the crumbling white pathway with the carelessness of custom, and, sailor as he had been, he was not sorry when the other side was reached, and he could stand in the security of the cutting and look back, and down into the gulf where the white waves foamed and growled among the boulders three hundred feet below.

"I've seen a many as did not care to cross that, first time they saw it," said old Tom with a chuckle.

"Well, I'm not surprised at that. It's apt to make one's head spin."

"I brought captain of brig up here and he wouldn't put a foot on it. Not for five hundred pounds, he said."

"It would have taken more than five hundred pounds to piece him together if he'd tumbled down there."

"That's so."

A young moon, and a clear sky still rarely light and lofty in the amber after-glow, gave them a safe passage back.

When they reached the house among the trees, Gard bethought him of his belongings.

"And my things from the quay?" he suggested.

"G'zammin! That boy has forgotten all about them, I'll be bound. I'll take the cart down myself."

"I'll go with you."

When they got back with the box and bag, which no one had touched since they were dropped on to the platform four hours before, they found that Nance and Bernel had got home and gone off to bed, having taken advantage of being across in Sark to call on some of their friends there.

Gard wondered how they would have fared if they had happened to be on the Coupée when the white horse went thundering across.

He dreamed that night that he was cautiously treading an endless white path that swung up and down in the darkness like a piece of ribbon in a breeze. And a great white horse came plunging at him out of the darkness, and just as he gave himself up for lost, a sweet firm face in a black sun-bonnet appeared suddenly in front of him, and the white horse squealed and leaped over them and disappeared, while the stones he had displaced went rattling down into the depths below.

CHAPTER V

HOW NANCE SHONE THROUGH HER MODEST VEILING

As soon as the old captain's time was up, Gard took up his work in the mines with energetic hopefulness.

His hopefulness was unbounded. His energy he tempered with all the tact and discretion his knowledge of men, and his experience in handling them, had taught him.

His father had been lost at sea the year after his son was born. His mother, a good and God-fearing woman, had strained every nerve to give her boy an education. She died when Stephen was fourteen. He took to his father's calling and had followed it with a certain success for ten years, by which time he had attained the position of first mate.

Then the owner of the Botallack Mine, in Cornwall, having come across him in the way of business, and been struck by his intelligence and aptitude, induced him by a lucrative appointment to try his luck on land.

The managers of the Sark Mines, seeking a special man for somewhat special circumstances, had applied to Botallack for assistance, and Stephen Gard came to Sark as the representative of many hopes which, so far, had been somewhat lacking in results.

But, as old Tom Hamon had predicted, he very soon found that he had laid his hand to no easy plough.

The Sark men were characteristically difficult, and made the difficulty greater by not understanding him—or declining to understand, which came to the same thing—when he laid down his ideas and endeavoured to bring them to his ways.

Some, without doubt, had no English, and their patois was quite beyond him. Others could understand him an they would, but deliberately chose not to—partly from a conservative objection to any change whatever, and partly from an idea that he had been imported for the purpose of driving them, and driving is the last thing a Sark man will submit to.

Old Tom Hamon, and a few others who had a financial interest in the mines, assisted him all they could, in hopes of thereby assisting themselves, but they were few.

As for the Cornishmen and Welshmen, the success or failure of the Sark Mines mattered little to them. There was always mining going on somewhere and competent men were always in demand. They were paid so much a week, small output or large, and without a doubt the small output entailed less labour than the large. They naturally regarded with no great favour the man whose present aim in life it was to ensure the largest output possible.

And so Gard found himself confronted by many difficulties, and, moreover, and greatly to the troubling of his mind, found himself looked upon as a dictator and an interloper by the men whom he had hoped to benefit.

Concerning the mines themselves he was not called upon for an opinion. The managers had satisfied themselves as to the presence of silver. If his opinion had been asked it would have confirmed them. But all he had to do was to follow the veins and win the ore in paying quantities, and he found himself handicapped on every hand by the obstinacy of his men.

Outside business matters he was very well satisfied with his surroundings.

In such spare time as he had, he wandered over the Island with eager, open eyes, marvelling at its wonders and enjoying its natural beauties with rare delight.

The great granite cliffs, with their deep indentations and stimulating caves and crannies; the shimmering blue and green sea, with its long slow heave which rushed in foam and tumult up the rock-pools and gullies; the softer beauties of rounded down and flower-and fern-clad slopes honeycombed with rabbit holes; the little sea-gardens teeming with novel life; in all these he found his resource and a certain consolation for his loneliness.

And in the Hamon household he found much to interest him and not a little ground for speculation.

Old Mrs. Hamon—Grannie—had promptly ordered him in for inspection, and, after prolonged and careful observation from the interior of the black sun-bonnet, had been understood to approve him, since she said nothing to the contrary.

It took him some time to arrive at the correct relationship between young Tom and Nance and Bernel, for it seemed quite incredible that fruit so diverse should spring from one parent stem.

For Tom was all that was rough and boorish—rude to Mrs. Hamon, coarse, and at times overbearing to Nance and Bernel, to such an extent, indeed, that more than once Gard had difficulty in remembering that he himself was only a visitor on sufferance and not entitled to interfere in such intimate family matters.

Tom was not slow to perceive this, and in consequence set himself deliberately to provoke it by behaviour even more outrageous than usual. Time and again Gard would have rejoiced to take him outside and express his feelings to their fullest satisfaction.

With Mrs. Hamon and Bernel he was on the most friendly footing, his undisguised sentiments in the matter of Tom commending him to them decisively.

But with Nance he made no headway whatever.

It was an absolutely new sensation to him, and a satisfaction the meaning of which he had not yet fully gauged, to be living under the same roof with a girl such as this. He found himself listening for her voice outside and the sound of her feet, and learned almost at once to distinguish between the clatter of her wooden pattens and any one else's when she was busy in the yard or barns.

Even though she held him at coolest arm's length, and repelled any slightest attempt at abridgment of the distance, he still rejoiced in the sight of her and found the world good because of her presence in it.

He did not understand her feeling about him in the least. He did not know that she had had to give up her room for him—that she detested the mines and everything tainted by them, and himself as head and forefront of the offence—that she regarded him as an outsider and a foreigner and therefore quite out of place in Sark. He only knew that he saw very little of her and would have liked to see a great deal more.

The very reserve of her treatment of himself—one might even say her passive endurance of him—served but to stimulate within him the wish to overcome it. The attraction of indifference is a distinct force in life.

There was something so trim and neat and altogether captivating to him in the slim energetic figure, in its short blue skirts and print jacket, as it whisked to and fro, inside and out, on its multifarious duties, and still more in the sweet, serious face, glimmering coyly in the shadow of the great sun-bonnet and always moulded to a fine, but, as it seemed to him, a somewhat unnatural gravity in his company.

And yet he was quite sure she could be very much otherwise when she would. For he had heard her singing over her work, and laughing merrily with Bernel; and her face, sweet as it was in its repression, seemed to him more fitted for smiles and laughter and joyousness.

He saw, of course, that brother Tom was a constant source of annoyance to them all, but especially to her, and his blood boiled impotently on her account.

He carried with him—as a delightful memory of her, though not without its cloud—the pretty picture she made when he came upon her one day in the orchard, milking—for, strictly as the Sabbath may be observed, cows must still be milked on a Sunday, not being endowed manna-like, with the gift of miraculous double production on a Saturday.

Her head was pressed into her favourite beast's side, and she was crooning soothingly to it as the white jets ping-panged into the frothing pail, and he stood for a moment watching her unseen.

Then the cow slowly turned her head towards him, considered him gravely for a moment, decided he was unnecessary and whisked her tail impatiently. Nance's lullaby stopped, she looked round with a reproving frown, and he went silently on his way.

It was another Sunday afternoon that, as he lay in the bracken on the slope of a headland, he saw two slim figures racing down a bare slope on the opposite side of a wide blue gulf, with joyous chatter, and recognized Nance and Bernel.

They disappeared and he felt lonely. Then they came picking their way round a black spur below, and stood for a minute or two looking down at something beneath them. Which something he presently discovered must be a pool of size among the rocks, for after a brief retiral, Nance behind a boulder and Bernel into a black hollow, they came out again, she lightly clad in fluttering white and Bernel in nothing at all, and with a shout of delight dived out of sight into the pool below.

He could hear their shouts and laughter echoed back by the huge overhanging rocks. He saw them climb out again and sit sunning themselves on the grey ledge like a pair of sea-birds, and Nance's exiguous white garment no longer fluttered in the breeze.

Then in they went again, and again, and again, till, tiring of the limits of the pool—huge as he afterwards found it to be—they crept over the barnacled rocks to the sea, and flung themselves fearlessly in, and came ploughing through it towards his headland. And he shrank still lower among the bracken, for though he had watched the distant little figure in white with a slight sense of sacrilege, and absolutely no sense of impropriety but only of enjoyment, he would not for all he was worth have had her know that he had watched at all, since he could imagine how she would resent it.

Nevertheless, these unconscious revelations of her real self were to him as jewels of price, and he treasured the memory of them accordingly.

He watched them swim back and disappear among the rocks, and presently go merrily up the bare slope again; and he lay long in the bracken, scarce daring to move, and when he did, he crept away warily, as one guilty of a trespass.

And glad he was that he had done so, for he had proof of her feeling that same night at supper.

Peter Mauger came sheepishly in again with Tom, and Tom, when he had satisfied the edge of his hunger, must wax facetious in his brotherly way.

"Peter and me was sitting among the rocks over against big pool s'afternoon and we saw things"—with a grin.

"Aw, Tom!" deprecated Peter in red confusion.

"An' Peter, he said he never seen anything so pretty in all his life as—"

"Aw now, Tom, you're a liar! I never said anything about it."

"You thought it, or your face was liar too, my boy. Like a dog after a rabbit it was."

"It was just like you both to lie watching," flamed Nance. "If you'd both go and jump into the sea every day you'd be a great deal nicer than you are; and if you'd stop there it would be a great deal nicer for us."

"Aw—Nance!" from Peter, and a great guffaw from Tom, while Gard devoted himself guiltily to his plate.

"You looked nice before you went in," chuckled Tom, who never knew when to stop, "but you looked a sight nicer when you came out and sat on rocks with it all stuck to you—"

"You're a—a—a disgusting thing, Tom Hamon, and you're just as bad, Peter Mauger!" and she looked as if she would have flown at them, but, instead, jumped up and flung out of the room.

Gard's innate honesty would not permit him to take up the cudgels this time. Inwardly he felt himself involved in her condemnation, though none but himself knew it.

But he had taken at times to glowering at Tom, when his rudeness passed bounds, in a way which made that young man at once uncomfortable and angry, and at times provoked him to clownish attempts at reprisal.

Mrs. Hamon bore with the black sheep quietly, since nothing else was possible to her, though her annoyance and distress were visible enough.

Old Tom was completely obsessed with his visions of wealth ever just beyond the point of his pick. He toiled long hours in the damp darknesses below seas, with the sounds of crashing waves and rolling boulders close above him, and at times threateningly audible through the stratum of rocks between; and when he did appear at meals he was too weary to trouble about anything beyond the immediate satisfaction of his needs. Besides, young Tom had long since proved his strength equal to his father's, and remonstrance or rebuke would have produced no effect.

As to Bernel, he was only a boy as yet, but he was Nance's boy and all she would have wished him.

In time he would grow up and be a match for Tom, and meanwhile she would see to it that he grew up as different from Tom in every respect as it was possible for a boy to be.

CHAPTER VI

HOW GRANNIE SCHEMED SCHEMES

Stephen Gard's experience of women had been small.

His mother had been everything to him till she died, when he was fourteen, and he went to sea.

When she was gone, that which she had put into him remained, and kept him clear of many of the snares to which the life of the young sailorman is peculiarly liable.

When he attained a position of responsibility he had had no time for anything else. And so, of his own experience, he knew little of women and their ways.

Less, indeed, than Nance knew of men and their ways. And that was not very much and tended chiefly to scorn and dissatisfaction, seeing that her knowledge was gleaned almost entirely from her experiences of Tom and Peter Mauger. Her father was, of course, her father, and on somewhat of a different plane from other men.

And so, if Nance was a wonder and a revelation to Gard, Gard was no less of, at all events, a novelty in the way of mankind to Nance.

His quiet bearing and good manners, after a life-long course of Tom, had a distinct attraction for her.

That he could burst into flame if occasion required, she was convinced. For, more than once, out of the corner of her eye and round the edge of her sun-bonnet, she had caught his thunderous looks of disgust at some of Tom's carryings-on.

She would, perhaps, have been ashamed to confess it but, somewhere down in her heart, she rather hoped, sooner or later, to see his lightning as well. It would be worth seeing, and she was inclined to think it would be good for Tom—and the rest of the family.

For Gard looked as if he could give a good account of himself in case of need. His well-built, tight-knit figure gave one the impression that he was even stronger than he looked.

If only he had been a Sark man and had nothing to do with those horrid mines! But all her greatest dislikes met in him, and she could not bring herself to the point of relaxing one iota in these matters of which he was unfortunately and unconsciously guilty.

The state of affairs at the mines improved not one whit as the months dragged on. There was a smouldering core of discontent which might break into flame at any moment—or into disastrous explosion if the necessary element were added.

Old Tom did his best, and stood loyally by the new captain and the interests of the mine and himself. But he was in a minority and could so far do no more than oppose vehement talk to vehement talk, and that, as a rule, is much like pouring oil on roaring flames.

Not many of those who were shareholders in the mine were also workers in it, and the workers met constantly at the house of a neighbour, who had turned his kitchen to an undomestic but profitable purpose by supplying drink to the miners at what seemed to the English and Welshmen ridiculously low prices.

In that kitchen the new captain and his new methods were vehemently discussed and handled roughly enough—in words. And hot words and the thoughts they excite, and wild thoughts and the words they find vent in, are at times the breeders of deeds that were better left undone.

To all financially interested in the mines the need for strictest economy and fullest efficiency was patent enough. It was still a case of faith and hope—a case of continual putting in of work and money, and, so far, of getting little out—except the dross which intervened between them and their highest hopes.

There was silver there without a doubt, and the many thin veins they came across lured them on with constant hope of mighty pockets and deposits of which these were but the flying indications.

And all putting in and getting nothing out results in stressful times, in business ventures as in the case of individuals. The great shafts sank deeper and deeper, the galleries branched out far under the sea, and there was a constant call for more and more money, lest that already sunk should be lost.

Mr. Hamon, disappointed in his view of raising money on the farm by Tom's obstinacy, in the bitterness of his spirit and the urgent necessities of the mines, conceived a new idea which, if he was able to carry it out, would serve the double purpose of satisfying his own needs at the recalcitrant Tom's expense.

"I must have more money for the mines," he said to his wife one day in private. "I'm thinking of selling the farm."

"Selling the farm?" gasped Mrs. Hamon, doubtful of her own hearing. For selling the farm is the very last resource of the utterly unfortunate. "Aye, selling the farm. Why not? It'll all come back twenty times over when we strike the pockets, and then we can live where we will, or we can go across to Guernsey, or to England if you like."

But Mrs. Hamon was silent and full of thought. She had no desire for wealth, and still less to live in Guernsey or in England, or anywhere in the world but Sark.

He had been a good husband to her on the whole, until this silver craze absorbed him. She had never found it necessary to counter his wishes before. But this idea of selling the farm cut to the very roots of her life.

For Nance's sake and Bernel's she must oppose it with all that was in her. If the farm were sold the money would all go into those gaping black mouths and bottomless pits at Port Gorey. The home would be broken up—an end of all things. It must not be.

"I should think many times before selling the farm if I were you," she said quietly, and left it there for the moment.

But old Tom, having made up his mind, and the necessities of the case pressing, lost no time over the matter.

"I've been speaking to John Guille about that business," he said, next day, in a confidently casual way.

"About—?"

"About the farm. He'll give me six hundred pounds for it and take the stock at what it's worth, and he's willing we should stop on as tenants at fifty pounds a year rent."

His wife was ominously silent. He glanced at her doubtfully.

"I shall stop on as tenant for the present and Tom can go on working it. When we reach the silver, and the money begins to come back, we can decide what to do afterwards."

Still his wife said nothing, but her face was white and set. It was hard for her to put herself in opposition to him, but here she found it necessary. He was going too far.

It was only when the silence had grown ominous and painful, that she said, slowly and with difficulty—

"I'm sorry to look like going against you, Tom, but I can't see it right you should sell the farm."

"It'll make no difference to you and the young ones. I'll see to that."

"It's not right and you mustn't do it."

"Mustn't do it!—And it's as good as done!"

"It can't be done until your mother and I consent, and we can't see it's a right thing to do."

"Can't you see that you're only saving the farm for Torn?" he argued wrathfully, bottling his anger as well as he could. "It's nothing to you and the young ones in any case."

"I know, but all the same it's not right. If it was to buy another farm it would be different, for you could leave it as you choose. But to throw away the money on those mines—"

This was a lapse from diplomacy and old Tom resented it.

"Throw the money away!" he shouted, casting all restraint to the winds. "Who's going to throw the money away? It's like you women. You never can see beyond the ends of your noses. I'll tell you what I'll do—I'll pay you out your dower right in hard cash. Will that satisfy you?"

If he died she would have a life interest in one-third of the farm, but could not, of course, will it to Nance or Bernel. If he sold the farm and paid her her lawful third in cash, she could do what she chose with it. It was therefore distinctly to her own interest to fall in with his plan.

But, dearly as she would have liked to make some provision, however small, for Nance and Bernel, her whole Sark soul was up in arms against the idea of selling the farm.

It would feel like a break-up of life. Nothing, she was sure, would ever be the same again.

"It's not right," she said simply.

"You're a fool—" and then the look on her quiet face—such a look as she might have worn if he had struck her—penetrated the storm-cloud of his anger. He remembered her years of wifely patience and faithful service, "—a foolish woman. A Sark wife should know which side of her bread the butter is on. Can't you see—"

"I know all that, Tom, but I hope you'll give up this notion of selling the farm. Your mother feels just as I do about it. We've talked it over—"

"I'll talk to her," and he went in at once to the old lady's room.

But Grannie gave him no time for argument.

"It's you's the fool, Tom," she said decisively, as he crossed the threshold. "There's not enough silver in Sark to make a plate for your coffin."

"I brought out more'n enough to make your plate and mine, myself to-day," he said triumphantly.

"Ah, bah! You'd have done better for yourself and for Sark if you'd let it lie."

"I'd have done better still if I'd got twice as much."

"If the good God set silver inside Sark, it was because He thought it was the best place for it, and it's not for the likes of you to be trying to get it out."

"What's it there for if it's not to be got out?"

"You mark me, Tom Hamon, no good will come of all this upsetting and digging out the insides of the Island—nenni-gia!"

"Pergui, mother, where do you think all the silver and gold in the world came from?"

"It didn't come out of our Sark rocks any way, mon gars."

"Good thing for us if it had, ma fé! But, see you here, mother, if I sell the farm it's not you and Nance that need trouble. If I pay out your dowers in hard cash you're both of you better off than you are now, and I'm better off too. It's only Tom could complain, and—"

"It's hard on the lad."

"Bidemme, it's no more than he deserves for his goings-on! Maybe it'll do him good to have to work for his living."

"And you would do that to get your bit more money to throw into those big holes?"

"Never you mind me. I'll take care of myself, and we'll see who's wisest in the end. Now, will you agree to it?"

"I'll talk it over with Nancy again," and the big black sun-bonnet nodded with sapient significance. "Send her to me."

"It's from you I got my good sense," said old Tom approvingly, and went off in search of his wife, while the clever old lady pondered deep schemes.

"Here's the way of it, Nancy," she said, when Mrs. Hamon came in. "He's crazy on these silver mines, and he's willing to pay out our dowers, yours and mine, so that he may throw the rest into the big holes at Port Gorey. Ch'est b'en! Your money and mine take more than half of what he gets. If you'll put yours to mine I'll make up the difference from what I've saved, and we'll retraite the farm, and it shall go to Nance and Bernel when the time comes."

"I can't help thinking it's rather hard on Tom," suggested Mrs. Hamon, with less vigour than before.

The idea appealed strongly to her maternal feelings and she had suffered much from Tom; still her instinct for right was there and was not to be stifled with a word.

"If you feel so when the time comes we could divide it among them, and till then Tom would have to behave himself," said the wily old lady, with a chuckle.

That again appealed strongly to Mrs. Hamon.

"Yes, I think I would agree to that," she said, after thinking it all over.

All things considered, Grannie's scheme was an excellent one and worthy of her.

By a curious anomaly of Sark law, though a man may not mortgage his property without the consent of his next-in-succession, he can sell it outright and do what he chooses with the proceeds. His wife has a dower right of one-third of both real and personal estate, into which she enters upon his death. The right, however, is there while he still lives, and must be taken into consideration in any sale of the property.

All property is sold subject to the "retraite"; in plain English, no sale is completed for six weeks, and within that time every member of the seller's family, in due order of succession, even to the collateral branches, has the right to take over, or withdraw, the property at the same price as has been agreed upon, paying in addition to the Seigneur the trézième or thirteenth part of the price, as by law provided.

If Grannie's scheme were carried out, therefore, she and Mrs. Hamon would become owners of the farm. Tom would be there on sufferance and might be kept within bounds or kicked out. Old Tom would have something more to throw into the holes at Port Gorey. And Nance and Bernel could be adequately provided for. An excellent scheme, therefore, for all concerned—except young Tom, who would have to behave himself better than he was in the habit of doing or suffer the consequences.

"Yes," said Nancy. "I don't see that I'd be doing right by Nance and Bernel not to agree to that. And if Tom behaves himself," at which Grannie grunted doubtfully, "he can have his share when the time comes."

CHAPTER VII

HOW GARD FOUGHT GALES AND TOM

So far the discussion as to the sale of the farm had been confined to the elders.

Young Tom had viewed John Guille's visits to the place with the lowering suspicion of a bull at a stranger's invasion of his field. He wondered what was going on and surmised that it was nothing to his advantage.

Words had been rare between him and his father since his refusal to lend himself to a loan on the farm, but his suspicion got the better of his obstinacy at last.

"What's John Guille want coming about here so much?" he demanded bluntly.

"I suppose he can come if he wants to. He's going to buy the farm."

"Going—to—buy—the—farm!... You—going—to—sell—the—farm—away— from—me?" roared young Tom, like the bull wounded to the quick.

"Ouaie, pardi! And why not? You had the chance of saving it and you wouldn't."

"If you do it, I'll—"

"Ouaie! You'll—"

"I'll—Go'zammin, I'll—I'll—"

"Unless you're a fool, mon gars, you'll be careful what you say or do. It'll all come back from the mines and you'll have your share if you behave yourself."

"— you and your mines!" was Tom's valedictory, and he flung away in mortal anger; anger, too, which, from a Sark point of view, was by no means unjustified. Selling the estate away from the rightful heir was disinheritance, a blow below the belt which most testators reserve until they are safe from reach of bodily harm.

Tom left the house and cut all connection with his family. He drifted away like a threatening cloud, and the sun shone out, and Stephen Gard, with the rest, found greater comfort in his room than they had ever found in his company.

So gracious, indeed, did the atmosphere of the house become, purged of Tom, that Gard, to his great joy, found even Nance not impossible of approach.

He had always treated her with extremest deference and courtesy, respecting, as far as he was able, her evident wish for nothing but the most distant intercourse.

But he was such a very great change from Tom!

She caught his dark eyes fixed on her at times with a look that reminded her of Helier Baker's black spaniel's, who was a very close friend of hers. They had neither dog nor cat at present at La Closerie, both having been scrimped by the silver mines, when old Tom's first bad attack of economy came on.

Then, at table, Gard was always quietly on the look-out to anticipate her wants. That was a refreshing novelty. Even Bernel, her special crony, thought only of his own requirements when food stood before him.

Now and again Gard began to venture on a question direct to her, generally concerning some bit of the coast he had been scrambling about, and she found it rather pleasant to be able to give information about things he did not know to this undoubtedly clever mine captain.

So, little by little, he grew into her barest toleration but apparently nothing more, and was puzzled at her aloofness and reserve, not understanding at all her bitter feeling against the mines and everything connected with them.

The first time he went to church with her and Bernel was a great white-stone day to him.

He had gone by himself once every Sunday, and done his best to follow the service in French, which he was endeavouring to pick up as best he could. And, if he could only now and again come across a word he understood, still the being in church and worshipping with others—even though it was in an unknown tongue—the sound of the chants and hymns and responses, and the mild austerity and reverent intonation of the good old Vicar, all induced a Sabbath feeling in him, and made a welcome change from the rougher routine of the week, which he would have missed most sorely.

On that special afternoon, he had been lying on the green wall of the old French fort, enjoying that most wonderful view over the shimmering blue sea, with Herm and Jethou resting on it like great green velvet cushions, and Guernsey gleaming softly in the distance, and Brecqhou and the Gouliot Head, and all the black outlying rocks fringed with creamy foam, till it should be time to go along to church.

When he heard voices in the road below and saw Nance and Bernel, he jumped up on the spur of the moment, and pushed through the gorse and bracken, and stood waiting for them.

"Will you let me join you?" he asked, as they came up, fallen shyly silent.

"We don't mind," said Bernel, and they went along together.

"This always strikes me afresh, each time I see it, as one of the most extraordinary places I've come across," said Gard, as they dipped down towards the Coupée.

"Wait till we're coming home," said Bernel hopefully.

"Why?"

"You see those clouds over there? That's wind—sou'-west—you'll see what it's like after church."

"Your gales are as extraordinary as all the rest—and your tides and currents and sea-mists. I suppose one must be born here to understand them. We have a fine coast in Cornwall, but I think you beat us."

"Of course. This is Sark."

"And does no one ever tumble over the Coupée in the dark?"

"N—o, not often, any way. Nance once saw a man blown over."

"That was a bad thing to see," said Gard, turning towards her. "How was it?"

"I was coming from school—"

"All alone?"

"Yes, all alone. The others had gone on; I'd been kept in, and it was nearly dark. It was blowing hard, and when I got to the first rock here I thought it was going to blow me over. So I went down on my hands and knees and was just going to crawl, when old Hirzel Mollet came down the other side with a great sheaf of wheat on his back. He was taking it to the Seigneur for his tithes. And then in a moment he gave a shout and I saw he was gone."

"That was terrible. What did you do?"

"I screamed and crawled back across the narrow bit to the cutting, and ran screaming up to the cottages at Plaisance, and Thomas Carré and his men came running down. But they could do nothing. They went round in a boat from the Creux, but he was dead."

"And how did you get home?"

"Thomas Carré took me across and I ran on alone, but it was months before I could forget poor old Hirzel Mollet."

"I should think so, indeed. That was a terrible thing to see."

The opening of the mines, and the influx of the Welsh and Cornishmen and their wives and children, with their new and up-to-date ideas of living and dressing, had wrought a great and not altogether wholesome change upon the original inhabitants.

All the week they were hard at work in their fields or their boats, but on Sunday the lonely lanes leading to Little Sark were thronged with sightseers, curious to inspect the mines and the latest odd fashions among the miners' wives and daughters.

Odd, and extremely useless little parasols, were then the vogue in England. The miners' women-folk flaunted these before the dazzled eyes of the Sark girls, and Sark forthwith burst into flower of many-coloured parasols.

The mine ladies dressed in printed cottons of strange and wonderful patterns. The Sark girls must do the same.

"Tiens!" ejaculated Nance more than once, as they walked. "Here is Judi Le Masurier with a new pink parasol!—and a straw bonnet with green strings!—and every day you'll see her about the fields without so much as a sun-bonnet on! And Rachel Guille has got a new print dress all red roses and lilac! Mon Gyu, what are we coming to!"

She had many such comments and still more unspoken ones. But Stephen Gard, glancing, whenever he could do so unperceived, at the trim but plainly-dressed little sun-bonneted figure by his side, vowed in his heart that the whole of these others rolled into one were not to be compared with her, and that he would give all the silver in the mines of Sark to win her appreciation and regard.

As they turned the corner at Vauroque, they came suddenly on a number of men lounging on the low wall, and among them Tom Hamon, pipe in mouth and hands in pockets.

As they passed he made some jocular remark in the patois which provoked a guffaw from the rest, and reddened Nance's face, and caused Bernel to glance up at Gard and jerk round angrily towards Tom.

"What did he say?" asked Gard, stopping.

But Nance hurried on and he could not but follow.

"What was it?" he asked again, as he caught up with her.

"If you please, do not mind him. It was just one of his rudenesses."

"They want knocking out of him."

"He is very rude," said Nance, and they passed the Vicarage and turned up the stony lane to the church.

Gard was surprised by the speedy verification of Bernel's weather forecast. Before the service was over the wind was howling round the building with the sounds of unleashed furies, and when they got out it was almost dark.

They bent to the gale and pressed on, Gard with a discomforting remembrance that the Coupée lay ahead.

As they passed Vauroque there seemed a still larger crowd of loafers at the corner, and again Tom's voice called rudely after them.

Gard turned promptly and strode back to where he was sitting on the wall, dangling his feet in devil-may-care fashion. Tom jumped down to meet him.

"Say that again in English, will you?" said Gard angrily.

"Go to—!" said Tom.

Then Gard's left fist caught him on the hinge of the right jaw, and he reeled back among the others who had jumped down to back him up.

"Well—? Want any more?" asked Gard stormily.

"You wait," growled Tom, nursing his jaw, "I'll talk to you one of these days."

"Whenever you like, you cur. What you need is a sound thrashing and a kick over the Coupée."

To his surprise none of the others joined in. But he did not know them.

They might guffaw at Tom's unseemly pleasantries, but they held him in no high esteem—either for himself or for his position, since word of the sale of La Closerie had got about.

Then they were a hardy crew and held personal courage and prowess in high respect. And in this matter there could be no possible doubt as to where the credit lay.

"Goin' to fight him, Tom?" drawled one, in the patois.

"— him!" growled Tom, but made no move that way.

And Gard turned and went over to Nance and Bernel, who were sheltering from the storm in lee of one of the cottages.

If he could have seen it, there was a warmer feeling in her heart for him than had ever been there before—a novel feeling, too, of respect and confidence such as she had never entertained towards any other man in all her life.

For that quick blow had been struck on her behalf, she knew; and it was vastly strange, and somehow good, to feel that a great strong man was ready to stand up for her and, if necessary, to fight for her.

She pressed silently on against the gale, with an odd little glow in her heart, and a feeling as though something new had suddenly come into her life.

The gale caught them at the Coupée, and the crossing seemed to Gard not without its risks.

Bernel bent and ran on through the darkness without a thought of danger.

Gard hesitated one moment and Nance stretched a hand to him, and he took it and went steadily across.

And, oh, the thrill of that first living touch of her! The feel of the warm nervous little hand sent a tingling glow through him such as he had never in his life experienced before. Verily, a white-stone day this, in spite of winds and darkness!

The gale howled like ten thousand demons, and the noise of the waves in Grande Grève came up to them in a ceaseless savage roar. Gard confessed to himself that, alone, he would never have dared to face that perilous storm-swept bridge. But the small hand of a girl made all the difference and he stepped alongside her without a tremor.

"B'en, Monsieur Gard, was I right?" shouted Bernel in his ear, as they stepped within the shelter of the cutting on the farther side.

"You were right. It's a terrible place in a gale."

"You wait," shouted Bernel. "We're not home yet."

"No more Coupées, any way," and they bent again into the storm.

They had not gone more than a hundred yards when, through some freakish funnelling of the tumbled headlands, the gale gripped them like a giant playing with pigmies, caught them up, flung them bodily across the road and held Gard and Bernel pinned and panting against the green bank, while Nance disappeared over it into the shrieking darkness.

"Good heavens!" gasped Gard, fearful lest she should have been blown over the cliffs, and wriggled himself up under the ceaseless thrashing of the gale and was whirled off the top into the field beyond.

There the pressure was less, and, getting on to his hands and knees to crawl in search of Nance, he found her close beside him crouching in the lee of the grassy dyke.

He crept into shelter beside her, and presently, in the lull after a fiercer blast than usual, she set off, bent almost double, and in a moment they were in comparative quiet. Nance crawled through a gap into the road and they found Bernel waiting for them.

"Knew you'd come through there. That's what that gap's made for," he shouted.

"I've been in many a storm but I never felt wind like that before," said Gard, as soon as his breath came back.

"If you'd stopped with me you'd have been all right," said Bernel. "There was no need for you to go after Nance. We've been through that lots of times, haven't we, Nance?"

"Lots."

"I shall know next time," said Gard, and to Nance it was a fresh experience to think of some one going out of his way to be of possible service to her.

CHAPTER VIII

HOW TOM WANTED TO BUT DIDN'T DARE

Before the six weeks allowed by Sark law for the retraiting of the property had expired, Grannie and Mrs. Hamon put in their claims, and it became generally known that they would become the new owners of La Closerie, in place of John Guille.

When the rumour at length reached Tom's ears, he, not unnaturally perhaps, set down the whole matter as a plot to oust him from his heritage and put Nance and Bernel in his place.

So his anger grew, and he was powerless. And the impotence of an angry man may lead him into gruesome paths. Smouldering fires burst out at times into devastating flames, and maddened bulls put down their heads and charge regardless of consequences.

When Tom Hamon asked Peter Mauger to lend him his gun to go rabbit-shooting one night, Peter, if he had been a thoughtful man, would have declined.

But Peter was above all things easy-going, and anything but thoughtful of such matters as surged gloomily in Tom's angry head, and he lent him his gun as a matter of course.

And Tom went off across the Coupée into Little Sark, nursing his black devil and thinking vaguely and gloomily of the things he would like to do. For to rob a man of his rights in this fashion was past a man's bearing, and if he was to be ruined for the sake of that solemn-faced slip of a Nance and that young limb of a Bernel, he might as well take payment for it all, and cut their crowing, and give them something to remember him by.

He had no very definite intentions. His mind was a chaos of whirling black furies. He would like to pay somebody out for the wrongs under which he was suffering—who, or how, was of little moment. He had been wounded, he wanted to hit back.

He turned off the Coupée to the left and struck down through the gorse and bracken towards the Pot, and then crept along the cliffs and across the fields towards La Closerie—still for three days his, in the reversion; after that, gone from him irrevocably—a galling shame and not to be borne by any man that called himself a man.

Should he lie in the hedge and shoot down the old man as he came in from those cursed mines which had started all the trouble? Or should he walk right into the house and shoot and fell whatever he came across? If he must suffer it would at all events be some satisfaction to think that he had made them suffer too.

From where he stood he could look right in through the open door, and could hear their voices—Nance and Bernel and Mrs. Hamon—the interlopers, the schemers, the stealers of his rights.

The shaft of light was eclipsed suddenly as Nance came out and tripped across the yard on some household duty.

He remembered how he used to terrify her by springing out of the darkness at her. She had helped to bring all this trouble about.

Why should he not—? Why should he not—?

And while his gun still shook in his hands to the wild throbbing of his pulses, Nance passed out of his sight into the barn.

The deed a man may do on the spur of the moment, when his brain is on fire, is not so readily done when it has to be thought about.

Then Mrs. Hamon came to the door, and called to Nance to bring with her a piece or two of wood for the fire.

Here was his chance! Here was the head and front of the offence, past, present, and future! If she had never come into the family there would have been no Nance, no Bernel, no selling of the farm, maybe. A movement of the arms, the crooking of a finger, and things would be even between them.

But—it would still be he who would have to pay—as always!

All through he had been the sufferer, and if he did this thing he must suffer still more—always he who must pay.

The man who hesitates is lost, or saved. When the contemplator of evil deeds begins also to contemplate consequences, reason is beginning to resume her sway.

Then he heard heavy footsteps and voices. His father and Stephen Gard.

Another chance! Gard he hated. There was a bruise on his right jaw still. And the old man!—he had cut him out of his inheritance by going crazy over those cursed mines.

"I'm sorry you have gone so far," Gard was saying as they passed. "If you had consulted me I should have advised against it. Mining is always more or less of a speculation. I would never, if I could help it, let any man put more into a mine than he can afford to lose."

"If you know a thing's a good thing you want all you can get out of it," said old Tom stoutly.

"Yes, if—" and they passed into the house, while Tom in the hedge was considering which of them he would soonest see dead.

Now they were all inside together. A full charge of small shot might do considerable and satisfactory damage.

But thought of the certain consequences to himself welled coldly up in him again, and he slunk noiselessly away, cursing himself for leaving undone the work he had come out to do.

On the common above the Pot, a terrified white scut rose almost under his feet and sped along in front of him. He blew it into rags, and was so ashamed of his prowess that he kicked the remnants into the gorse and went home empty-handed.

CHAPTER IX

HOW OLD TOM FOUND THE SILVER HEART

One of the first things Stephen Gard had seen to, when he got matters into his own hands, was the safeguarding of the mines from ever-possible irruption of the sea. The great steam pumps kept the workings reasonably clear of drainage water, but no earthly power could drain the sea if it once got in.

The central shafts had sunk far below sea-level. The lateral galleries had, in some cases, run out seawards and were now extending far under the sea itself.

From the whirling coils of the tides and races round the coast, he judged that the sea-bed was as seamed and broken and full of faults as the visible cliffs ashore.

In bad weather, the men in those submarine galleries and the outbranching tunnels could hear the crash of the waves above their heads, and the rolling and grinding of the mighty boulders with which they disported.

If, by chance, the sea should break through, the peril to life and property would be great.

He therefore caused to be constructed and fitted inside each tunnel, at the point where it branched from its main gallery, a stout iron door, roughly hinged at the top and falling, in case of need, into the flange of a thick wooden frame. The framework was fitted to the opening on the seaward side, in a groove cut deep into the rock round each side and top and bottom. The heavy iron door, when open, lay up against the roof of the tunnel and was supported by two wooden legs. If the sea should break through, the first rush of the water would sweep away the supporting legs, the iron door would fall with a crash into the flange of the wooden frame, and the greater the pressure the tighter it would fit.

So the weight of the sea would seal the iron door against the wooden casement, which would swell and press always tighter against the rock, and that boring would be closed for ever. And if any man should be inside the tunnel when the sea broke through, there he must stop, drowned like a rat in its hole, unless by a miracle he could make his way along the tunnel before the trap-door fell.

Gard never ceased to enjoin the utmost caution on the men who undertook these outermost experimental borings.

His strict injunctions were to cease work at the first sign of water in these undersea tunnels, make for the gallery, close the trap, and await events.

Believing absolutely in the existence of one or more great central deposits whence all these thin veins of silver had come, and hoping to strike them at every blow of his pick, old Tom Hamon was the keenest explorer and opener of new leads in the mine.

"The silver's there all right," he said, time and again, "it only wants finding," and he pushed ahead, here and there, wherever he thought the chances most favourable.

He took his rightful pay along with the rest for the work he did, but it was not for wages he wrought. Ever just beyond the point of his energetic pick lay fortune, and he was after it with all his heart and soul and bodily powers.

For months he had been following up a vein which ran out under the sea, and grew richer and richer as he laid it bare. He believed it would lead him to the mother vein, and that to the heart of all the Sark silver. And so he toiled, early and late, and knew no weariness.

His tunnel, in places not more than three and four feet high and between two and three feet wide, extended now several hundred feet under the sea, and was fitted at the gallery end with the usual raised iron door.

It was hot work in there, in the dim-lighted darkness, in spite of the fact that the sea was close above his head. Fortunately, here and there, he had come upon curious little chambers like empty bubbles in one-time molten rock, ten feet across and as much in height, some of them, and curiously whorled and wrought, and these allowed him breathing spaces and welcome relief from the crampings of the passage.

When he had broken into such a chamber it needed, at times, no little labour to rediscover his vein on the opposite side. But he always found it in time, and broke through the farther wall with unusual difficulty, and went on.

The men generally worked in pairs, but old Tom would have no one with him. He did all the work, picking and hauling the refuse single-handed. The work should be his alone, his alone the glory of the great and ultimate discovery.

The rocks above him sweated and dripped at times, but that was only to be expected and gave him no anxiety. Alone with his eager hopes he chipped and picked, and felt no loneliness because of the flame of hope that burned within him. Above him he could hear the long roll and growl of the wave-tormented boulders—now a dull, heavy fall like the blow of a gigantic mallet, and again a long-drawn crash like shingle grinding down a hillside. But these things he had heard before and had grown accustomed to.

And so it was fated that, one day, after patiently picking round a great piece of rock till it was loosened from its ages-old bed, he felt it tremble under his hand, and leaning his weight against it, it disappeared into space beyond.

That had happened before when he struck one of the chambers, and he felt no uneasiness. If there had been water beyond, it would have given him notice by oozing round the rock as he loosened it. The brief rush of foul gas, which always followed the opening of one of these hollows, he avoided by lying flat on the ground until he felt the air about him sweeter again.

Then, enlarging the aperture with his pick, he scrambled through into this chamber now first opened since time began.

It was like many he had seen before, but considerably larger. Holding his light at arm's length, above his head, a million little eyes twinkled back at him as the rays shot to and fro on the pointed facets of the rock crystals which hung from the roof and started out of the walls and ground.

The gleaming fingers seemed all pointed straight at him. Was it in mockery or in acknowledgment of his prowess?

For, in among the pointing fingers, it seemed to him that the silver-bearing veins ran thick as the setting of an ancient jewel, twisted and curling and winding in and out so that his eyes were dazzled with the wonder of it all.

"A man! A man at last! Since time began we have awaited him, and this is he at last!" so those myriad eyes and pointing fingers seemed to cry to him.

And up above, the roar and growl of the sea sounded closer than ever before.

But he had found his treasure and he heeded nought beside. Here, of a surety, he said to himself, was the silver heart from which the scattered veins had been projected. He had found what he had sought with such labours and persistency. What else mattered?

And then, without a moment's warning—the end.

No signal crackings, no thin jets or streams from the green immensity beyond.

Just one universal collapse, one chaotic climacteric, begun and ended in the same instant, as the crust of the chamber, no longer supported by the in-pent air, dissolved under the irresistible pressure of the sea.

Where the sparkling chamber had been was a whirling vortex of bubbling green water, in which tumbled grotesquely the body of a man.

The water boiled furiously along the tunnel and foamed into the gallery. The wooden supports of the iron door gave way; the door sank slowly into its appointed place.

Old Tom Hamon was dead and buried.

CHAPTER X

HOW YOUNG TOM FOUND HIS MATCH

The news spread quickly.

Tom Hamon heard it as he sat brooding over his wrongs and cursing the chicken-heartedness and fear of consequences which had robbed him of his revenge.

He started up with an incredulous curse and tore across the Coupée to the mines to make sure.

But there was no doubt about it. Old Tom was dead: the six weeks were still two days short of their fulfilment; the property was his; his day had come.

He walked straight to La Closerie, and stalked grimly into the kitchen, where, as it happened, they were sitting over a doleful and long-delayed meal.

Mrs. Hamon had been too overwhelmed by the unexpected blow to consider all its bearings. Grannie, looking beyond, had foreseen consequences and trouble with Tom, and had sent for Stephen Gard and given him some elementary instruction relative to the laws of succession in Sark.

Tom stalked in upon them with malevolent triumph. They had tried their best to oust him from his inheritance and the act of God had spoiled them. He felt almost virtuous.

But his natural truculence, and his not altogether unnatural exultation at the frustration of these plans for his own upsetting, overcame all else. Of regret for their personal loss and his own he had none.

"Oh—ho! Mighty fine, aren't we, feasting on the best," he began. "Let me tell you all this is mine now, spite of all your dirty tricks, and you can get out, all of you, and the sooner the better. Eating my best butter, too! Ma fé, fat is good enough for the likes of you," and he stretched a long arm and lifted the dish of golden butter from the board—butter, too, which Nance and her mother had made themselves after also milking the cows.

"Put that down!" said Gard, in a voice like the taps of a hammer.

"You get out—bravache! Bretteur! I'm master here."

"In six weeks—if you live that long. Until things are properly divided you'll keep out of this, if you're well advised."

"I will, will I? We'll see about that, Mister Bully. I know what you're up to, trying to fool our Nance with your foreign ways, and I won't have it. She's not for the likes of you or any other man that's got a wife and children over in England—"

This was the suddenly-thought-of burden of a discussion over the cups one night at the canteen, soon after Gard's arrival, when the possibility of his being a married man had been mooted and had remained in Tom's turgid brain as a fact.

"By the Lord!" cried Gard, starting up in black fury, "if you can't behave yourself I'll break every bone in your body."

And Nance's face, which had unconsciously stiffened at Tom's words, glowed again at Gard's revelation of the natural man in him, and her eyes shone with various emotions—doubts, hopes, fears, and a keen interest in what would follow.

The first thing that followed was the dish of butter, which hurtled past Gard's head and crashed into the face of the clock, and then fell with a flop to the earthen floor.

The next was Tom's lowered head and cumbrous body, as he charged like a bull into Gard and both rolled to the ground, the table escaping catastrophe by a hair's-breadth.

Mrs. Hamon had sprung up with clasped hands and piteous face. Nance and Bernel had sprung up also, with distress in their faces but still more of interest. They had come to a certain reliance on Gard's powers, and how many and many a time had they longed to be able to give Tom a well-deserved thrashing!

Through the open door of her room came Grannie's hard little voice, "Now then! Now then! What are you about there?" but no one had time to tell her.

Gard was up in a moment, panting hard, for Tom's bull-head had caught him in the wind.

"If you want ... to fight ... come outside!" he jerked.

"— you!" shouted Tom, as he struggled to his knees and then to his feet. "I'll smash you!" and he lowered his head and made another blind rush.

But this time Gard was ready for him, and a stout buffet on the ear as he passed sent him crashing in a heap into the bowels of the clock, which had witnessed no such doings since Tom's great-grandfather brought it home and stood it in its place, and it testified to its amazement at them by standing with hands uplifted at ten minutes to two until it was repaired many months afterwards.

Tom got up rather dazedly, and Gard took him by the shoulders and ran him outside before he had time to pull himself together.

"Now," said Gard, shaking him as a bull-dog might a calf. "See here! You're not wanted here at present, and if you make any more trouble you'll suffer for it," and he gave him a final whirl away from the house and went in and closed the door.

Tom stood gazing at it in dull fury, thought of smashing the window, picked up a stone, remembered just in time that it would be his window, so flung the stone and a curse against the door and departed.

"I'm sorry," said Gard, looking deprecatingly at Nance. "I'm afraid I lost my temper."

"It was all his fault," said Nance. "Did he hurt you?"

"Only my feelings. He had no right to say such things or do what he did."

"It's always good to see him licked," said Bernel with gusto. "Nance and I used to try, but he was too big for us."

Mrs. Hamon had gone in with a white face to explain things to Grannie.

She came back presently and said briefly to Gard, "She wants you," and he went in to the old lady.

"You did well, Stephen Gard," she chirped. "Stand by them, for they'll need it. He's a bad lot is Tom, and he'll make things uncomfortable when he comes here to live. When Nancy takes her third of what's left of the house, that'll be only two rooms, so you'll have to look out for another, and maybe you'll not find it easy to get one in Little Sark. If you take my advice you'll try Charles Guille at Clos Bourel, or Thomas Carré at the Plaisance Cottages by the Coupée, they're kindly folk both. I've told Nancy to get Philip Tanquerel of Val Creux to help her portion the lots, and it'll be no easy job, for Tom will choose the best and get all he can."

They were agreeably surprised to hear no more of Tom, but learned before long that, on the strength of his unexpected good fortune, he had gone over to Guernsey to pass, in ways that most appealed to him, the six weeks allowed by the law for the settlement of his father's affairs.

Within that six weeks Philip Tanquerel of Val Creux had, on Mrs. Hamon's behalf, to allot all old Tom's estate, house, fields, cattle, implements, furniture, into three as equal portions as he could contrive with his most careful balancing of pros and cons. For, with Solomon-like wisdom, Sark law entails upon the widow the apportionment of the three lots into which everything is divided, but allows the heir first choice of any two of them, the remaining lot becoming the widow's dower.

No light undertaking, therefore, the apportionment of those lots, or the widow may be left with only bedrooms to live in, and an ill proportion of grazing ground for her cattle and herself to live upon. For, be sure that when it comes to the picking of these lots, even the best of sons will pick the plums, and when such an one as Tom Hamon is in question it is as well to mingle the plums and the sloes with an exactitude of proportionment that will allow of no advantage either way.

CHAPTER XI

HOW GARD DREW NEARER TO HIS HEART'S DESIRE

Gard's isolation was brought home to him when he endeavoured to find another lodging in Little Sark.

Accommodation was, of course, limited. Many of the miners had to tramp in each day from Sark. There was still, in spite of all his tact and efforts, somewhat of a feeling against him as a new-comer, an innovator, a tightener of loose cords, and no one offered to change quarters to oblige him. And so, in the end, he took Grannie's advice and found a room in one of the thatch-roofed cottages which offered their white-washed shoulders to the road just where it rose out of the further side of the Coupée into Sark.

They were quiet, farmer-fisher folk who lived there, having nothing to do with the mines and little beyond a general interest in them.

When not at work, he was thrown much upon himself, and if in his rambles he chanced upon Bernel Hamon it was a treat, and if, as happened all too seldom, upon Nance as well, an enjoyment beyond words.

But Nance was a busy maid, with hens and chickens, and cows and calves, and pigs and piglets claiming her constant attention, and it was only now and again that she could so arrange her duties as to allow of a flight with Bernel—a flight which always took the way to the sea and developed presently into a bathing revel wherein she flung cares and clothes to the winds, or into a fishing excursion, in which pleasure and profit and somewhat of pain were evenly mixed.

For, though she loved the sea and ate fresh-caught fish with as much gusto as any, she hated seeing them caught—almost as much as she hated having her fowls or piglets slaughtered for eating purposes, and never would touch them—a delicacy of feeling at which Bernel openly scoffed but could not laugh her out of.

She had sentiments also regarding the rabbits Bernel shot on the cliffs, but being wild, and she herself having had no hand in their upbringing and not having known them intimately, she accepted them as natural provision, though not without compunctions at times concerning possible families of orphans left totally unprovided for.

When she did permit herself a few hours off duty she did it with a whole-hearted enjoyment—approaching the naïve abandon of childhood—which, to Gard's sober restraint, when he was graciously permitted to witness it, was wholly charming.

By degrees, and especially after her father's tragic death, Nance's feelings towards the stranger had perceptibly changed.

He might be an alien, an Englishman; but he was at all events a Cornishman, and she had heard say that the men of Cornwall and of the Islands and of the Bretagne had much in common, just as their rugged coasts had. And England, after all, was allied to the Islands, belonged to them in fact, and was indeed quite as essential a part of the Queen's dominions as the Islands themselves, and to harbour unfriendly feeling towards your own relations—unless indeed, as in the case of Tom, they had given you ample cause—would be surely the mark of a small and narrow mind.

And he might be a miner; and mines, and most miners, were naturally hateful to her. But he had been a sailor, and was miner only by accident as it were, and she knew that he loved the sea. Allowance, she supposed, must be made for men getting twists in their brains—like her father. He had gone crazy over these mines though he had been sensible enough in other matters.

What her careful, surreptitious observation of him, from the depths and round the wings of her sun-bonnet, told her was that he was an upright man, and true, and bold, with a spirit which he kept well in hand but which could blaze like lightning on occasion, and a strength which he could turn to excellent purpose when the need arose.

And—and—she admitted it shyly to herself and not without wonder, and found herself dwelling upon it as she sang softly to the ping-pang of the milk into the pail, or the swoosh of it in the churn—he thought of her, Nance Hamon—perhaps he even admired her a little—any way he was certainly interested in her, and in his shy reserved way he showed a desire for her company which she no longer found pleasure in defeating as she had done at first.

Undoubtedly an odd feeling, this, of being cared for by an outside man—- but withal tending to increase of self-esteem and therefore not unpleasing.

Peter Mauger, indeed—but then she had never looked upon Peter as anything but Peter, and the shadow of Tom had always obscured him to her. Stephen Gard was a man, and a different kind of a man from Peter altogether.

She remembered, with a slight reddening still of the warm brown cheeks whenever she thought of it—how, on the previous Sunday afternoon, she and Bernel had gone running over the downs through the waist-high bracken towards Brenière, the tide in their favourite pool below the rocks being too high for bathing. And on the slope above the Cromlech they had come suddenly on Gard, lying there looking out over the sea towards L'Etat.

He had jumped up at sight of them and stood hesitating a moment.

"Going for a bathe?" he asked, knowing the usual course of their proceedings.

"Yes, we were," said Bernel. "You going?" with a glance at the towel Gard had brought out on the chance of a dip.

"I'd thought of it, but your tides and currents here are so troublesome—"

"Oh, we know all about 'em. They're all right when you know."

"I suppose so, but—" with a look at Nance, "I'll clear out."

"You're not coming?"

"Your sister wouldn't like it."

"Nance?" with a look of surprise. "She won't mind. Will you, Nance?"

Then it was her turn to hesitate, for bathing with Bernel was one thing, and with Mr. Gard quite another.

"You'll show me another time, Bernel," said Gard, picking up his towel. "I wouldn't like to spoil your fun now."

"But you wouldn't. Would he, Nance?"

"I don't mind—if you'll give me the cave."

"All the caves you want," said Bernel, scornful at such unusual stickling on the part of his chum.

"Quite sure you don't mind?" asked Gard, doubtful still.

"If I have the cave. It's generally the one who gets there first, and Bern goes quicker than I do."

"Of course. You're only a girl," laughed Bernel, as he raced on down the slope.

And Nance laughed too at his brotherly depreciation, and Gard, who had never regarded her as only a girl, and whose thoughts of her were very absorbing and uplifting, happening to catch her eye, laughed also, and so they went down towards the sea in pleasant enough humour and the nearest approach to good-fellowship they had yet attained.

Nance disappeared round a corner, and the next he saw of her she was swimming boldly out towards Brenière point, and in a moment he and Bernel were after her.

"Don't go past the point," jerked Bernel.

"She's gone."

"She's a fish and knows her way," and just then they ploughed into what at first looked to Gard like a perfectly smooth spot amid the troubled waters, and then he was lifted from below and flung awry and out of his stroke, and tossed and tumbled till he felt as helpless as a dead fish. Then a fresh coil of the bubbling tide whirled him to one side and he was out again in the safety of the dancing waves.

"You see?" cried Bernel. "That's what it's like," and shot into it headlong.

And Gard, treading water quietly at a safe distance, saw how, every here and there, great crowns of water came surging up from below, with such lunging force that they rose in some cases almost a foot above the neighbouring level of the sea, and he wondered how any swimmer could make way through them. And yet Nance had cleft them like a seal, and he could hardly make out her brown head bobbing among the distant waves.

"Is it safe for her?" he cried after Bernel, but the boy's only reply was a scornful wave of the arm as he pressed on to join her.

Gard had an ample swim, and was dressed and sitting on a rock, when they came leisurely in, and it seemed to him that never in his life had he seen anything half so pretty as those shining coils of chestnut hair with the sea-drops sparkling in them, and the bright energetic face below, browned with sun and wind, rosy-brown now with her long swim, and beaded like her hair with pearly drops.

As she swept along below, she gave just one quick up-glance, and then, with completest ignorance of his presence, turned her head to Bernel and chattered away to him with most determined nonchalance.

She and Bernel used the long effective side-stroke almost entirely, and the little arm that flashed in and out so tirelessly was as white as the garment that fluttered in wavy convolutions about the lithe little body below.

Gard, as he watched her, felt like a discoverer of hidden treasure, overwhelmed and intoxicated with the wonder of unexpected riches. He had come to this wild little land of Sark after silver, and he said to himself that he had found a pearl beyond price.

In a minute or two they were scrambling up the slope and flung themselves down beside him for a rest, feeling the strain of unusual exertion now that the brace and tonic of the water was off them.

"You are bold swimmers," said Gard.

"She's a fish in the water," said Bernel, "and she made me swim almost as soon as I could walk."

"You see," said Nance, in her decisive little way, "many of our Sark men won't learn to swim. They think it's mistrusting God. But that seems to me foolish. Every man who goes down to the sea ought to be able to swim—besides, it's terribly nice."

"Yes, surely, Sark men ought to be able to swim, and they have certainly no lack of opportunity. But it's a dangerous coast for those who don't know it. Look at that now," and he nodded to the foaming race in front of them, between Brenière and a gaunt rocky peak which rose like a mountain-top out of the lonely sea. "Why, it must be running five or six miles an hour."

From where they sat the sea seemed perfectly calm, a level plain of deepest blue, with pale green streaks under the rocks and dark purple patches further out, its surface just furrowed with tiny wind-ripples, and underneath, a long slow heave like the breathings of the spirit of the deep. But, smooth as the blue plain seemed, wave met rock with roar and turmoil, and between that outlying peak and the shore the waters tore and foamed with wild white crests—tumbling green ridges that were never two seconds the same. While all along the great black base of the peak the white waves rushed like mighty rockets, flinging long white arms up its ragged sides and crashing together at the end in dazzling bursts of foam.

"Wonderful!" said Gard. "I've lain here for hours watching it."

"I've swum it," said Nance quietly.

"So've I," said Bernel.

"Never! You two? I wonder you came back alive!"

"On the slack it's not so bad, and at half ebb."

"And what is there to see when you get there?"

"Oh, just rocks, and puffins and gulls. You can hardly walk without stepping on them. Do you remember how we sat and watched the baby gulls coming out, Nance?"

"Yes," nodded Nance. "And you nearly got your fingers bitten off by a puffin when you felt in its hole."

"Ma dé, yes! They do bite."

"What do you call the rock?" asked Gard, nodding across at it.

"L'Etat," said Nance. "Mr. Cachemaille once told me that it had most likely at one time been joined on to Little Sark by a Coupée, just the same as Little Sark is joined to Sark. That's the Coupée, that shelf under water where the tide runs so fast. Some day, he said, perhaps our Coupée will go and we'll be an island just as L'Etat is."

"It won't be this week," said Bernel philosophically.

"It looks like the top of a high mountain just sticking up out of the water," said Gard, fascinated by the ceaseless rush of those monstrous waves in an otherwise calm sea.

"I suppose that is what it is," said Nance. "It's far worse at the other end. You can't see it from here. No matter how smooth the sea is it seems to tumble down over some cliff under water and then come shooting up again, and it throws itself at the rocks and sends the spray up into the sky."

"I'd like to go and see it," said Gard. "But I don't think I would like to swim. Could one get a boat?"

"We have a boat with Nick Mollet in the bay below here," said Bernel. "But he's generally out fishing and you're always busy."

"I'll take a holiday some day and you shall take me over."

Time came when they went, but it was hardly a holiday undertaking.

CHAPTER XII

HOW NANCE CAME UP THE MAIN SHAFT WITHOUT GOING DOWN IT

It was a few days after this that Gard had another proof of Nance's and Bernel's fearlessness and prowess in the waters they had conquered into friendliness.

Bernel was a great fisherman. He could wheedle out rock-fish by the dozen while envious miners sat about him tugging hopefully at empty lines.

He had gone down one afternoon to the overhanging wooden slip at Port Gorey, and had excellent sport, until a sudden shift of the wind to the south-west began piling the waters into the gulf on an incoming tide. Then he drew in his lines and sat dangling his legs for a few minutes, before gathering up his catch and going home.

Nance saw him from the other headland and came tripping round to see how he had fared.

"Bern," she cried, as she came up. "Tell that man he's not safe down there. The waves are bad there sometimes."

"Hi, you!" cried Bernel, to a miner who had been watching his success and had then climbed down seaward over the furrowed black ledges, hoping to do better there. "Come back! It's not safe there."

But the fisherman, intent on his sport, either did not, or would not, hear him.

"Oh, well, if you won't," said Bernel.

And then, without warning, a wave greater than any that had gone before it, hurled itself up the rocks and came roaring over the black ledges into the bay, and the man was gone.

Nance and Bernel had straightened up instantly at the sound of its coming.

Their eyes swept the rocks, and caught a glimpse of the dark body tumbling with the cascade of foam into Port Gorey.

"Oh, Bern!" cried Nance, with up-clasped hands.

But Bernel, loosing his belt and kicking off his breeches with a glance at the derelict, launched himself clear of the pier with a shout. And Nance, seeing the bulk of the man, and careless of everything but Bernel who seemed so very small compared with him, threw off her sun-bonnet and linen jacket, loosed a button, and was gone like a white flash after the two of them.

Gard was in the assay office not far away. He heard the shout and ran out just in time to see Nance go, and running to the slip he saw their clothes lying and the meaning of it all.

Bern had hold of the miner by the collar of his coat, and was doing his best with one hand to tow him to the shingle at the head of the gulf, the almost drowned one splashing wildly and doing his utmost to get hold of and drown his rescuer. Every now and again Bernel found it necessary to let go in order to keep out of his way.

Nance swam steadily up and the sinking one made a frantic clutch at her.

"Lie quiet or you shall drown," she cried. "Do you hear? Lie quiet and you are safe! See!" and she held his right hand while Bernel took his left and the man found himself no longer sinking, and they struck out for the shingle.

Others of the miners had run down with ropes, but ropes were useless in that deep gulf. Nance and Bernel were doing the only thing possible, and Gard saw that they were all right now that the man had ceased to struggle.

He picked up Bernel's things, and Nance's, with a curious feeling of delight and a touch of shyness, her sun-bonnet, her little linen jacket, her woollen skirt, her neat little wooden sabots, and ran swiftly with them to the shaft at the head of the gulf.

They would make for the adit, he thought, and so gain the shaft and come up by the ladders, if, indeed, John Thomas was in any state to climb ladders.

"Bring some brandy," he shouted to one of the men, and ran on. Nance was more to him than all the miners in Sark, and it was not brandy she would be wanting, he knew, but her clothes.

And, since a man needs both his hands to go down almost perpendicular ladders, he left at the top all that she would not instantly need and took only the little jacket and the woollen skirt. These he rolled into a bundle as he ran, and gripped in his teeth as he began the descent, and rejoiced all the way down in this close intimacy with her clothing. Indeed, on one of the stages, when he stopped for a moment's breathing, he kissed the little garments devoutly, and then laughed shamefacedly at himself for his foolishness, and glanced round quickly lest any should have witnessed it.

So down, down, till he came to the level, and crept along the adit to the shore.

They had dragged John Thomas up on to the shingle, and he lay there half-dead and fuller of water than was his custom.

Nance looked up quickly at the sound of Gard's feet, and the paled-brown of her face flushed red at sight of him, and then a grateful gleam lighted it as he dropped her things into her hand and bent over John Thomas, who was showing signs of life in a dazed and water-logged fashion.

"You did splendidly, you two," he said to Bernel. "It's a grand thing to save a man's life, even if it's only John Thomas," for John Thomas had found this land of free spirits too much for him, and had become a soaker and an indifferent workman.

"He'll be all right after a bit," he added. "I told them to send down some brandy," at which John Thomas groaned heavily to show his extremity. "As soon as it comes, Bernel, you help Nance up the ladders. Then run home both of you. Your things are at the top, Bernel. And here comes the brandy. Now, up you go! Do you think you can manage the ladders?" he asked Nance.

"I'll manage them," and they crept away into the darkness of the adit, and Nance thought she had never been in such a hideous place in her life.

CHAPTER XIII

HOW GARD REFUSED AN OFFER AND MADE AN ENEMY

They had been most gratefully and graciously free from Tom since his father's death, but he reappeared a day or two before the end of the six weeks, and brought with him a wife from Guernsey—not even a Guernsey woman, however, but a Frenchwoman from the Cotentin—black-haired, black-eyed, good-looking, after the type that would please such an one as Tom Hamon—somewhat over-bold of face and manner for the rest of the family.

Philip Tanquerel had had to bring all his sagacity to bear on his difficult task of apportioning the lots, and Tom, who knew every inch of the ground and all its capacities, grinned viciously now and again at the acumen displayed in the divisions.

The allotment of the house-room had presented difficulties.

The great kitchen at La Closerie occupied the whole centre third of the ground floor, the remaining thirds of the space on each side being taken up with the rarely-used best room and three bedrooms, all pretty much of a size, and all opening into the kitchen. Up above, under the sloping thatch was the great solie or loft, entered from the outside through the door-window in the gable by means of a short wooden ladder.

Grannie's dower rights, when Tom's grandfather died, had obtained for her the two rooms constituting one-third of the house on the south side of the kitchen, and certain rights of use of the kitchen itself. As she needed only one room, she had bartered off the other and her kitchen rights to her son and his wife in exchange for food and attendance, and the arrangement had worked excellently.

But, on her first glimpse of young Tom's quick-eyed, bold-faced Frenchwoman, she had vowed she would have none of her; and in the end, as the result of some chaffering, it was arranged that Tom and his wife should have the kitchen and all the rooms north of it, while Mrs. Hamon and Nance and Bernel had the room next Grannie's for a kitchen, and the great loft for bedrooms, all the necessary and duly specified alterations to be made at Tom's expense, and Mr. Tanquerel to see them carried out at once. Grannie's other room was to become their sitting-room also and they were to provide for her as hitherto. By boarding up the doors leading to the kitchen, and making a new entrance to their own rooms, the families were therefore entirely separated, to every one's complete satisfaction.

The division of the furniture and kitchen utensils gave Mrs. Hamon all she needed. Tom, of course, took as droit d'ainesse , before the division, the family clock—which still bore signs of strife, and had refused to go since that night when Gard's buffet had sent him headlong into it; and the farm-ladders and the pilotins—the stone props on which the haystacks were built; and in addition to his own full share, as between himself and Nance and Bernel, he exacted from them to the uttermost farthing the extra seventh part of the value of all they received—an Island right, but honoured more in the breach than in the observance, and one which, in its exercise, tended to label the exerciser as unduly mean and grasping.

Beyond that, everything was so fairly well balanced that Tom found himself unable to secure all he had hoped, and so deemed himself ill-used, and did not hesitate to express himself in his usual forcible manner.

To obtain some of the things he specially wanted, Tanquerel had so arranged the lots that he must sacrifice others, and these little matters rankled in his mind and obscured his purview.

There was a good deal of unhappy wrangling, but in the end Mrs. Hamon and Nance found themselves with a large cornfield, one for pasture, and one for mixed crops, potatoes, beans and so on, besides rights of grazing and gorse-cutting on a certain stretch of cliff common.

They had also a pony and two cows, and two pigs and a couple of dozen hens and a cock—quite enough to keep Nance busy; and to them also fell an adequate share of the byres and barns, and the free use of the well.

Tom, however, still looked upon them as interlopers, and grudged them every stick and stone, and hoof and claw. If they had never come into the family all would have been his. Whatever they had they had snatched out of his mouth.

If it had not been for Philip Tanquerel the alterations agreed on would never have been completed. He got down the carpenter and mason from Sark, stood over them, day by day, till the work was done, and then referred them to Tom for payment—and a pleasant and lively time they had in getting it.

The conditions resulting from all this were just such as have prevailed in hundreds of similar cases, such as are almost inevitable from the minute divisions and sub-divisions of small properties. When ill-feeling has prevailed beforehand it is by no means likely to be lessened by the unavoidable friction of such a distribution.

The open ill-feeling was, however, all on Tom's side. The others had suffered him at closer quarters the greater part of their lives. It was to them a mighty relief to be boarded off from him, and to feel free at last from his unwelcome incursions.

He never spoke to any of them, and when they passed one another on their various farm duties a black look and a muttered curse was his only greeting.

By means of what fairy tales concerning himself, or his position, or Sark, he had induced the lively-eyed Julie to marry him, we may not know. But Mrs. Tom very soon let it be known that she considered herself woefully misled, and quite thrown away upon such a place as Sark, and still more so upon this ultima thule of Little Sark, which she volubly asserted was the very last place le bon Dieu had made, and the condition in which it was left did Him little credit.

She, at all events, showed no disinclination to chat with her neighbours. Very much the contrary. None of them could pass within range of her eyes and tongue without a greeting and an invitation to talk.

"Tiens donc, Nancie, ma petite!" she would cry, at sight of Nance. "What a hurry you are in. It is hurry and scurry and bustle from morning till night with you over there. The hens? Let them wait, ma garche, 'twill strengthen their legs to scratch a bit, and 'twill enlighten your mind to hear about Guernsey and Granville. Oh the beautiful country! Mon Dieu, if only I were back there!"

They all—except, perhaps, Grannie—felt for her—lonely in a strange land—and were inclined to do what they could to make her more contented. But she desired them chiefly as listeners, and the things she had to tell were little to their taste, and less to her credit from their point of view, though she herself evidently looked upon them as every-day matters, and calculated to inspire these simple island-folk with the respect due to a woman of the greater world outside.

Grannie's views of her grand-daughter-in-law had never altered from the first moment she set eyes on her.

When Mrs. Tom came in to hear herself talk, one afternoon when Tom was away fishing, the old lady simply sat and stared at her from the depths of her big black sun-bonnet, and never opened her lips or gave any sign of interest or hearing.

"Is she deaf?" asked Mrs. Tom after a while.

"Dear me, no. Grannie hears everything," said Mrs. Hamon, with a smile at thought of all the old lady would have to say presently.

"Nom d'un nom, then why doesn't she speak? Is it dumb she is?"

"Neither deaf nor dumb—nor yet a fool," rapped Grannie, so sharply that the visitor jumped.

And during the remainder of her visit, no matter to whom she was talking or what she was saying, Julie's snapping black eyes would inevitably keep working round to the depths of the big black sun-bonnet, and at times her discourse lost point and trailed to a ragged end.

"It's my belief that old woman next door is a witch," she said to her husband later on.

"She's an old devil," he said bluntly. "She'll put the evil eye on you if you don't take care."

"She ought to be burnt," said Mrs. Tom.

"All the same," said Tom musingly, "she's got money, so you'd best be as civil to her as she'll let you."

"Mon Dieu! My flesh creeps still at the way she looked at me. She has the evil eye without a doubt."

And Grannie?—"Mai grand doux! What does a woman like that want here?" said she. "A wide mouth and wanton eyes. La Closerie has never had these before—a Frenchwoman too!"—with withering contempt. For, odd as it may seem, among this people originally French, and still speaking a patois based, like their laws and customs, on the old Norman, there is no term of opprobrium more profound than "Frenchman."

Madame Julie flatly refused to subject herself to further peril from Grannie's keen but harmless gaze, and contented herself with such opportunities of enlarging Nance's outlook on life as casual chats about the farm-yard afforded, and found time heavy on her hands.

Ennui, before long, gave place to grumbling, and that to recrimination; and from what the others could not help hearing, through the boarded-up doors and the floor of the loft, Tom and his wife had a cat-and-dog time of it.

Gard had moved over to Plaisance with great regret. But nothing else was possible under the altered circumstances at La Closerie, so he made the best of it.

It was some consolation to learn that they also missed him.

"Everything's different," grumbled Bernel, one day when they met. "Tom and his wife quarrel so that we can hear them through the walls. And Grannie sits by the hour without opening her mouth. And mother and Nance are as quiet as if they were going to be sick. And I'm getting green-mouldy. Seems as if we'd got to the end of things, and nothing was ever going to happen again. I think I'll go to Guernsey."

"Do you think they'd like—I mean, would they mind if I came in for a chat now and then? It's pretty lonely up at Plaisance too."

"Oh, they'll mind and so will I. When'll you come?"

"I'll look in to-night as I come from the mines—if you're sure—"

"You come and try, and if you don't like it you needn't come again"—with a twinkle of the eye.

Nance did not strike him as looking as though she were going to be sick, when he went in that night, nor did her mother.

Grannie indeed had little to say, but then she was never over-talkative, and when Gard more than once looked at her, and wondered if she had fallen asleep, he always found the keen old eyes wide open, and eyeing him watchfully as ever out of the depths of the big black sun-bonnet.

Mrs. Hamon asked about his new quarters, and his quiet shake of the head and simple—"They're kindly folk, but it's somehow very different"—told its own tale.

"They're a bit short-handed, you see," he added, "and so they're all kept busy, and at times, I'm afraid, they wish me further."

"And you go all that way back for your dinner each day?" asked Mrs. Hamon thoughtfully.

"Well, I have tried taking it with me, but it's not very satisfactory."

"What would you say to coming here for it, as you used to? I think we could manage it, Nance. What do you say?"

"We could manage it all right," said Nance, "if—" and then, in spite of herself, she could not keep that telltale mouth of hers in order, and the attempt to repress a smile only emphasized the dimples at the corners. For Gard's face was as eager as a dog's at sight of a rat.

"It will save me such a lot of time," he explained—at which Nance dimpled again as she went out to feed her chickens, and left them to complete the new arrangement.

And if it had cost Gard every penny of his salary he would still have rejoiced at it, and considered his bargain a good one. As it was, it cost him no more than the trouble of rearranging his terms with the good folks at Plaisance, and it gave a new zest and enjoyment to life since it ensured a meeting with Nance at least once each day.

And not with Nance only!

Madame Julie, very weary of herself, and Tom, and her surroundings, and Sark, and life in general as understood in Sark, very soon became conscious of the regular visits next door of the best-looking young man she had yet seen in the Island, and was filled with curiosity concerning him.

"He's after that slip of a Nance," she said to herself. "And he has his own share of good looks, has that young man."—And then came the inevitable, "Mon Dieu, but I wish Tom had been made like that!"

To get a better view of him—and perhaps not without a vague idea of ulterior interest and amusement for herself—anything to add a dash of colour to the prevailing greyness of her surroundings—she was leaning on the gate next day when he came striding up to his dinner, and gave him, "Bon jour, m'sieur!" with much heartiness and the full benefit of her black eyes and white teeth.

"'Jour, madame!" and he whipped off his hat and passed on into the house.

"That was Madame Tom, I suppose, who was leaning over the gate, as I came in," he said, as they ate.

"I expect so," said Mrs. Hamon. "She generally seems to have time on her hands."

"When Tom's not there," snapped Grannie. "Got her hands full enough when he is."

"I should imagine Tom would not be too easy to get on with at times. Maybe he'll settle down now he's married."

"Doesn't sound like settling down sometimes," chirped the old lady again.

"Oh? I'm sorry to hear that. She doesn't look bad-tempered."

"Tom's got more'n enough for the two of them."

"I'm afraid she finds it a change from what she's been accustomed to," said Mrs. Hamon quietly. "She came in once or twice, but her talk is of things that don't interest us, and ours is of things that don't interest her, so we can't get as friendly as we would like to be."

"And Tom?"

"Tom considers us all robbers, as he always has done. He gives us his blackest face whenever he sees any of us."

"That's unpleasant, seeing you're such close neighbours."

"Yes, it's unpleasant, but we can't help it. It's just Tom. How is your work getting on?"

"Not as I would wish," said Gard, with a gloomy wag of the head. "Your Sark men are difficult—very difficult, and the others who ought to know better, and who do know better"—with more than a touch of warmth—"go on as though I was a slave-driver."

"Sark men are hard to drive," said Mrs. Hamon sympathetically.

"They know perfectly well that I want only what is just and right to the shareholders. They expect their pay to the last penny, but when I insist on a proper return for it they look at me as if they'd like to knock me on the head. It's disheartening work. I've been tempted at times to throw it all up and go back to England"—at which Nance's heart gave so unusual a little kick that she had difficulty in frowning it into quietude, and just then Bernel came in with his gun and a couple of rabbits.

"Who's going to England?" he asked. "I'll go too."

"No you won't," said Nance sharply. "We want you here."

"It's as dull as Beauregard pond and as dirty, since the m—aw—um!" with a deprecatory glance at Gard.

"You'd find most busy places just as dirty," said Gard.

"Then I'll go to sea. That's clean at all events."

"Let's hope things will brighten a bit. You wouldn't find the fo'c'sle of a trader as comfortable as La Closerie, my boy,"—and they fell to on their dinner and left the matter there.

"Dites-donc, Nannon, ma petite," said Mrs. Tom to Nance, a day or two later, "who is the joli gars who comes each day to see you?"

"Mr. Gard from the mines comes up here to get his dinner, if that's what you mean."

"Oh—ho! He comes for his dinner, does he? And is that all he comes for, little Miss Modesty?"

"That's all," said Nance solemnly.

"Oh yes, without a doubt, that's all. I think I'll ask him next time I see him. Why doesn't he go home for his dinner like other people?"

"He's living at Plaisance now and it's far to go. He used to live here, you know."

"Ma foi, no, I didn't know. He used to live here? And why did he go to Plaisance then?"

"We hadn't room for him, you see."

"But, Mon Dieu, we have room and to spare! There are those two bedrooms empty. Why shouldn't he—"

But Nance shook her head at that.

"Why then?" demanded Mrs. Tom, with visions of some one besides Tom to talk to of an evening—a good-looking, sensible one too. "Why?"

"He and Tom don't get on well together—"

"Pardi, I'm not surprised at that. It would need an angel out of heaven to get on with him sometimes. What induced me ever to marry such a grumbler I don't know. I wonder if Monsieur What-is-it?—Gard— would come back if I could arrange it?"

But Nance shook her head again.

"Ah—ha, ma garche, and you would sooner he did not—is it not so?"

"I'm quite sure he and Tom would never get on together, and I don't think Mr. Gard would come."

"It's worth trying, however. He would be some one to talk to of an evening any way."

And so, when Tom came in that evening, she tackled him on the subject.

"Say then, mon beau,"—and as she said it she could not but contrast his slouching bulk with the straight, well-knit figure of the other—"why should we not take in a lodger as all the rest do? Our two rooms there are empty and—"

"Who's the lodger?"

"There is one comes up every day to dinner next door, and would stop there altogether if they had the room. Tiens, what's this his name is? He's from the mines—"

"You mean Gard—the manager," scowled Tom.

"That's it—Monsieur Gard. Why shouldn't he—"

"Because I'd break his head if I got the chance, and he knows it. Comes up there to dinner, does he? How long's he been doing that?"

"For a week now. Couldn't you get over your bad feeling? It would be money in our pockets."

"No, I couldn't, and he wouldn't come if you asked him."

"Will you let me try?"

"I tell you he won't come."

"In that case there's no harm in trying. If I can persuade him, will you promise to be civil to him, and not try to break his head?"

"He won't come, I tell you."

"And I say he may."

"And you'll nag and nag till you get your own way, I suppose."

"Of course. What's the use of a woman's tongue if she can't get her own way with it? Will you promise to behave properly if he comes?"

"I'll behave if he behaves," he growled sulkily. "But we'll neither of us get the chance. He won't come."

"Eh bien, we'll see!"

And when Gard came up to dinner next day, she was leaning over the gate waiting for him, very tastefully dressed according to her lights, and with an engaging smile on her face.

"Dites donc, Monsieur Gard," she said pleasantly. "Our little Nannon was telling me you regretted having to live so far away. Why should you not come back and occupy your old room? It is lying empty there, and I would do my very best to make you comfortable, and you would be close to your friends all the time then, instead of having to go across that frightful Coupée."

"It is very kind of you, madame," and he stared back at her in much surprise, and found himself wondering what on earth had made her marry such a man as Tom Hamon. For she was undeniably good-looking and had all a Frenchwoman's knack of making the very best of all she had—abundant black hair, very neatly twisted up at the back of her head; white teeth and full red lips; straight, well-developed figure very neatly dressed; and large black eyes which looked capable of so many things, that they found it difficult to settle for any length of time to any one expression.

"It is very kind of you, madame," said Gard, "but—" and he stood looking at her and hesitating how to put it.

"You mean about Tom," she laughed. "But that is all past. I have spoken to him, and he promises to behave himself quite properly if you will come. Voilà!"

Just for a moment the possibilities of the suggestion caught his mind. He would be near Nance all the time. He would be saved much tiresome walking to and fro. Especially he would be saved that passage of the Coupée, which at night, even with a lantern, was not a thing one easily got accustomed to, and on stormy nights was enough to make one's hair fly. Then this woman was very different from his present landlady, and would probably, he thought, have different notions of comfort.

The quick black eyes caught something of what was in him: and he, as suddenly, caught something of what lurked, consciously or unconsciously, in them, and a little tremor of repugnance shook his heart and braced him back to reason.

He shook his head. "It would not do, madame. He and I would never get on together, no matter how hard we tried. I thank you for the offer all the same," and he made as though to pass her.

"I wish you would come," she said, and laid a pleading hand on his arm. "I'm sure he would try to behave. I can generally manage him except when he's been drinking. Then I'm afraid of him, and wish some one else was at hand. But that's only when he's been out all night at the fishing, and it's soon over and done with. Do come, monsieur!"—It was almost a whisper now, and she leaned towards him—the rich dark face—the great solicitous eyes.

But she had mistaken her man. Perhaps she had not met many like him.

He shook off her hand almost brusquely.

"It is impossible, madame. I could not," and he pushed past just as Nance came to the door.

She had seen him coming, heard their voices outside, and wondered what was keeping him.

She turned back into the house when she saw Julie, wondering still more. For Gard's face was disturbed, and had in it something of the look she had seen more than once when he had faced Tom in his tantrums.

And, glancing past him, she had seen what he had not—Julie's face when he turned his back on her.

"Mon Gyu!" gasped Nance to herself, and went in wondering.

"She and Tom wanted me to take my old room again, and I refused," was all he said.

"Tom wanted you to go there?" said Mrs. Hamon in amazement.

"So she said."

Grannie's disparaging sniff was charged with libel.

"Well?" asked Tom of his wife, when he came in later on with Peter Mauger, who had come over for supper. "Got your lodger?"

"No."

"That's what I told you," with a provocative laugh.

"Oh, he'd have come quick enough."

"Would, would he? Then why didn't he?"

"I wouldn't trust myself alone in the house with that man."

"Ah!" said Tom, staring at her. "Always thought he was a bad lot myself, didn't I, Peter?"

Peter nodded.

"It's a wonder to me that Mrs. Hamon lets him run after that girl of hers as she does," said Julie.

"If I catch him up to any of his tricks I'll break his head for him."

"Maybe it would be a good thing for little Nance if you did."

"Knew he was a toad as soon as I set eyes on him, so did Peter. Didn't you, Peter?"

Peter nodded.

"What d'he say to you?" demanded Tom.

"Didn't say much. Asked if you were much away at the fishing and that. But the way he looked at me!—I've got the shivers down my back yet," and a virtuous little shudder shook her and made a visible impression on Peter.

"Peter and me'll maybe have a word with him one of these days, won't we, Peter?"

"Maybe," said Peter.

"We don't want toads like Gard running off with any of our Sark girls, do we, Peter?"

"No," said Peter.

"Mr. Gard had better look out for himself or take himself off before somebody does it for him. There's plenty wouldn't mind giving him a crack on the head and slipping him over the Coupée some dark night."

As to such extreme measures Peter offered no opinion. He looked vaguely round the big kitchen as though in search of something that used to be there, and said—

"How about supper?"

CHAPTER XIV

HOW THEY WENT THROUGH THE DARKNESS OF THE NARROW WAY

One dark night Gard sauntered down the cutting towards the Coupée, enjoying a last pipe before turning in.

This had become something of a habit with him. The people of Plaisance, hard at work all day in the fields, went early to bed and left him to follow when he pleased. And to stand securely in that deep cleft, just where the protecting walls broke off short and left the narrow path to waver on into the darkness, was always fascinating to him.

When the moon flooded the gulf on the left with shimmering silver, and the waves broke along the black rocks below in crisp white foam like silver frost, he would stand by the hour there and never tire of it.

The moon cast such a mystic glamour over those great voids of darkness and over the headlands, melting softly away, fold behind fold, on the right, while Little Sark became a mystery land into which the white path rambled enticingly and invited one to follow.

And to him, as his eyes followed it till it disappeared over the crown of the ridge, it was more than a mystery land—a land of promise, rich in La Closerie and Nance.

Always within him, as he watched, was the feeling that if the sweet slim figure should come tripping down the moonlit path towards him, he would be in no way astonished. When he stood there, watching, it seemed to him that it would be entirely fitting for her to come so, in the calm soft light that was as pure and sweet as herself.

And at times his eye would light on the grim black pile of L'Etat, lying out there in the silvery shimmer like some great monumental cairn, a rough and rugged heap of loneliness and mystery—the grimmer and lonelier by reason of the twinkling brightness of its setting. And then his thoughts would play about the lonely pile, and come back with a sense of homely relief to the fairy path which Nance's little feet had trod, in light and dark, and storm and shine, since ever she could walk.

He pictured her as a tiny girl running fearlessly across the grim pathway to school, dancing in the sunshine, bending to the storm, and all alone when she had been kept in—he wondered with a smile what she had been kept in for.

He thought of her, as he had seen her, walking to church, her usually blithe spirit tuned to sedateness by the very fact, and, to him, delightfully stiffened by the further fact that she, almost alone among her friends and school-fellows, wore Island costume, while all the rest flaunted it in all the colours of the rainbow. And he laughed happily to himself, for very joy, at thought of the sweet elusive face in the shadow of the great sun-bonnet. There was not a face in all Sark to compare with it, nor, for him, in all the world.

But this night, as be stood there pulling slowly at his pipe and thinking of Nance, was one of the black nights.

Later on there would be a remnant of a moon, but as yet the sky above was an ebon vault without a star, and the gulfs at his feet were pits of darkness out of which rose the voices of the sea in solemn rhythmic cadence.

Down in Grande Grève, on his right, the waves rolled in almost without a sound, as though they feared to disturb the darkness. From the intervening moments he could tell how slowly they crept to their curve. Their fall was a soft sibilation, a long-drawn sigh. The ever-restless sea for once seemed falling to sleep.

And then, as he listened into the darkness, a tiny elfish glimmer flickered in the void below, flickered and was gone, and he rubbed his eyes for playing him tricks. But the next wave broke slowly round the wide curve of the bay in a crescent of lambent flame, and a flood of soft, blue-green fire ran swelling up the beach and then with a sigh drew slowly back, and all was dark again. Again and again—each wave was a miracle of mystic beauty, and he stood there entranced long after his pipe had gone dead.

And as he stood gazing down at the wonder of it, his ear caught the sound of quick light footsteps coming towards him across the Coupée, and he marvelled at the intrepidity of this late traveller. If he had had to go across there that night, he would have gone step by step, with caution and a lantern; whereas here was no hesitation, but haste and assurance.

It was only when she had passed the last bastion, and was almost upon him, that he made out that it was a girl.

His heart gave a jump. She had been so much in his thought. Yet, even so, it was almost at a venture that he said—

"Nance?"

And yet, again, he had learned to recognize her footsteps at the farm, and where the heart is given the senses are subtly acute, and she had slackened her pace somewhat as she drew near.

"Yes; I am going to the doctor."

"Why—who—?"

"Grannie is ill—in pain. He will give me something to ease her." He had turned and was walking by her side.

"I am sorry. You will let me go with you?"

"There is no need at all—"

"No need, I know; but all the same it would be a pleasure to me to see you safely there and back."

She hurried on without speaking. If there had been any light, and he had dared to peep inside the black sun-bonnet, he might perhaps have found the hint of a smile overlaying her anxiety on Grannie's account.

By the ampler feel of things, and the easing of the slope, he knew they were out of the cutting, and presently they were passing Plaisance.

"If you would sooner I did not walk with you, I will fall behind; but I couldn't stop here and think of you going on alone," he said.

"That would be foolishness," she said gently. "But there is really no need. I have no fears of ghosts or anything like that."

"There might be other kinds of spirits about," he said quietly. "And when men drink as some of my fellows do, they are no respecters of persons. But this is surely very sudden. Your grandmother seemed all right at dinner-time."

"She had bad pains in the afternoon, and they have been getting worse. She did not want to have the doctor, but the things she took did her no good, and mother said I had better go and ask him for something more."

"And where is Bernel?"

"He went to the fishing with Billy Mollet, and he was not back."

"And suppose the doctor is not in?"

"They will know where he is, and I will go after him."

"Did you see those wonderful waves of fire as you came across the Coupée?"

"I have seen them often. When there is more sea on, and it breaks on the rocks, it is finer still. It is something in the water, Mr. Cachemaille told me."

"I heard your footsteps down there on the Coupée, but I couldn't see a sign of you till you were almost against me."

"I saw from the other side that some one was there, but I could not see who."

"You have most wonderful eyes in Sark."

"It is never quite dark to me on the darkest night. I suppose it is with being used to it."

"You'll have to help me across the Coupée."

"And how will you get back?"

"The moon will be up, and then I can see all right. I don't need much light, but I've not been brought up to see through solid black."

The doctor was fortunately in, and knew by ample experience what would ease Grannie's pains. So presently they were hurrying back along the dark road.

As they turned the corner by Vauroque an open doer cast a great shaft of light across the darkness, and there, just as on a previous occasion, on the wall lounged half-a-dozen men, and among them was Tom Hamon, who had come up to have a drink with his friend Peter.

At sight of him, Nance bent her head and tried to shrink into herself as she hurried past.

But Tom had seen her, and the sight of her alone with Gard at that time of night roused the virtuous indignation, and other more potent spirits, within him.

He sprang down into the road, shouting what sounded like a spate of curses in the patois.

Gard stopped and turned, with a keen recollection of the same thing having happened before. He remembered too how that occasion ended.

But Nance laid an entreating hand on his arm.

"Please—don't!"

Her voice sounded a little strange to him. If he had been able to see her face now he would have found it pallid, in spite of its usual healthy brown bloom.

She stood entreatingly till he turned and went on with her.

"He is evidently aching for another thrashing," he said grimly, as he stalked beside her.

And presently they were in the cutting, and the unnerving vastness of the gulfs opened out on either side. Gard felt like a blindfolded man stumbling along a plank.

He involuntarily put out a groping hand and took hold of her cloak. A little hand slipped out of the cloak and took his in charge, and so they went through the darkness of the narrow way.

He breathed more freely when the further slope was reached, and only then became aware that the hand that held his was all of a tremble. The next moment he perceived that she was sobbing quietly.

"Nance!" he cried. "What is it? You are crying. Is it anything I—"

"No, no, no!" sobbed the wounded soul convulsively.

"What then? Tell me!"

"I cannot. I cannot."

"Nance—dear!" and he sought her hand again and stood holding it firmly. "It is like stabs in my heart to hear you sobbing. I would give my life to save you from trouble. Do you believe me, dear?"

"Yes, yes—"

"And you can trust me, dear, can you not? You distrusted me at first, I know, but—"

"Oh, I do trust you, and I know you are good. And it is that that makes it so wicked of him to say such things about us—"

In her excitement she had let slip more than she intended. She stopped abruptly.

"Tom?"

She did not speak, but the wound welled open in another sob.

"Don't trouble about him, dear! I don't know what he said, but if it was meant to make you doubt me, it was not true. You are more to me than anything in the world, Nance, and I have never loved any other woman—except my mother. Do you believe me?"

"Yes—oh, yes! I cannot help believing you. Oh, I wish sometimes that Tom was dead. When I was very little I used to pray each night to God to kill him."

"I'll teach him to leave you alone."

"I must go now. Grannie is waiting for her medicine."

He took the little hand under his arm and pressed it close to his side, and they pushed on down the dark lanes till they came in sight of the lights of La Closerie.

Then he bent into the sun-bonnet and sealed his capture of the virginal fortress by a passionate kiss on the tremulous little lips. And she, with the frankness of a child, reached up and kissed him warmly back.

"Good-night, dear, and God bless you!" he said fervently.

"Can you find your way in the dark?"

"There is the moon. I shall be all right."

She bent her head and ran on towards the lights. He watched her go in at the door, and turned and went back along the lane, and his heart was high with the joy that was in him.

CHAPTER XV

HOW TWO FELL OUT

It was but a thin strip of a moon that had risen above the evening mists—a mere sickle of red gold—but such as it was it sufficed to lift the pall of darkness from the earth and set the black sky back into its proper place.

To Gard the night had suddenly become spacious and ample, and the peaceful slip of a moon, which grew paler and brighter every minute, was full of promise.

He was so full of Nance that he had almost forgotten Tom and his scurrilous insolences.

He crossed the Coupée without any difficulty, enjoyed over again the recollection of that last crossing, and stood in the cutting on the Sark side for a moment to marvel at the change an hour had made in his outlook on things in general

Tom? Why, he could almost forgive Tom, for it was he who had helped to bring matters to a head—unconsciously, indeed, and probably quite against his wish. Still, he had been the instrument—the drop of acid in the solution which had crystallized their love into set form and made it visible, and fixed it for life.

Truly, he was half inclined to consider himself under obligation to Tom—if only his boorishness could be kept in check for the future. For, of a certainty, he was not going to allow Nance to be made miserable by his loutish insolences.

He had climbed the cutting and was on the level, when he heard heavy footsteps coming towards him, and the next moment he was face to face with the object of his thoughts.

Possibly Tom had expected to meet him and had been preparing for the fray, for he opened at once with a volley of patois which to Gard was so much blank cartridge.

"Oh—ho, le velas—corrupteur! Amuseur! Séducteur! Ou quais noutre fille? Quais qu'on avait fait d'elle d'on?"

"Quite finished?" asked Gard quietly, as the other came to a stop for want of breath. "Say it all over again in English, and I'll know what you're talking about."

"English be—!" he broke out afresh, in a turgid mixture of tongues. "Séducteur, amuseur! Where's our Nance? Gaderabotin, what have you done with the girl? I know you, corrupteur! Running after men's wives—and our Nance, too! See then—you touch la garche and I'll—"

"See here! We've had enough of this," said Gard, gripping him by the shoulders and shaking him. "If you weren't drunk I'd thrash you within an inch of your life, you brute. Come back when you're sober, and I'll give you a lesson in manners."

Tom had been struggling to get his arms up. At last he wrenched himself free and came on like a bull. One of his flailing fists caught Gard across the face, flattening his nose and filling one eye with stars; the other hand, trying to grip his opponent, ripped open his coat, tearing away both button and cloth.

"You lout!" cried Gard, his blood up and dripping also from his nose. "If you must have it, you shall;" and he squared up to him to administer righteous punishment.

And then the futility of it came upon him. The man was three-parts drunk, in no condition for a fight, scarce able to attempt even to defend himself.

No punishment of Tom drunk would have the slightest moral effect on Tom sober. He would remember nothing about it in the morning, except that he had been knocked about.

When he received his next lesson in deportment it was Gard's earnest desire and hope that it might prove a lasting and final one.

So he decided to postpone it, and contented himself with warding and dodging his furious lunges and rushes, and gave him no blow in return. Until, at last, after one or two heavy falls of his own occasioning, Tom gave it up, spluttered a final commination on his opponent, and turned to go home.

He went blunderingly down into the hollow way, and Gard stood watching him in doubt.

It seemed hardly possible he could cross the Coupée in that state, and he felt a sort of moral responsibility towards him. Much as he detested him, he had no wish to see him go reeling over into Coupée bay.

So he set off after him to see him safely across, and Tom, hearing him coming, groped in the crumbling side wall till he found a rock of size, and sent it hurling up the path with another curse.

Then he blundered on, and Gard followed. And Tom stopped again by one of the pinnacles and sought another rock, and flung it, and it dropped slowly from point to point till it landed on the shingle three hundred feet below.

He stood there in the dim light, cursing volubly in patois and shaking his fist at Gard; but at last, to Gard's great relief, he humped his back and stumbled away up the cutting on the further side.

And Gard, very sick of it all, and with an aching head and a very tender nose, but withal with a warm glow at the heart which no aches or pains could damp down, turned and went home to bed.

CHAPTER XVI

HOW ONE FELL OVER

Gard's first waking thoughts next morning were of Nance entirely.

He would see her at dinner-time. How would he find her? Last night the disturbance of her feelings had shaken her out of herself somewhat, and shown her to him in new and delightful lights.

If, this morning, she should be to some extent withdrawn again into her natural modest shell, he would not be surprised; and he made up his mind, then and there, to be in no wise disappointed. Last night was a fact, a delightful fact, on which to build the rosy future.

It was a long time to wait till dinner-time to see her. What if he went round that way, before going to work, just to inquire if Tom got home all right.

And then the feeling of discomfort in his eye and nose, as though the one had shrunk to the size of a pin-point and the other had grown to the bulk of a turnip—brought back the whole matter, and on further consideration he decided not to go to the farm till the proper time. If he came across Tom, the fray would inevitably be resumed at once, and his right eye, at the moment, showed a decided disinclination to open to its usual extent, or to perform any of the functions properly demanded of a right eye contemplating battle.

He must get up at once and bathe it and bring it to reason.

Raw beef, he believed, was the correct treatment under the circumstances. But raw beef was almost as obtainable as raw moon, and even raw mutton he did not know where he could procure, nor whether it would answer the purpose.

So he bathed his bruises with much water, and reduced their excesses to some extent, but not enough to escape the eye of his hostess when he appeared at breakfast.

"Bin fighting?" she queried dispassionately.

"A one-sided fight. Tom Hamon was drunk last night and hit me in the face, but he was not in a condition to fight or I'd have taught him better manners."

"He's a rough piece," with a disparaging shake of the head. "It'd take a lot to knock him into shape. Try this," and she delved among her stores, and found him an ointment of her own compounding which took some of the soreness out of his bruises.

But black eyes and swollen noses are impertinently obtrusive and disdainful of disguise, and the captain's battle-flags provoked no little jocosity among his men that morning.

"Run up against su'then, cap'n?" asked John Hamon the engineer, who was one of the few who sided with him.

"Yes, against a drunken fist in the dark. When it's sober I'm going to give it a lesson in manners."

"Drunken fisses is hard to teach. You'll have your hands full, cap'n."

It seemed an unusually long morning, but dinner-time came at last and he hastened across to the farm, eager for the first sight of the sweet shy face hiding in the big sun-bonnet.

Quite contrary to his expectations Nance came hurrying to meet him. She had evidently been on the watch for him. Still more to his surprise, her face, instead of that look of shy reserve which he had been prepared for, was full of anxious questioning. The large dark eyes were full of something he had never seen in them before.

"Why—Nance—dear! What is the matter?" he asked quickly.

"Did you meet Tom again last night? Oh," at nearer sight of his bruised face, "you did, you did!"

"Yes, dear, I did. Or rather he met me—as you see."

"Did you fight with him?" she panted.

"He was too drunk to fight. He ran at me and gave me this, and my first inclination was to give him a sound thrashing. Then I saw it would be no good, in the condition he was in, so I just kept him at arm's length till he tired of it. He went off at last, and I was so afraid he might tumble off the Coupée that I followed him, and he hurled rocks at me whenever he came to a stand. But he got across all right, and I went back and went to bed. Now, what's all the trouble about?"

"He never came home," she jerked, with a catch in her voice which thought only of Tom had never put there.

"Never came home?"

"And they're all out looking for him."

"I wonder if he went back to Peter Mauger's.... If he tried to cross that Coupée again—in the condition he was in—"

"He didn't go back to Peter's. Julie went there first of all to ask."

"Good Lord, what can have become of him?"

The answer came unexpectedly round the corner of the house—Julie Hamon, in a state of utmost dishevelment and agitation, which turned instantly to venomous fury at the sight of Gard and Nance.

Her black hair seemed all a-bristle. Her black eyes flamed. Her dark face worked like a quicksand. Her skirts were wet to the waist. Her jacket was open at the top, as though she had wrenched at it in a fit of choking. Her strong bare throat throbbed convulsively. Her hands, half closed at her side, looked as though they wanted something to claw.

"Did you do it?" she cried hoarsely, stalking up to Gard.

"Do what?"

"Kill him."

"Tom?... You don't mean to say—"

"You ought to know. He's there in the school-house, broken to a jelly and his head staved in. And they say it's you he fought with last night. The marks of it are on your face"—her voice rose to a scream—"Murderer! Murderer! Murderer!"

"You wicked—thing!" cried Nance, pale to the lips.

"You—you—you!" foamed Julie. "You're as bad as he is. Because my man tried to save you from that—murderer—"

"Oh, you—wicked!—You're crazy," cried Nance, rushing at her as though to make an end of her.

And Julie, mad with the strain of the night's anxieties and their abrupt and terrible ending, uncurled her claws and struck at her with a snarl—tore off her sun-bonnet, and would have ripped up her face, if Gard had not flung his arms round her from the back and dragged her screaming and kicking towards her own door.

Mrs. Hamon had come running out at sound of the fray. Gard whirled the mad woman into her own house and Mrs. Hamon followed her and closed the door.

Gard turned to look for Nance.

She was nervously trying to tie on her sun-bonnet by one string.

"Nance, dear," he said, "you don't believe I had anything to do with this?"

"Oh no, no! I'm sure you hadn't. But—"

"But?" he asked, looking down into the pale face and bright anxious eyes.

"Oh, they may say you did it. They will think it. They are sure to think it, and they are so—"

"Don't trouble about it, dear. I know no more about it than you do, and they cannot get beyond that. Promise me you won't let it trouble you."

"Oh, I will try. But—"

"Have no fears on my account, Nance. I will go at once and tell them all I know about it."

He pressed her hands reassuringly, and she went into the house with downcast head and a face full of forebodings, and he set off at once for Sark.

CHAPTER XVII

HOW TOM WENT TO SCHOOL FOR THE LAST TIME

Mrs. Tom had had a troubled night. Anxiety at her husband's continued absence had in due time given way to anger, and anger in its turn to anxiety again.

In a state of mind compounded of these wearing emotions, she had set out in the early morning to find out what had become of him; if he was sleeping off a drunken debauch at Peter Mauger's, to give them both a vigorous piece of her mind; if he was not there, to find out where he was; in any case to vent on some one the pent-up feelings of the night.

Vigorous hammering on Peter Mauger's door produced first his old housekeeper, and presently himself, heavy-eyed, dull-witted, and in flagrant dishabille, since Mrs. Guille had but a moment ago shaken him out of the sleep of those who drink not wisely over-night, with the information that a crazy woman wanted him at the door.

"Where's Tom?" demanded Julie, ready to empty the vials of her wrath on the delinquent as soon as he was produced.

But Peter's manner at once dissipated that expectation.

"Tom?" he said vaguely, and gazed at her with a bovine stupidity that jarred her strained nerves like a blow.

"Yes, Tom—my husband, fool! Where is he?" she asked sharply.

"Where is he?" scratching his tousled head to quicken his wits. "I d'n know."

"You don't know? What did you do with him last night, you drunken fool?"—by this time the neighbours had come out to learn the news.

Peter gaped at her in astonishment, his muddled wits and aching head beginning dimly to realize that something was wrong.

"Tom left here ... last night ... t'go home," he nodded emphatically.

"Well, he never got home," snapped Julie. "And you'd best get your clothes on and help me find him. You were both as drunk as pigs, I suppose. If he's lying dead in a ditch it's you that'll have the blame."

"Aw now, Julie!"

"Don't Julie me, you fool! Get dressed and do something."

"I'll come. You wait," and he went inside, and put his head into a basin of water, and threw on his clothes, and came out presently looking anxious and disturbed now that his sluggish brain had begun to work.

"Where you been looking?" he asked.

"Nowhere. I expected to find him here."

"We had a glass or two and then he started off home. He could walk all right.... Did you.... You didn't see anything wrong ... anything ... at the Coupée?" he asked, with a quick anxious look at her.

"No, I didn't. What do you mean? Oh, mon Dieu!" and she started down the road at a run, with Peter lumbering after her and the neighbours in a buzzing tail behind.

The cold douche had cooled Peter's hot head, the running quickened his blood and his thoughts, a sudden grim fear braced his brain to quite unusual activity.

As he ran he recalled the events of the night before; their meeting with Gard and Nance; Tom's scurrilous insults.

If Tom and Gard had met again—Gard would be sure to see Nance home. Had he met Tom on his way back? And if so—if so—and ill had come to Tom—why, Gard might get the blame. And—and—in short, though by zig-zag jerks as he ran—if Gard were out of the way for good and all, Nance's thoughts might turn to one nearer home. He would be sorry if ill had come to Tom, of course. But if Gard could be got rid of he would be most uncommonly glad.

And as he panted after Julie, head down with the burden of much thinking, just before he reached the sunk way to the Coupée, his eye lighted on something in the road that caused him to stop and bend—a button with a scrap of blue cloth attached. He picked it up hastily and put it in his pocket. On a white stone just by it there were some red-brown spots. He pushed it with his foot to the side of the road and was down into the cutting before the heavy-footed neighbours came up.

Julie was ranging up and down the narrow pathway, searching the depths with a face like a hawk, hanging on to the rough sides of the pinnacles, and bending over in a way that elicited warning cries from the others as they came streaming down.

But keenest search of the western slope revealed nothing amid its tangle of gorse and blackberry bushes, and the eastern cliff fell so sheer, and had so many projecting lumps and underfalls, that it was impossible to see close in to the foot.

And then one, nimbler witted than the rest, climbed out along the common above the northern cliff, whereby, when he had come to the great slope, he took the Coupée cliff in flank, and could spy along its base.

And suddenly he stopped, and stiffened like a pointer sighting his bird, peered intently for a moment, and gave tongue.

The chase was ended. That they had sought, and feared to find, was found.

They came hurrying up, and clustered like cormorants on the slope, Julie among them, her face grim and livid in its black setting, her eyes blazing fiercely.

The finder pointed it out. They all saw it—a huddled black heap close in under the cliff.

Elevated by his discovery, the finder maintained his reputation by doing the only thing that could be done. He left them talking and sped away across the downs, across the fields, towards Creux harbour.

He might, if he had known it, have found a boat nearer at hand, Rouge Terrier way or in Brenière Bay. But he was a Sark man, and a farmer at that, and knew little and cared less, of the habits of Little Sark.

And the rest, falling to his idea, streamed after him, for that which lay under the cliff could only be gotten out by boat.

So to the Creux, panting the news as he went. And there, willing hands dragged a boat rasping down the shingle, and lusty arms, four men rowing and one astern sculling and steering at the same time, sent her bounding over the water as though it were life she sought, not death. For, though no man among them had any smallest hope of finding life in that which lay under the cliff, yet must they strain every muscle, till the labouring boat seemed to share their anxiety to get there and learn the worst.

So, out past the Lâches, with the tide boiling round the point; past Derrible, with its yawning black mouths; past Dixcart with its patch of sand; under the grim bastions of the Cagnon; the clean grey cliffs and green downs above, all smiling in the morning sun; the clear green water creaming among the black boulders, hissing among their girdles of tawny sea-weeds, cascading merrily down their rifted sides; round the Convanche corner, so deftly close that the beauty of the water cave is bared to them, if they had eye or thought for anything but that which lies under the cliff in Coupée Bay. And not a word said all the way—not one word. Jokes and laughter go with the boat as a rule, and high-pitched nasal patois talk; but here—not a word.

The prow runs grating up the shingle, the heavy feet grind through it all in a line, for none of them has any desire to be first. Together they bend over that which had been Tom Hamon, and their faces are grim and hard as the rocks about them. Not that they are indifferent, but that any show of feeling would be looked upon as a sign of weakness.

Under such circumstances men at times give vent to jocularities which sound coarse and shocking. But they are not meant so—simply the protest of the rough spirit at being thought capable of such unmanly weakness as feeling.

But these men were elementally silent. One look had shown them there was nothing to be done but that which they had come to do—to carry what they had found back to the waiting crowd at the Creux.

They had none of them cared much for this man. He was not a man to make close friends. But death had given him a new dignity among them, and the rough hands lifted him, and bore him to the boat as tenderly as though a jar or a stumble might add to his pains.

And so, but with slower strokes now, as though that slight additional burden, that single passenger, weighed them to the water's edge, they crawl slowly back the way they came, logged, not with water, but with the presence of death.

The narrow beach between the tawny headlands is black with people. Up above, on the edge of the cliff, another crowd peers curiously down.

The Sénéchal is there at the water's edge, Philip Guille of La Ville, and the Greffier, William Robert, who is also the schoolmaster, and Thomas Le Masurier the Prévôt, and Elie Guille the Constable, and Dr. Stradling from Dixcart, and the dark-faced, fierce-eyed woman who cannot keep still, but ranges to and fro in the lip of the tide, and whom they all know now as the wife—the Frenchwoman, though some of them have never seen her before.

A buzz runs round as the boat comes slowly past the point of the Lâches. The woman stops her caged-beast walk and stands gazing fiercely at it, as if she would tear its secret out of it before it touched the shore.

The watchers on the cliff have the advantage. Something like a thrill runs through them, something between a sigh and a groan breaks from them.

The woman wades out to meet the boat. She sees and screams, and chokes. The wives on the beach groan in sympathy.

The body is lifted carefully out and laid on the cool grey stones, and the woman stands looking at it as a tiger may look at her slaughtered mate.

"Stand back! Stand back!" cries the Sénéchal to the thronging crowd; and to the Constable, "Keep them back, you, Elie Guille!" to which Elie Guille growls, "Par madé, but that's not easy, see you!"

The Doctor straightens up from his brief examination, and says a word to the Sénéchal, and to the men about him.

A rough stretcher is made out of a couple of oars and a sail, and the sombre procession passes through the gloomy old tunnel into the Creux Road, and wends its way up to the school-house for proper inquiry to be made as to how Tom Hamon came by his death.

And close behind the stretcher walks the dark-faced woman, with her eyes like coals of fire, and her dress dragged open as though to stop her from choking.

"Mon Dieu! Mon Dieu! Mon Dieu! Mon Dieu!" she says in perpetual iteration, through her clenched teeth. But to look at her face and eyes you might think it was rather the devil she was calling on.

For, ungracious as their lives had been in many respects, yet this violent breaking of the yoke has left the survivor sore and wounded, and furious to vent her rage on whom at present she knows not.

She is not allowed inside the school-house—hastily cleared of its usual occupants, who dodge about among the crowd outside, enjoying the unlooked-for holiday with gusto in spite of its gruesome origin— and so she prowls about outside, and the neighbours talk and she hears this, that, and the other, and presently, with bitter, black face and rage in her heart, she goes off home to find out Stephen Gard if she can, and accuse him to his face of the murder of her husband.

CHAPTER XVIII

HOW PETER'S DIPLOMACY CAME TO NOUGHT

Peter Mauger had kept himself carefully beyond the range of Julie's wild black eyes. In the state she was in there was no knowing what she might do or say. And the words even of a mad woman sometimes stick like burrs. He began to breathe more freely when she whirled away home.

The Sénéchal and Constable came out of the school-house at last with very grave faces.

"The Doctor says his head was staved in with the blows of some round blunt thing like a mallet," said the Sénéchal to the gaping crowd, "and we must hold a proper inquiry. Any of you who saw Tom Hamon last night will be here at two o'clock to tell us all you know. Tell any others who know anything about it that they must be here too," and he went back into the school-house, and the buzzing crowd dispersed, with plenty to buzz about now in truth.

Peter Mauger went thoughtfully home. He had had no breakfast, and was feeling the need of it, and he had something in his mind that he wanted to think out.

And as he ate he thought, slowly and ruminatingly, and with many pauses, when his jaws stopped working to give his mind freer play, but still very much to the purpose, and as soon as he had done he set out to put his project into execution.

Just beyond the Coupée he met Gard hurrying towards Sark, and the state of Gard's nose and eye, and his torn coat, caught his eye at once.

"What's this about Tom Hamon?" asked Gard hastily.

"He's dead."

"His wife has just told me so. But how did it happen?"

"They're going to find out at school-house at two o'clock. Any that saw him last night are to be there. You'd better be there."

"I'm going now."

"All right," said Peter, and went on his way into Little Sark.

His way took him to La Closerie. But he was not anxious to meet Mrs. Tom, so he hung about behind the hedges till Nance happened to come out of the house, and then he whistled softly and beckoned to her to come to him.

Her face was very pale and troubled, and he saw she had been crying.

"I want to speak to you," he said.

"What is it?"

"Come round here. It's important."

"What is it?" she asked wearily again, when she had joined him behind the green dyke.

"It's this, Nance. You—you know I want you. I've always wanted you—"

"Oh—don't!" she cried, with protesting hand. "This is no time. Peter Mauger, for—"

"Wait a bit! Here's how it is. Doctor says Tom was killed by some one beating his head in with a hammer or something of the kind. Now who beat his head in? Who would be most likely to beat his head in? Not me, for we were mates. Some one that hated him. Some one that he was always quarrelling with—" Her face had grown so white that there was no colour even in the trembling lips. She stared at him with terrified eyes.

"You know who I mean," he said. "If it wasn't him that did it I don't know who it was."

"It wasn't," she jerked vehemently.

"You'd wish so, of course. But—Look here!—I'm pretty sure they met again last night after—"

"Yes, they met, and Tom tried to fight him—"

"Ah—then!"

"And he's gone up at once, as soon as he heard that Tom was found, to tell them all about it."

"Aw!"—decidedly crestfallen at the wind being taken out of his sails in this fashion. "I—I thought—maybe I could help him—"

"Oh you did, did you?"—plucking up heart at sight of his discomfiture. "And how were you going to help him?"

"If he's gone to make a clean breast of it it's all up, of course. If he'd kept it to himself—"

"He might have run away, you mean?"

"Safest for him, maybe. Up above Coupée there's a stone with blood on it. And I picked up this beside it," and he hauled out the button and the bit of blue cloth he had found. "I thought, maybe if he knew about these he might think it safest to go."

"Then every one would have the right to say he'd done it, and he didn't. He knew no more about it than you did."

"I didn't know anything about it."

"Well, neither did he, and he's not the kind to run away."

"Aw, well—I done my best. You'll remember that, Nance. You know what the Sark men are. He'd be safest away. You tell him I say so," and he pouched his discounted piece of evidence and turned and went, leaving Nance with a heavy heart.

For, as Peter said, she knew what the Sark men were—a law unto themselves, and slow to move out of the deep-cut grooves of the past, but, once stirred to boiling point, capable of going to any lengths without consideration of consequences.

And therein lay Gard's peril.

CHAPTER XIX

HOW THE SARK MEN FELT ABOUT IT

Every soul in the Island that could by any means get there, was in or outside the school-house, mostly outside, long before the clock struck two. Never in their lives had they hurried thither like that before.

A barricade of forms had been made across the room. Within it, at the school-master's table, sat the Sénéchal, Philip Guille, and the Doctor, and old Mr. Cachemaille, the Vicar, ageing rapidly since the tragic death of his good friend, the late Seigneur; beside them stood the Prévôt and the Greffier, behind them lay the body of Tom Hamon covered with a sheet.

It was a perfect day, with a cloudless blue sky and blazing sun, and all the windows were opened wide. Those inside dripped with perspiration, but felt cold chills below their blue guernseys each time they looked at that stark figure with the upturned feet beneath the cold white sheet.

Outside the barricade stood Elie Guille, the Constable, and his understudy Abraham Baker, the Vingténier, to keep order and call the witnesses.

The Seigneur, Mr. Le Pelley, was away or he would undoubtedly have been there too. In his absence the Sénéchal conducted the proceedings.

In the front row of school-desks, scored with the deep-cut initials of generations of Sark boys, sat the dead man's widow, tense and quivering, her eyes consuming fires in deep black wells, her face livid, her hands clenched still as though waiting for something to rend.

More than one of the men who sat beside her at the desk found, with a grim smile, his own name looking up at him out of the maltreated board. And one nudged his neighbour and pointed to the name of Tom Hamon, cut deeper than any of the others and with the N upside down.

Very briefly the Sénéchal stated that they were there to find out, if they could, how Tom Hamon came by his death, and added very gravely, in a deep silence, that after a most careful examination of the body the Doctor was of opinion that death had been caused, not by the fall from the Coupée, which accounted for the dreadful bruises, but by violent blows on the head with a hammer or some sueh thing prior to the fall. They wanted to find out all about it.

The Doctor stood up and confirmed what the Sénéchal had said, went somewhat more into detail to substantiate his opinion, and ended by saying, "The head, as it happens, is less bruised than any other part of the body, except on the crown, and that is practically beaten in, and not, I am prepared to swear, by a fall. These wounds were the immediate cause of death, and they were made before he fell down the rocks. Besides, he went down feet first. The abrasions on the legs and thighs prove that beyond a doubt. Then again, the base of the skull is not fractured, as it most certainly would have been if he had fallen on his head. Death was undoubtedly the result of those wounds in the head. It is impossible for me to say for certain with what kind of weapon they were made, but it was probably something round and blunt."

"Now," said the Sénéchal, when the Doctor had finished, and the hum and the growl which followed had died down again, "will any of you who know anything about this matter come forward and tell us all you know?"

Stephen Gard stood up at once and all eyes settled on him. Then Peter Mauger was pushed along from the back, with friendly thumps and growling injunctions to speak up. But the looks bestowed on Gard were of quite a different quality from those given to Peter, and the men at the table could not but notice it.

"We will take Peter Mauger first. Let him be sworn," said the Sénéchal, and Gard sat down.

The Greffier swore Peter in the old Island fashion—"Vous jurez par la foi que vous devez à Dieu que vous direz la vérité, et rien que la vérité, et tous ce que vous connaissez dans cette cause, et que Dieu vous soit en aide! (You swear by the faith which you owe to God that you will tell the truth, and only the truth, and all that you know concerning this case, and so help you God!)"

Peter put up his right hand and swore so to do.

"Now tell us all you know," said the Sénéchal.

And Peter ramblingly told how he and Tom had been drinking together the night before, and how Tom had started off home and he had gone to bed.

"Were you both drunk?"

"Well—"

"Very well, you were. Did you think it right to let your friend go off in that condition when he had to cross the Coupée?"

"I've seen him worse, many times, and no harm come to him."

"Well, get on!"

He told how Mrs. Tom woke him up in the morning, and how they had all gone in search of the missing man.

"Was it you that found him?"

"No, it was Charles Guille of Clos Bourel. But I found something too."

"What was it?"

"This"—and from under his coat he drew out carefully the white stone with its red-brown spots, and from his pocket the button and the scrap of blue cloth. And those at the back stood up, with much noise, to see.

The men at the table looked at these scraps of possible evidence with interest, as they were placed before them.

"Where did you find these things?"

"Between Plaisance and the Coupée."

"What do you make of them?"

"Seemed to me those red spots might be blood. The other's a button torn off some one's coat."

"Have you any idea whose blood and whose coat?"

"The blood I don't know. The button, I believe, is off Mr. Gard's coat,"—at which another growl and hum went round.

"And you know nothing more about the matter?"

"That's all I know."

"Very well. Sit down. Mr. Gard!" and Gard pushed his way among unyielding legs and shoulders, and stood before the grave-faced men at the table.

They all knew him and had all come to esteem what they knew of him. They knew also of his difficulties with his men, and that there was a certain feeling against him in some quarters. Not one of them thought it likely he had done this dreadful thing. But—there was no knowing to what lengths even a decent man might go in anger. All their brows pinched a little at sight of his torn coat and missing button.

He was duly sworn, and the Sénéchal bade him tell all he knew of the matter.

"That button is mine," he said quietly, holding out the lapel of his coat for all to see. "If there is blood on that stone it is mine also"—at which a growling laugh of derision went round the spectators.

Gard flushed at this unmistakable sign of hostility. The Sénéchal threatened to turn them all out if anything of the kind happened again, and Gard proceeded to recount in minutest detail the happenings of the previous night—so far as they concerned himself and Tom Hamon.

"What were you doing down at the Coupée at that time of night?" asked the Sénéchal.

"I had been having a smoke and was just about to turn in when I met Miss Hamon hurrying to the Doctor's for some medicine. I asked her permission to accompany her, and then took her home to Little Sark. It was when I was coming back that I met Tom Hamon."

"Yes, little Nance came to me about half-past ten," said the Doctor, "I remember I asked her if she was not afraid to go all that way home alone, and she said she had a friend with her."

"Was there any specially bad feeling between you and Tom Hamon?"

"There had always been bad feeling, but any one who knows anything about it knows that it was not of my making."

"Will you explain it to us?"

"If you say I must. One does not like to say ill things of the dead."

"We want to get to the bottom of this matter, Mr. Gard. Tell us all you know that will help us."

"Very well, sir, but I am sorry to have to go into that. It all began through Tom's bad treatment of his stepmother and step-sister and brother when I lived at La Closerie. I took sides with them and tried to bring him to better manners. We rarely met without his flinging some insult after me. They were generally in the patois, but I knew them to be insults by his manner and by the way they were greeted by those who did understand."

"Had you met last night before you met near the Coupée?"

"We passed Tom by La Vauroque as we came from the Doctor's. He shouted something after us, but I did not understand it."

"You don't know what it was that he said?" an unfortunate question on the part of the Sénéchal, and quite unintentionally so on his part. It necessitated the introduction of matters Gard would fain have kept out of the enquiry.

"Well," he said, with visible reluctance, "I learned afterwards, and by accident, something of what he said or meant."

"How was that, and what was it?"

"Is it necessary to go into that? Won't it do if I say it was a very gross insult?"

The three at the table conferred for a moment. Then the Sénéchal said very kindly, "I perceive we are getting on to somewhat delicate ground, Mr. Gard, but, for your own sake. I would suggest that no occasion should be given to any to say that you are hiding anything from the court."

"Very well, sir, I have nothing whatever to hide, and I have still less to be ashamed of. I found Miss Hamon was weeping bitterly at what her brother had said, and I tried to get her to tell me what it was, but she would not. I said I knew it was something against me, but I hoped by this time she had learned to know and trust me. I told her her sobs cut me to the heart and that I would give my life to save her from trouble. In a word, I told her I loved her, and in the excitement of the moment she dropped a word or two that gave me an inkling of what Tom had said. It was casting dirt at both her and myself. Then, as I came home, I met Tom as I have told you."

The Sénéchal considered the matter for a moment. He did not for one moment believe that Gard had had any hand in the killing of Tom Hamon. But he could not but perceive the hostile feeling that was abroad, and his desire was, if possible, to allay it.

"It is, I should think," he said gravely, "past any man's believing that, after asking Tom's sister to marry you, you should go straight away and kill Tom, even in the hottest of hot blood, though men at such times do not always know what they are doing. But you, from what I have seen and heard of you, are not such a man. I am going to ask you one question in the hope that your answer may have the effect of setting you right with all who hear it. Before God—had you any hand in the death of this man?—have you any further knowledge of the matter whatever?"

"Before God," said Gard solemnly, his uplifted right hand as steady as a rock, "I had no hand in his death. I know nothing more whatever about the matter."

"I believe you," said the Sénéchal.

"And I," said the Doctor.

"And I," said the Vicar gravely, and with much emotion.

But from the spectators there rose a dissentient murmur which caused the Vicar to survey his unruly flock with mild amazement and disapproval—much as the shepherd might if his sheep had suddenly shed their fleeces and become wolves.

And Julie Hamon sprang to her feet with blazing eyes, pointed a shaking hand at Gard, and screamed:

"Murderer! Murderer! Murderer!"

CHAPTER XX

HOW SARK CRAVED BLOOD FOR BLOOD

Stephen Gard walked slowly down the road towards Plaisance in the lowest of spirits.

This strange people amongst whom he had fallen, possessed, in pre-eminent degree, what in these later times is known as the defects of its qualities.

Black sheep there were, of course, as there are in every community, who seemed all defects and possessed of no redeeming qualities whatever. But, taken as a whole, the men of Sark were simple, honest according to their lights, brave and hardy, very tenacious of their own ideas and their island rights, somewhat stubborn and easier to lead than to drive, and withal red-blooded, as the result of their ancestry, and given to a large despite of foreigners, in which category were included all unfortunates born outside the rugged walls of Sark.

He had done his best among them, both for their own interests and those of the mines, but no striving would ever make him other than a foreigner; and in the depression of spirit consequent on the trying experiences of the day, he gloomily pondered the idea of giving up his post and finding a more congenial atmosphere elsewhere.

Still, he was a Cornishman, and dour to beat. And, if he had incurred unreasonable dislike, he had also lighted on the virgin lode of Nance's love and trust, and that, he said to himself with a glow of gratitude, outweighed all else.

He had left the school-house at once when he had given his evidence, and had heard no more of what had taken place there. The bystanders had let him pass without any open opposition, but their faces had been hard and unsympathetic, and he recognized that life among them would be anything but a sunny road for some time to come.

If the people at Plaisance had told him to clear out and find another lodging he would not have been in the least surprised. But they had no such thought. In common with all who really got to know him, they had come to esteem and like him, and they had no reason to believe that he had had anything to do with Tom Hamon's death.

He had pondered these matters wearily till bed-time, and he turned in at last sick of himself, and Sark, and things generally. But his brain would not sleep, and the longer he lay and the more he tossed and turned, the wearier he grew.

Sleep seemed so impossible that he was half inclined to get up and dress and go out. The cool night air and the freshness of the dawn would be better than this sleepless unresting. Suddenly there came a sharp little tap on his window.

A bird, he thought, or a bat.

The tap came again—sharp and imperative.

He got up quietly and went to the window. The night was still dark. As he peered into it a hand came up again and tapped once more and he opened the window.

"Mr. Gard!"—in a sharp whisper.

"Nance! What is it, dear? Anything wrong?"

"I want you—quick."

"One minute!" and he hastily threw on his things and joined her outside.

"What is it, Nance?" he asked anxiously, wondering what new complication had arisen.

"I'll tell you as we go. Come!" and they were speeding noiselessly down the road to the Coupée.

There she took his hand, as once before, to lead him safely across, and her hand, he perceived, was trembling violently.

They were half way along the narrow path when the hollow way in front leading up into Little Sark resounded suddenly with the tramp of heavy feet.

"Mon Dieu! Mon Dieu!" panted Nance, and he could feel her turn and look round like a hunted animal.

"Quick!" she whispered. "Behind here! and oh, grip tight!" and she knelt and crawled on hands and knees round the base of the nearest pinnacle.

In those days the pinnacles which buttress the Coupée were considerably higher and bulkier than they are now, and along their rugged flanks the adventurous or sorely-pressed might find precarious footing. But it was a nerve-racking experience even in the day-time when the eye could guide the foot. Now, in the ebon-black night, it was past thinking of.

Dazed by the suddenness and strangeness of the whole matter, and without an inkling of what it all meant, Gard clung like a fly to the bare rock and tried his hardest not to think of the sheer three hundred feet that lay between him and the black beach below.

In grim and menacing silence, save for the crunch of their heavy feet on the crumbling pathway, the men went past, a dozen or more, as it seemed to Gard. When the sound of them had died in the hollow on the Sark side, Nance whispered, "Quick now! quick!"

They crawled back into the roadway, and she took his hand in hers again which shook more than ever, and they sped away into Little Sark.

"Now tell me, Nance. What is it all about?" he panted, as she nipped through an opening in a green bank and led the way towards the eastern cliffs over by the Pot.

"Oh—it's you they want," she gasped, and he stopped instantly and stood, as though he would turn and go back.

"It is no use," she jerked emphatically, between breaths, and dragged impatiently at his arm. "You don't know our Sark men.... They do things first and are sorry after.... Bernel heard them planning it all.... The men from Sark were to meet these ones, and then—"

"But," he said angrily, "running away looks like—"

"No, no! Not here.... And it is only for a time. The truth will come out, but it would be too late if they had got you."

"What would they have done with me?"

"Oh—terrible things. They are madmen when they are angry."

He had yielded to her will, and they were speeding swiftly along the downs. The path was quite invisible to him. He tripped and stumbled at times on tangled roots of gorse and bracken, but she kept on swiftly and unerringly, as though the night were light about her.

"Where are you taking me?" he asked, as they crept past the miners' cottages on the cliff above Rouge Terrier.

"To Brenière.... To L'Etat.... Bernel went on to find a boat."

And presently they were out on the bald cliff-head, and slipping and sliding down it till they came to the ledge, below which Brenière spreads out on the water like a giant's hand.

Between her panting breaths Nance whistled a low soft note like the pipe of a sea-bird. A like sound came softly up from below, and slipping and stumbling again, they were on the beach among mighty boulders girt with dripping sea-weed.

Another low pipe out of the darkness, and they had found the boat and tumbled into it, wet and bruised, and breathless.

"Dieu merci!" said Bernel, and pulled lustily out to sea.

The swirl of the tide caught them as they cleared Brenière Point, and Gard crawled forward to take an oar. Nance did the same, and so set Bernel free to scull and steer, the arrangement which dire experience has taught the Sark men as best adapted to their rock-strewn waters and racing currents.

Gard's mind was in a tumult of revolt, but he sensibly drove his feelings through his muscles to the blade of his oar, and said nothing. Nance and Bernel were not likely to have gone to these lengths without what seemed to them sufficient reason.

And he remembered Nance's trembling arm on the Coupée, and her agonies of fear on his account, and so came by degrees to a certain acceptance of their view of matters, and therewith a feeling of gratitude for their labours and risks on his behalf. For he did not doubt that, should the self-appointed administrators of justice learn who had baulked them of their prey, they would wreak upon them some of the vengeance they had intended for himself.

He saw that it was no light matter these two had undertaken, and as he thought it over, and told the black welter under his oar what he thought of these wild and hot-headed Sark men, his gratitude grew.

The thin orange sickle of a moon rose at last, high by reason of the mists banked thick along the horizon, and afforded them a welcome glimmer of light—barely a glimmer indeed, rather a mere thinning of the clinging darkness, but enough for Bernel's tutored eye.

He took them in a cautious circuit outside the Quette d'Amont, the eastern sentinel of L'Etat, and so, with shipped oars, by means of his single scull astern, brought them deftly to the riven black ledges round the corner on the south side.

It is a precarious landing at best, and the after scramble up the crumbling slope calls for caution even in the light of day. In that misleading darkness, clinging with his hands and climbing on the sides of his feet, and starting at startled feathered things that squawked and fluttered from under his groping hands and feet, Gard found it no easy matter to follow Nance, though she carried a great bundle and waited for him every now and again. When he looked down next day upon the way they had come he marvelled that they had ever reached the top in safety.

"Wait here!" she said at last, when they had attained a somewhat level place, and before he had breath for a word she was away down again.

She was back presently with another bundle, and he started when she thrust into his hands a long gun, and bade him pick up the first bundle and follow her. The feel of the gun brought home to him, as nothing else could have done, her and Bernel's views of possible contingencies.

He followed her stumblingly along the rough crown of the ridge, till she dipped down a rather smoother slope and came to a stand before what seemed to him a heap of huge stones.

"There is shelter in here," she said. "And these things are for your comfort. We will bring you more to eat in a day or two—"

"Nance, dear," he said, dropping the gun and the bundle, and laying his hand on her slim shoulder. "I have become a sore burden to you—"

"Oh no, no!" she said hastily. "You would have done as much for me, and it is because—"

"For you, dear? I would give my life for you, Nance, and here it is you who are doing everything, and running all these risks for me."

"It is because I know they are in the wrong. It may be only a day or two, and they will thank me when they find out their mistake."

"Well, I thank you and Bernel with my whole heart. Please God I may some time be able to repay you!"

"If you are safe, that is all we want. Now I must go. We must get back before they miss us."

"God keep you, dear!" and he bent and kissed her, and as before she kissed him back with the frankness of a child.

He was about to follow her when she turned to go, but she said imperatively, "Stop here, or you may lose yourself in the dark. And in the day-time do not walk on the ridge or they may see you—"

"And the gun? What is that for?"

"If they should come here after you, you will keep them off with it," she said, with a spurt of the true Island spirit. "It is your life they seek, and they are in the wrong. But no one ever comes here, and you will not need it. Now, good-bye! And God have you in His keeping!"

"And you, dearest—and all yours!"—and she was gone like a flitting shadow.

And while he still stood peering into the darkness into which she had merged, she suddenly materialized again and was by his side.

"I forgot. Bernel told me to tell you it throws a little high. But I hope you won't need it. And there is fresh water among the rocks at the south end there."

He caught her to him again, and kissed her ardently, and then she was gone.

He strained his ears, fearful of hearing her slip or fall in the darkness, but she went without displacing a stone, and he was alone with the sickly moon, and the sombre sky, and the voices of the rising tide along the grim black ledges of his sanctuary.

CHAPTER XXI

HOW LOVE TOOK LOVE TO SANCTUARY

It all seemed monstrous strange to him, now that he had time to think of the actual fact apart from the difficulties of its accomplishment.

An hour ago he was lying in his bed at Plaisance, in low enough spirits, indeed, at the outlook before him, but his gloomiest thought had never plumbed depths such as this.

He wondered briefly if so extreme a step had been really necessary.

And then he heard again the purposeful tramp of those heavy feet on the Coupée, and fathomed again the menace of them.

And he felt Nance's guiding hand trembling violently in his once more, and he said to himself that she and Bernel knew better than he how the land lay, and that he could not have done other than he had done.

Then he became aware that the dew was drenching him, and so he bent and groped in the dark for the shelter Nance had spoken of.

The strip of moon had paled as it rose, the huge white stones glimmered faintly in it, and a darker patch below showed him where the entrance must be. He crept into the darker patch on his hands and knees, bumping his head violently, but once inside found room to sit upright. Snaking out again, he laid hold of the two bundles and the gun, and dragged them into shelter.

What the bundles contained he could not tell in the dark, but one felt like a thick woollen cloak, and the other like a blanket, and among their contents he felt a loaf of bread, and a bottle and a powder-flask. So he rolled himself up in the blanket and the cloak, and lay wondering at the strange case in which he found himself, and so at last fell asleep.

He woke into a dapple of light and shade which filled his wandering wits with wonder, till, with a start, he came to himself and remembered.

The place he was in was something like a stone bee-hive, about eight feet across from side to side, with a rounded sloping roof rising at its highest some four feet from the ground, and the great blocks of which it was built fitted so ill in places that the sun shot the darkness through and through with innumerable little white arrows of light. The dark opening of the night was now a glowing invitation to the day. He shook off his wraps and crawled out into the open.

And what an open!

He drew deep breaths of delight at the magnificence of his outlook—its vastness, its spaciousness, its wholesome amplitude and loneliness. He felt like a new man born solitary into a new world.

The sky, without a cloud, was like a mighty hollowed sapphire, in which blazed the clear white sun; and the vast plain of the sea, sweeping away into infinity, was a still deeper blue, with here and there long swathes of green, and here and there swift-speeding ruffles purple-black.

A brisk easterly breeze set all the face of it a-ripple, and where the dancing wavelets caught the sun it glanced and gleamed like sheets of molten silver.

"A silver sea! A silver sea!" he cried aloud, and into his mind there flashed an incongruous comparison of the bountifulness of Nature's silver with the pitiful grains they hacked out of her rocks with such toil and hardship.

Away to the south across the silver sea the Jersey cliffs shone clear in the sunshine, and on the dimpling plain between, the black Paternosters looked so like the sails of boats heading for Sark that he remembered suddenly that he was in hiding, and dropped to cover alongside the great stones of his shelter.

But careful observation of the square black objects showed him that they did not move, and anyway they were much too far away to see him. So he took courage again, and, full of curiosity concerning his hiding-place, he crept up the southern slope till he reached the ridge of the roof, so to speak, and lay there looking over, entranced with the beauty of the scene before him.

The whole east coast of Sark right up to the Burons, off the Creux, lay basking in the morning light. Dixcart and Derrible held no secrets from him; he looked straight up their shining beaches. Their bold headlands were like giant-fists reaching out along the water towards him. Brenière, the nearest point to his rock, was another mighty grasping hand, but between it and him swept a furious race of tossing, white-capped waves, with here and there black fangs of rock which stuck up through the green waters as though hungering for prey.

He could just see the upper part of the miners' cottages on the cliff above Rouge Terrier, but, beyond these and the ruined mill on Hog's Back, not another sign of man and his toilsome, troublesome little works. But for these, Sark, in its utter loneliness, might have been a new-found island, and he its first discoverer.

Ranging on, his eye rested on the shattered fragments of Little Sark, scattered broadcast over the sea about its most southerly point—bare black pinnacles, ragged ledges, islets, rocklets, reefs, and fangs, every one of which seemed to stir the placid sea to wildest wrath. Elsewhere it danced and dimpled in the sunshine, with only the long slow heave in it to tell of the sleeping giant below, but round each rock, and up the sides of his own huge pyramid, it swept in great green combers shot with bubbling white, and went tumbling back upon itself in rings of boiling foam.

Beyond, he saw the rounded back of Jethou, and just behind it the long line of houses in Guernsey.

He lay long enjoying it all, with the warm sun on his back, and the brisk wind toning his blood, but no view, however wonderful, will satisfy a man's stomach. He had fed the day before mostly on most unsatisfying emotions, and now he began to feel the need of something more solid. So he crept back along the slope to find out what there was for breakfast.

His stores lay about the floor of his resting-place, just as he had turned them out in the night; a couple of long loaves, a good-sized piece of raw bacon, and another of boiled pork which he thought he recognized, some butter in a cloth, a bottle which looked as if it might contain spirits, the powder-flask, and a small linen bag containing bullets, snail-shot, and percussion caps. These, with Bernel's gun and the blanket, and the old woollen cloak, which he recognized as Mr. Hamon's roquelaure, and his pipe, and the tobacco he happened to have in his pouch, constituted, for the time being, his worldly possessions.

He spread his cloak and blanket in the sun to dry and air, and, doubtful whether his rock would supply any further provision or when more might reach him from Sark, he proceeded to make a somewhat restricted meal of bread and cold pork.

The raw bacon suggested something of a problem. To cook it he must have a fire. To have a fire he must have fuel; his tinder-box he always carried, of course, for the new matches had not yet penetrated to Sark. Moreover, to light a fire might be dangerous as liable to attract attention, unless he could do it under cover where no stray gleams could get out.

He pondered these matters as he ate, spinning out his exiguous meal to its uttermost crumb to make it as satisfying as possible.

He saw his way at once to perfecting his cover. All about him where he sat, the grey rock pushed through a thin friable soil like the bones of an ill-buried skeleton. And everywhere in the scanty soil grew thick little rounded cushions, half grass, half moss, varying in size from an apple to a foot-stool, which came out whole at a pluck or a kick. After breakfast he would plug up every hole in his shelter, and pile half-a-dozen sizeable pieces outside with which to close the front door. Then, if he could find anything in the shape of fuel, he saw his way to a dinner of fried bacon, but it would have to be after dark when the smoke would be invisible.

But first he must find out about his water supply.

Down at the south end, Nance had said. That must be over there, on that almost-detached stack of rocks, where the waves seemed to break loudest.

So, after another crawl up to the ridge to make certain that no boats were about—for he had frequently seen them fishing in the neighbourhood of L'Etat—he crept down the flank of his pyramid almost to sea-level to get across to the outer pile.

He had to pick his way with caution across a valley of black rocks, rifted and chasmed by the fury of the waves. He could imagine—or thought he could, but came far short of it—how the great green rollers would thunder through that black gully in the winter storms.

There were great wells lined all round with rich brown sea-weeds, and narrow chasms in whose hidden depths the waters swooked and gurgled like unseen monsters, and whose broken edges, on which he had to step, were like the rough teeth of gigantic saws set up on end alongside one another.

He crawled across these rough serrations and scaled the rifted black wall in front, and came at once on a number of shallow pools of rain-water lying in the hollows of a mighty slab.

But the moment his head rose above the level of the steep black wall his ears were filled with a deafening roaring and rushing, supplemented by most tremendous dull thuddings which shook the stack like the blows of a mighty flail.

From behind a further wall there rose a boiling mist, through which lashed up white jets of spray which slanted over the rocks beyond in a continuous torrent.

He crawled to the further wall and looked over into a deep black gully, some fifteen feet wide and perhaps thirty feet deep, into which, out of a perfectly calm sea, most monstrous waves came roaring and leaping, till the whole chasm was foaming and spuming like an over-boiling milk-pan. In the middle of the chasm, for the further torment of the waters, was jammed a huge black rock, against which the incoming green avalanche dashed itself to fragments and went rocketing into the air. The solid granite at the further end was cleft from summit to base by a tiny rift a foot wide through which the boiling spume poured out to the sea beyond.

But the marvel was where those gigantic waves came from. Save for the dancing wind-ripples and its long, slow internal pulsations, the sea was as smooth as a pond to within twenty yards of the rocks. Then it suddenly seemed to draw itself together, to draw itself down into itself indeed, like a tiger compressing its springs for a leap, and then, with a rush and a roar, it launched itself at the rocks with the weight of the ocean behind it, and hurtled blindly into the chasm where the black rock lay.

It was a most wonderful sight, and Gard sat long watching it, then and later, fascinated always and puzzled by that extraordinary self-compression and sudden upleap of the waters out of an otherwise placid sea.

It was but one more odd expression of Nature's fantastic humour, and the nearest he could come to an explanation of it was that, in the sea bed just there, was some great fault, some huge chasm into which the waters fell and then came leaping out to further torment on the rocks.

It was as he was returning to his own quarters by a somewhat different route across the valley of rocks, that he lighted on another find which contented him greatly.

In one of the saw-toothed chasms he saw a piece of wood sticking up, and climbed along to get it as first contribution to his fire. And when he got to it, down below in the gully, he found jammed the whole side of a boat, flung up there by some high spring tide and trapped before it could escape. Excellent wood for his firing, well tarred and fairly dry. He hauled and pulled till he had it all safely up, and then he carried it, load after load, to his house, and laid it out in the sun to dry still more.

He worked hard all day, keeping a wary outlook for any stray fishermen.

First he culled a great heap of the thin wiry grass which seemed the chief product of his rock, and spread it also to dry for a couch. There was no bracken for bedding, no gorse for firing. The grass would supply the place of the one, the broken boat the other.

Then he made good all the holes in his walls and roof, except one in the latter for the escape of the smoke, and built a solid wall of the tufted cushions round the seaward side of his doorway, as a screen against his light being seen, and as a protection from the south-west wind if it should blow up strong in the night.

He found it very strange to be toiling on these elemental matters, with never a soul to speak to. He felt like a castaway on a desert island, with the additional oddness of knowing himself to be within reach of his kind, yet debarred from any communication with them on pain, possibly, of death.

At times he felt like a condemned criminal, yet knew that he had done no wrong, and that it was only the mistaken justice of a simple people that wanted blood for blood, and was not over-heedful as to whose blood so long as its own sense of justice was satisfied.

But, he kept saying to himself, things might have been worse with him, very much worse, but for Nance and Bernel. And before long, any day, the matter might be cleared up and himself reinstated in the opinion of the Sark men.

Even that would leave much to be desired, but possibly, he thought, if they found they had sorely misjudged him in this matter, they might realize that they had done so in other matters also, and that he had only been striving to do his duty as he saw it.

And then, wherever else his thoughts led him, there was always Nance, and the thought of Nance always set his heart aglow and braced him to patient endurance and hope.

He retraced, again and again, all the ways they had travelled together in these later days, recalled her every word and look, felt again the trembling of her hand—for him—on the Coupée, heard again the tremors of her voice as she urged him to safety. And those sweet ingenuous kisses she had given him! Yes, indeed, he had much to be grateful for, if some things to cavil at, in fortune's dealings.

But, behind all his fair white thought of Nance, was always the black background of the whole circumstances of the case, and the grim fact of Tom Hamon's death, and he pondered this last with knitted brows from every point of view, and strove in vain for a gleam of light on the darkness.

Could the Doctor be mistaken, and was Tom's death the simple result of his fall over the Coupée? The Doctor's pronouncement, however, seemed to leave no loophole of hope there.

If not, then who had killed Tom, and why?

He could think of no one. He could imagine no reason for it.

Tom had been a bully at home, but outside he was on jovial terms with his fellows—except only himself. He had to acknowledge to himself the seeming justice of the popular feeling. If any man in Sark might, with some show of reason, have been suspected of the killing of Tom Hamon, it was himself.

Once, by reason of overmuch groping in the dark, an awful doubt came upon him—was it possible that, in some horrible wandering of the mind, of which he remembered nothing, he had actually done this thing? Done it unconsciously, in some over-boiling of hot blood into the brain, which in its explosion had blotted out every memory of what had passed?

It was a hideous idea, born of over-strain and overmuch groping after non-existent threads in a blind alley.

He tried to get outside himself, and follow Stephen Gard that night and see if that terrible thing could have been possible to him.

But he followed himself from point to point, and from moment to moment, and accounted for himself to himself without any lapse whatever; unless, indeed, his brain had played him false and he had gone out of the house again after going into it, and followed Tom and struck him down.

With what? The Doctor said with some blunt instrument like a hammer. Where could he have obtained it? What had he done with it?

The idea, while it lasted, was horrible. But he shook it off at last and called himself a fool for his pains. He had never harboured thought of murder in his life. He had detested Tom, but he had never gone the length of wishing him dead. The whole idea was absurd.

All these things he thought over as, his first essential labours completed, he lay under the screen of the ridge and watched the sun dropping towards Guernsey in a miracle of eventide glories.

Below him, the long slow seas rocketted along the ragged black base of his rock with mighty roarings and tumultuous bursts of foam, and on the ledges the gulls and cormorants squabbled and shrieked, and took long circling flights without fluttering a wing, to show what gulls could do, or skimmed darkly just above the waves and into them, to show that cormorants were never satisfied. And now and again wild flights of red-billed puffins swept up from the water and settled out of his sight at the eastern end of the rock, and he promised himself to look them up some other day if opportunity offered.

From the constant tumult of the seas about his rock, except just at low water, he saw little fear of being taken by surprise, even if his presence there became known. Twice only in the twenty-four hours did it seem possible for any one to effect a landing there, and at those times he promised himself to be on the alert.

He lay there till the sun had gone, and the pale green and amber, and the crimson and gold of his going had slowly passed from sea and sky, and left them grey and cold; till a single light shone out on Sark, which he knew must be in one of the miners' cottages, and many lights twinkled in Guernsey; till beneath him he could no longer see the sea, but only the white foam fury as it boiled along the rocks. Then he crept away to his burrow, rejoicing in the thought of the companionship of a fire and hot food.

CHAPTER XXII

HOW THE STARS SANG OF HOPE

It took Gard some time to get his fire started, and when it did blaze up, with fine spurts of gas from the tar, and vivid blue and green and red flames from the salted wood, the little stone bee-hive glowed like an oven and presently grew as hot as one. The smoke escaped but slowly through the single hole in the roof, and at last he could stand it no longer, and crept out into the night until his fire should have burned down to a core of red ashes over which he could grill his dinner.

And what a night! He had seen the stars from many parts of the earth and sea, but never, it seemed to him, had he seen such stars as these, so close, so large, so wonderfully clean and bright. And, indeed, glory of the heavens so supreme as that is possible only far away from man, and all the works and habitations of man, and all his feeble efforts at the mitigation of the darkness. Nay, for fullest perception, it may be that it is necessary for a man to be not only alone in the profundity of Nature's night, but to be lifted somewhat out of himself and his natural darkness by extremity of joy, or still more of need.

The milky way was as white as though a mighty brush dipped in glittering star-dust had been drawn across the velvet dome. The larger stars, many of which were old acquaintances and known to him by name, seemed to swing so clear and close that they took on quite a new aspect of friendliness and cheer. The smaller—I write as he thought—a mighty host, an innumerable company quite beyond his ken, still spoke to him in a language that he had never forgotten.

Long ago, when he was quite a little boy, he had come upon a great globe of the heavens, a much-prized curiosity of his old schoolmaster. Upon it appeared all the principal stars linked up into their constellations, the shadowy linking lines forming the figures of the Imaginary Ones associated with them in the minds of the ancients. There, on the varnished round of the globe, ranged the Great and Little Bears, and the Dogs, and the Archer, and the Flying Horse, the Lion, and the Crab, and the Whale, and the Twins, and Perseus and Andromeda, and Cassiopeia. And up there, on the dark inner side of the mighty dome, he seemed to see them all again, and time swung back with him for a moment, and he was a boy once more.

And, gazing up at them all, their steady shine and many-coloured twinklings led him to wonder as to the how and the why of them. From the stars to their Maker was but a natural step, and so he came, simply and naturally, to thought of the greatness of Him who swung these innumerable worlds in their courses, and, from that, to His goodness and justice.

Memories of his mother came surging back upon him, and of all her goodness and all she had taught him. She had had a mighty, simple trust in the goodness of God, and had passed it on to her boy, though his rough contact with the world had overworn it all to some extent.

Still, it was all there, and now it all came back to him through the hopeful twinkling eyes of those innumerable stars.

"Have courage and hope!" they sang; and though all his little world, save those two or three who knew him best, was against him, he stood there with his face turned up to the stars, and believed in his heart that all would yet be well.

And when at last he turned back to things of earth, he found the stars still twinkling in the sea, as though they would not let him go even though he gave up looking at them. They gleamed and glanced in the smooth-rolling waves till the deep seemed sown with phosphorescence, as on that night in Grand Grève; the night Nance came upon him so suddenly in the dark and he went on with her to get Grannie's medicine.

Was it possible that that blessed night, that terrible night, was barely forty-eight hours old? So much had happened since then, such incredible things! It seemed weeks ago. It seemed like a dream; horrid, fantastic, wonderfully sweet.

Within that tiny span of hours he had come to the knowledge of Nance's love for him. Oh those sweet, frank kisses! If he had died last night; if the hot heads in their madness had killed him to balance Tom Hamon's account—still he would have lived: for Nance had kissed him.

And within the half of that short span he had been judged a murderer, had had to flee for his life, and would, without a doubt, have lost it but for Nance.

She had undertaken a mighty risk for him—for him! And she had shown him that she loved him, for she had kissed him with her heart in her lips.

And, grateful as he was for all the rest, it was still the recollection of those sweet kisses that he thought of most.

So "Hope! Hope!" sang the stars, and his heart was high because his conscience was clean and Nance had kissed him.

When at last he crawled into his burrow, his fire was only white ashes, and he would not trouble to relight it.

He broke off a piece of bread, and ate it slowly, and thought of Nance, and promised himself the larger breakfast. Then he rolled himself in his cloak, and slept more soundly than an alderman after a civic feast.

CHAPTER XXIII

HOW NANCE SENT FOOD AND HOPE TO HIM

Next morning, when he crawled out of his burrow, Gard found everything swathed in dense white mist. Upon which he promptly lit his fire, and in due course enjoyed a more satisfying meal than he had eaten since he landed on the rock.

Then he decided to take advantage of the screening mist to explore such parts of his prison-house as were not available to him at other times. So he walked along the ridge, secure from observation since he could not himself see down to the water from it, though the rushings and roarings along the black ledges below never ceased.

Every nook and ledge of the out-cropping rock on the south side of the ridge was occupied by lady gulls in all stages of their maternal duties. From the surprise they expressed at his intrusion, and the way they stuck to their nests, they were evidently quite unused to man and his ways, and it was all he could do to avoid stepping on them and their squawking families as he picked his way along.

He clambered down the eastern slope nearest Sark, and found the ground there covered with a fairly deep soil, and green growths that were strange to him. The soil was perforated with holes which at first he ascribed to rabbits, but when he inserted his hand into one he got such a nip from an unusually strong beak that he changed his mind to puffins, and, standing quite still for a time, he presently saw the members of the colony come creeping out behind their great red bills and scurry off across the water in search of breakfast.

Then the great semi-detached pinnacle below attracted him, and he scrambled down amid the complaints of a great colony of gulls and cormorants but found the tide still too full for him to cross the intervening chasm. Those wonderful great green waves out of a smooth sea came roaring along the sides of the island and met full tilt in the chasm below him, as they leaped exultant from their conflict with the rocks. They hurled themselves against one another in wildest fury, and the foam of their meeting boiled white along the ledges, and dappled all the sea.

As he crawled through the lank wet grass and soft spongy soil, he found himself suddenly confronted with a great barrier of fallen rocks; as though, at some period of its existence, the north end of the island had tapered to a gigantic peak which, in the fulness of its time, had come down with a crash, and now lay like a titanic wall from summit to sea-board. Huge and forbidding, of all shapes and sizes, the mighty fragments barred his course like a menace, and he attacked them warily, drawing himself with infinite caution from one to another; over this one, under this, deftly between these two, lest an unwary weighting should start them on the movement that might grind him to powder.

The fog increased their forbidding aspect tenfold. He could not see a foot before him, and could only worm his way among them, testing each before he trusted it, and finding at times monsters become but mediocre when his hand was on them. More than once he had to rest his hands on cautiously-tried ledges and swing his legs forward and grope with his feet for foothold, and whether the space below was trifling, or whether it ran to incredible depth, he could not tell.

It was a mighty relief to him to come out at last on the other side of the wall, and to find himself on the great north slope which faced Sark, and so was closed to him in clear weather.

The long thin grass grew rankly here, and was beaded with moisture, but he pushed along with an eerie feeling at the wildness of it all.

The mist clung close about him, but had suddenly become luminous. He felt as though he were packed loosely all round with cotton wool on which a strong light was shining. It gave him a feeling of light-headedness. Everything was light about him, and yet he could not see more than a couple of feet before his face. The waves roared hoarsely below him, and once he had unknowingly got so low down that a monstrous white arm, reaching suddenly up out of the depths, seemed about to lay hold on him and drag him back with it into the turmoil.

He was panting and full of mist when at last he climbed the second great rock barrier and rounded the corner towards the south.

And as he sat resting there, the whiff of a westerly breeze tore a long lane in the white shroud, and for a moment he saw, as through a telescope, the houses of Guernsey gleaming in bright sunshine. Then it closed again, and presently began to drift past him in strange whorls and spirals, like hurrying ghosts wrapped hastily in filmy garments, which loosed at times and trailed slowly over the rocks and caught and clung to their sharp projections. Then the sun completed the rout, and the mist-ghosts swept away towards France, harried by the west wind like a flock of sheep before the shepherd's dog.

In the afternoon the heat grew so intense that he was driven to the wells in the valley of rocks for a bathe, for there was no shelter available, and his bee-hive was like an oven.

None of the pools was large enough for a swim, and it was more than a man's life was worth to venture among the boiling surges of the outer rocks. But he could at all events get under water, if it was only to sit there and cool off.

So he stripped, and was just about slipping into a deep still bath, emerald green, with a fringe of amber weeds all round its almost perpendicular sides, when, glancing down to make sure of an ultimate footing, his eye lighted with a shock of surprise on a pair of huge eyes looking straight up at him out of the water. They were violet in colour, protuberant, and malevolent beyond words.

He sat down suddenly on the baking black rock, with a cold shiver running down his back in spite of the scorch of the sun. The utter cold malignity of those great violet eyes, and the thought of what would have happened if he had stepped into that pool, made him momentarily sick.

He had seen small devil-fish in the pools in Sark, but never one approaching this in size. He crept away at last, leaving it in possession, and found a pool clear of boulders or caving hollows, and sat in it with no great enjoyment, wondering if the great unwholesome beast in the other would be likely to climb the cliff and come upon him in the night. He thought it unlikely, but still the idea clung to him and caused him no little discomfort. He blocked his door that night with great green cushions, though he felt doubtful if they would be effective against the wiles and strength of a devil-fish, if half that he had heard of them was true.

In the middle of the night—for he went to bed early, having nothing else to do, except to watch the stars—he woke with a cold start, feeling certain that hideous creature had crawled up the slope and was feeling all round his house for an entrance.

Certainly something was moving about outside, and feeling over the stones in an uncertain, searching kind of a way. And when you have been wakened up from a nightmare in which staring devil-eyes played a prominent part, something may be anything, and as like as not the owner of the eyes.

But even devil-fishes in their most advanced stages have not yet attained the power of human speech. If they speak to one another what a horrible sound it must be!

It was with a sigh of relief, and a sudden unstringing of the bow, that he heard outside—

"Mr. Gard!" and with a lusty kick, which expressed some of his feeling, he sent his doorway flying and crawled out after it.

The myriad winking stars lifted the roof of the world and the darkness somewhat, sufficient at all events for him to make out that it was not Nance.

"You, Bernel?" he queried, as the only possible alternative.

"Yes, Mr. Gard. I've brought you some more things to eat."

"Good lad! I'm a great trouble to you. Where is Nance? In the boat?"

"No, she couldn't come. That Julie's watching her like a cat. It was she and Peter stirred up the men against you. All day yesterday the whole Island was out looking for you, dead or alive, and very much puzzled as to what had become of you. And Julie's got a suspicion that we know. They searched the house for you in spite of mother and Grannie, but they won't forget Grannie in a hurry, and I don't think they'll come back," and he laughed at the recollection of it.

"What did Grannie do?"

"She just looked at them from under that big black sun-bonnet, and muttered things no one heard. But her eyes were like points of burning sticks, and they all crept out one after another, afraid of they didn't know what. But Julie's been on the watch all day, and would hardly let us out of her sight. But she couldn't watch us both when we were not together. So Nance got a bundle of things ready for you, and then went out with another bundle and Julie followed her, and I slipped off here."

"Bernel, I don't know how to thank you all! What should I have done without you?"

"You'd have been dead, most likely. It's not that they cared much for Tom, you know, but they don't like the idea of a Sark man being killed by a foreigner and no one paying for it."

"But I'm not a foreigner—"

"Yes you are, to them. Of course you're not a Frenchman, but all the same you're not a Sark man. Good thing for you you'd lived with us and we'd got to know you and like you."

"Yes, that was a good thing indeed. I'm only sorry to have brought you trouble and to be such a trouble to you."

"If we thought you'd done it of course we wouldn't trouble. But we know you couldn't have."

"Nothing fresh has turned up?"

"Nothing yet. But Nance says it will, sure. Truth must out, she says."

"It's a weary while of coming out sometimes, Bernel. And I can't spend the rest of my life here, you know."

"She said you were to keep your heart up. You never know what may happen."

"Tell her I can stand it because of all her goodness to me. If I hadn't her to think of I might go mad in time."

"I've brought you a rabbit I snared. Nance cooked it."

"That was good of her. Can you eat puffins' eggs?"

"They want a bit of getting used to," laughed the boy. "But they're better cooked than raw."

"I can cook them. I found part of an old boat, and I've plugged up all the holes in the shelter, and I only light a fire at night. Could I fish here?"

"Too big a sea close in. I've got some in the boat. I put out a line as I came across. I'll leave you some."

"And have you a bottle—or a bailing-tin? Anything I could bring home some water from the pools in? I have to go over there every time I need a drink, and in the dark it's not possible."

"You can have the bailer. It's a new one and sound."

"Now tell me, Bernel, if they find out I'm here what will they do?"

"They might come across and try and take you, unless they cool down; and that won't be so long as that Julie and Peter talk as they do. She makes him do everything she tells him. He's a sheep."

"And if they come across, what do you and Nance expect me to do?"

"You've got my gun," said the boy simply.

"Yes, I've got your gun. But do you expect me to kill some of them?"

"They'd kill you," said Bernel, conclusively. On second thoughts, however, he added, "But you needn't kill them. Wing one or two, and the rest will let you be. With a gun I could keep all Sark from landing on L'Etat."

"Suppose they come in the night? How many landing-places are there?"

"There's another at the end nighest Guernsey, but it's not easy. And it's only low tide and half-ebb that lets you ashore here at all."

"How about your boat?"

"She's riding to a line. Tide's running up that way, but I'd better be off."

They stumbled through the darkness and the sleeping gulls, which woke in fright, and volubly accused one another of nightmares and riotous behaviour—and Bernel hauled in his boat, and handed Gard the tin dipper and three good-sized bream.

"If you can't eat them all at once, split them open and dry them in the sun," he said. "They'll keep for a week that way."

"Tell Nance I think of her every hour of the day, and I pray God the truth may come out soon."

"I'll tell her. It'll come out. She says so," and he pulled out into the darkness and was gone.

And the Solitary went back to his shelter, secure in the knowledge that the tide was on the rise, and half-ebb would not be till well on into next day. And he thought of Nance, and of Bernel, and of all the whole matter again; white thoughts and black thoughts, but chiefly white because of Nance, and Nance was a fact, while the black thoughts were shadows confusing as the mist.

He could only devoutly hope and pray that a clean wind might come and put the shadows to flight and let the sun of truth shine through.

CHAPTER XXIV

HOW HE SAW STRANGE SIGHTS

Living thus face to face with Nature, and drawn through lack of other occupation into unusually intimate association with her, Gard found his lonely rock a centre of strange and novel experience.

Situated as he was, even small things forced themselves largely upon his observation and wrought themselves into his memory. He found it good to lose himself for a time in these visible and tangible actualities, rather than in useless efforts after an understanding of the mystery of which he was the victim and centre.

He had given over much time to pondering the subject of Tom Hamon's death, but had come no nearer any reasonable solution of it. That hideous doubt as to himself in the matter recurred at times, but he always hastened to dissipate it by some other interest more practical and palpable, lest it should bring him to ultimate belief in its possibility, and so to madness.

And so he spent hours watching that wonderful roaring cauldron on the south stack where his water pools were. Other hours in study of the social and domestic economies of gulls and cormorants. He saw families of awkward little fawn-coloured squawkers force their way out of their shells under his very eyes, while indignant mothers told him what they thought of him from a safe distance.

He bathed regularly in the heat of the day, but always after careful inspection of his chosen pool, and one day fled in haste up the black rocks at sight of the tip of a long, quivering, flesh-coloured tentacle coming curling round a rock in the close neighbourhood of the pool in which he was basking.

That monster under the rock gave him many a bad dream. It seemed to him the incarnation of evil, and those horrible, bulging, merciless eyes stuck like burrs in his memory.

One day, when he had been watching the cauldron, and filling his tin dipper at the freshwater pools, as he came to descend the black wall leading to the valley of rocks, he witnessed a little tragedy.

Down below, on the edge of the pool where the octopus dwelt, a silly young cormorant was standing gazing into the water, so fascinated with something it saw there that it forgot even to jerk its head in search of understanding.

Gard stood and watched. He saw a tiny pale worm-like thing come creeping up the black rock on which the cormorant squatted. The cormorant saw it too, and he was hungry, as all cormorants always are, even after a full meal. So presently he made a jab at it with his curved beak, and in a moment the pale worm had twisted itself tightly round his silly neck, and dragged him screaming and fluttering under the water.

Another day, when he was coming down by the break in the cliff, where some great winter wave had bitten out such a slice that the top had come tumbling down, he saw the monster sunning itself on the flat rock by the side of its pool, like a huge nightmare spider.

The moment he appeared its great eyes settled on his as though it had been waiting only for him. And when he stopped, with a feeling of shuddering discomfort at its hugeness—for its body seemed considerably over a foot in width, while its arms lounging over the rocks were each at least six feet long, and looked horribly muscular—he could have sworn that one of the great devil-eyes winked familiarly at him, as though the beast would say, "Come on, come on! Nice day for a bathe! Just waiting for you!"

He could see the loathsome body move as it breathed, swinging comfortably in the support of its arms.

In a fury of repulsion he stooped to pick up a rock, but when he hurled it the last tentacle was just sliding into the pool, and it seemed to him that it waved an ironical farewell before it disappeared.

More than once fishing-boats hovered about his rock, but kept a safe distance from the boiling underfalls, and he always lay in hiding till they had gone.

But he saw more gracious and beautiful things than these.

As he lay one morning, looking over the ridge at the Sark headlands shining in the sun—with a strong west wind driving the waves so briskly that, Sark-like, they tossed their white crests into the air in angry expostulation long before they met the rocks, and went roaring up them in dazzling spouts of foam—his eye lighted on a gleam of unusual colour on the racing green plain. It came again and again, and presently, as the merry dance waxed wilder still, every white-cap as it tossed into the air became a tiny rainbow, and the whole green plain was alive with magical flutterings, of colours so dazzling that it seemed bestrewn with dancing diamonds. A sight so wonderful that he found himself holding in his! breath lest a puff should drive it all away.

That same evening, too, was a glory of colour such as he had never dreamed of. The setting sun was ruby; red, and the cloud-bank into which he sank was all rimmed with red fire that seemed to corruscate in its burning brilliancy.

To Gard indeed, in the somewhat peculiar state of mind induced by his sudden cutting-off from his kind and flinging back upon himself, it seemed as though the blood-red sun had fallen into a vast consuming fire behind that dark, fire-rimmed cloud, and that that was the end of it, and it would never rise again.

The sky, right away into the farthest east, was flaming red with a hint of underlying smoke below the glow. The sea was a weltering bath of blood, and the cliffs of Sark, save for the gleam of white foam at their feet, shone as red as though they had just been bodily dipped in it.

His lonely rock, when he looked round at it in wonder, was all unfamiliarly red. There was a red fantastic glow in the very air, and he himself was as red as though he had in very fact killed Tom Hamon, and drenched himself with his blood.

So startling and unnatural was it all, that he found himself wondering fearfully if these outside things were really all blood-red, or whether something had gone wrong with his brain and eyes, and only caused them to look so to him alone, or whether it was indeed the end of all things shaping itself slowly under his very eyes. And in that thought and fear he was not by any means alone.

But the wonderful red, which in its universality and intensity had become overpowering and fearsome, faded at last, and he hailed its going with a sigh of relief. His eyes and his brain were all right, he had not killed Tom Hamon, and this was not the earth's last sunset.

And again that night, as he sat on the ridge on sentinel duty till the rising tide should lock the doors of his castle, the sea all round him shone with phosphorescence; every breaking wave along the black plain was a lambent gleam of lightning, and where they tore up the sides of his rock they were like flames out of a fiery sea, so that he sat there looking down upon a weltering band of nickering green and blue fires, which clung to the black ledges and dripped slowly back into the seething gleam below.

It was all very strange and very awesome, and he wondered what it might portend in the way of further marvels.

And he had not long to wait.

Far away in the Atlantic a cyclone had been raging, and carrying havoc in its skirts. Now it was whirling towards Europe, and the puffins crept deep into their holes, and the gulls circled with disconsolate cries, and the cormorants crouched gloomily in lee of their snuggest ledges, and all nature seemed waiting for the blow.

Gard was awakened in the morning by the gale tearing at the massive stones of his shelter as though it would carry them bodily into the sea.

And when he crawled out, flat like a worm, the wind caught him even so, and he had to grimp to earth and anchor himself by projecting pieces of rock.

Such seas as these he had never imagined round Sark; forgetting that behind Guernsey lay thousands of miles of waters tortured past endurance and racing now to escape the fury of the storm.

A white lash of spray came over him as he lay, and soaked him to the skin, and, turning his face to the storm, he saw through the chinks of his eyes a great wavering white curtain between him and the sky line. The south-west portion of his island, where his freshwater pools were, and the valley of rocks, were all awash, the mighty waves roaring clean over the south stack, and rushing up into the black sky in rockets of flying spray. The tide had still some time to run, and he feared what it might be like at its fullest. It seemed to him by no means impossible that it might sweep the whole rock bare.

CHAPTER XXV

HOW HE LIVED THROUGH THE GREAT STORM

It was a fortunate thing for Gard that the storm—the great storm from which, for many a year afterwards, local events in Sark dated—came when it did; two days after Bernel's visit and the replenishment of his larder. For if he had been caught bare he must have starved.

Eight whole days it lasted, with only two slight abatements which, while they raised his hopes only to dash them, still served him mightily.

During the first days he spent much of his time crouched in the lee of his bee-hive, watching the terrific play of the waves on his own rock and on the Sark headlands.

He wondered if any other man had seen such a storm under such conditions. For he was practically at sea on a rock; in the midst of the turmoil, yet absolutely unaffected by it.

On shipboard, thought of one's ship and possible consequences had always interfered with fullest enjoyment of Nature's paroxysms. It was impossible to detach one's thoughts completely and view matters entirely from the outside. But here—he was sure his rock had suffered many an equal torment—there was nothing to come between him and the elemental frenzy. Nothing but—as the days of it ran on—a growing solicitude as to what he was going to live on if it continued much longer.

Never was Sark rabbit so completely demolished as was that one that Nance had cooked and sent him. Before he had done with it he cracked the very bones he had thrown away, for the sake of what was in them, and finally chewed the softer parts of the bones themselves to cheat himself into the belief that he was eating.

That was after he had devoured every crumb of his bread, and finished his three fishes to the extreme points of their tails.

He was, I said, in the very midst of the turmoil yet unaffected by it. But that was not so in some respects.

Bodily, as we have seen, the storm bore hardly upon him, since rabbit-bones and fish-tails can hardly be looked upon as a nutritious or inviting dietary.

But mentally and spiritually the mighty elemental upheaval was wholly crushing and uplifting.

As he cowered, with humming head, under the fierce unremitting rush of the gale, and felt the great stones of his shelter tremble in it, and watched the huge green hills of water, with their roaring white crests, go sweeping past to crash in thunder on the cliffs of Sark, he felt smaller than he had ever felt before—and that, as a rule, and if it come not of self-abnegation through a man's own sin or folly, is entirely to his good; possibly in the other case also.

To feel infinitely small and helpless in the hands of an Infinitely Great is a spiritual education to any man, and it was so to this man.

He felt himself, in that universal chaos, no more than a speck of helpless dust amid the whirling wheels of Nature's inexplicable machinery, and clung the tighter to the simple fundamental facts of which his heart was sure—behind and above all this was God, who held all these things in His hand. And over there in Sark was Nance, the very thought of whom was like a coal of fire in his heart, which all the gales that ever blew, and all the soddened soaking of ceaseless rain from above and ceaseless spray from below, could not even dim.

For long-continued and relentless buffeting such as this tells upon any man, no matter what his strength of mind or body to begin with; and a perpetually soaked body is apt in time to sodden the soul, unless it have something superhuman to cling to, as this man had in his simple trust in God and the girl he loved.

In all those stressful days, so far as he could see, the tides—which in those parts rise and fall some forty feet, as you may see by the scoured bases of the towering cliffs—seemed always at the full, the westerly gale driving in the waters remorselessly and piling them up against the land without cessation, and as though bent on its destruction.

Great gouts of clotted foam flew over his head in clouds, and plastered his rock with shivering sponges. The sheets of spray from his south-west rocks lashed him incessantly. His shelter was as wet inside as out, as he was himself.

He felt empty and hungry at times, but never thirsty; his skin absorbed moisture enough and to spare. But, chilled and clammed and starving, on the fifth day when he had crawled into his wet burrow for such small relief as it might offer from the ceaseless flailing without, he broached his bottle of cognac and drank a little, and found himself the better of it.

On the evening of the third day his hopes had risen with a slight slackening of the turmoil. He was not sure if the gale had really abated, or if it was only that he was growing accustomed to it. But under that belief, and the compulsion of a growling stomach, he crawled precariously round to the eastern end of the rock where the puffins had their holes, lying flat when the great gusts snatched at him as though they were bent on hurling him into the water, and gliding on again in the intervals. And there, with a piece of his firewood he managed to extort half-a-dozen eggs from fiercely expostulating parents. The end of his stick was bitten to fragments, but he got his eggs, and was amazed at the size of them compared with that of their producers.

The sight of the great wall of tumbled rocks on his right, and the sudden remembrance of his previous passage over it, set him wondering if it might not be possible to find better shelter in some of those fissures across which he had had to swing himself by the hands on the previous occasion. For this was the leeward side of the island, and the huge bulk of it rose like a protecting shoulder between him and the gale, whereas his bee-hive, on the exposed flank of the rock, got the full force of it. So he scooped a hole in the friable black soil and deposited his eggs in it and crawled along to the wall.

The tumbled fragments looked much less fearsome than they had done in the fog. He found no difficulty in clambering among them now, when he could see clearly what he was about, and he wormed his way in and out, and up and down, but could not light on any of those tricky spaces which had seemed to him so dangerous before.

And then, as he crawled under one huge slab, a black void lay before him, of no great width but evidently deep. It took many minutes' peering into the depths to accustom his eyes to the dimness.

Then it seemed to him that the rough out jutting fragments below would afford a holding, and he swung his feet cautiously down and felt round for foothold.

Carefully testing everything he touched, he let himself down, inch by inch, assured that if he could go down he could certainly get up again.

At first the gale still whistled through the crevices among the boulders, but presently he found himself in a silence that was so mighty a change from the ceaseless roar to which he was becoming accustomed, that he felt as though stricken with deafness. Up above him the light filtered down, tempered by the slab under which he had come, and enabled him still to find precarious hand and foot hold.

But presently his downward progress was barred by a rough flooring of splintered fragments, and he stood panting and looked about him.

His well was about twenty feet deep, he reckoned, and there were gaping slits here and there which might lead in towards the rock or out towards the sea. He had turned and twisted so much in his descent that it took him some time to decide in which direction the sea might lie and in which the rock. And, having settled that, he wriggled through a crevice and wormed slowly on.

He was almost in the dark now, and could only feel his way. But he was used to groping in narrow places, and a spirit of investigation urged him on.

Half an hour's strenuous and cautious worming, and a thin trickle of light glimmered ahead. He turned and worked his way back at once.

There was no slit opposite the one he had tried, but presently, half-way up the well, he made out an opening like the mouth of a small adit. His back had been to it as he came down, and so he had missed it.

He climbed up and in, and felt convinced in his own mind that this was no simple work of nature. Nature had no doubt begun, but man had certainly finished it. For the floor level was comparatively free from harshness, and the outjutting projections of the sides and roof had been tempered, and progress was not difficult.

It was very narrow, however, and very low, and quite dark. He could only drag himself along on his stomach like a worm. But he pushed on with all the ardour of a discoverer.

Was it silver? Was it smugglers? Or what? Wholly accidental formation he was sure it was not, though he thought it likely that man's handiwork had only turned Nature's to account.

The fissure had probably been there from the beginning of time, or it might be the result of numberless years of the slow wearing away of a softer vein of rock, but some man at some time had lighted on it, and followed it up, and with much labour had smoothed its natural asperities and used it for his own purposes. And he was keen to learn what those purposes were.

To any ordinary man, accustomed to the ordinary amplitudes of life, and freedom to stretch his arms and legs and raise his head and fill his lungs with fresh air, a passage such as this would have been impossible. Here and there, indeed, the walls widened somewhat through some fault in the rook, bur for the most part his elbows grazed the sides each time he moved them.

Even he, used as he was to such conditions, began at last to feel them oppressive. The whole mighty bulk of L'Etat seemed above and about him, malignantly intent on crushing him out of existence.

He knew that was only fancy. He had experienced it many times before. But the nightmare feeling was there, and it needed all his will at times to keep him from a panic attempt at retreat, when the insensate rock-walls seemed absolutely settling down on him, and breathing was none too easy.

But going back meant literally going backwards, crawling out toes foremost; for his elbows scraped the walls and his head the roof, and turning was out of the question. The men who had made and used that narrow way had undoubtedly gone with a purpose, and not for pleasure. And he was bound to learn what that purpose was.

So he set his teeth, and wormed himself slowly along, with pinched face and tight-shut mouth, and nostrils opened wide to take in all the air they could and let out as little as possible. And, even at that, he had to lie still at times, pressed flat against the floor, to let some fresher air trickle in above him.

But at last he came to what he sought, though no whit of it could he see when he got there. By the sudden cessation of the pressure on his sides and head, he was aware of entrance into a larger space, and, with forethought quickened by the exigences of his passage, he lay for a moment to pant more freely and to think.

His body was in the passage. He knew where the passage led out to. What lay ahead he could not tell.

If it was a chamber, as he expected, there might quite possibly be other passages leading out of it. And so it would be well to make sure of recognizing this one again before he loosed his hold on it. So he pulled off one boot, and feeling carefully round the opening, placed it just inside as a landmark.

Then he groped on along the right-hand wall to learn the size of the chamber, and was immediately thankful that his own passage was safely marked, for he came on another opening, and another, and another, and labelled them carefully in his mind, "One, two, three."

It was truly eerie work, groping there in that dense darkness and utter silence, and trying to the nerves even of one who had never known himself guilty of such things. But, being there, he was determined to learn all he could.

He clung to his right-hand wall as to a life-rope. If he once got mazed in a place like that he might never taste daylight and upper air again.

Of the size of the chamber he could so far form no opinion. He would have given much for a light. His flint and steel were indeed in his pocket, but he was sodden through and through, and had no means whatever of catching a spark if he struck one.

Then, as he groped cautiously along past the third opening, his progress was stayed, and not by rock.

He was on his knees, his hands feeling blindly, but with infinite enquiry, along the rough rock wall, when he stumbled suddenly over something that lay along the ground. Dropping his hands to save himself from falling, they lighted on that which lay below, and he started back with an exclamation and a shudder. For what he had felt was like the hair and face of a man.

He crouched back against the wall, his heart thumping like a ship's pump, and the blood belling in his ears, and sat so for very many minutes; sat on, until, in that silent blackness, he could hear the dull, far-away thud of the waves on the outer walls of the island.

Then, by degrees, he pulled himself together. If it was indeed a man, he was undoubtedly dead, and therefore harmless; and having learned this much he would know more.

So presently he groped forward, felt again the round head and soft hair, and below it and beyond it a heap of what felt like small oblong packages done up in wrappings of cloth and tied round with cord.

He picked one up and handled it inquisitively, with a shrewd idea of what might be, or might have been, inside. The cord was very loose, as though the contents had shrunk since it was tied. As he fumbled with it in the dark, it came open and left him no possible room for doubt as to what those contents were. He sneezed till the top of his head seemed like to lift, and the tears ran down his cheeks in an unceasing stream. What had once been tobacco had powdered into snuff, and his rough handling of the package had scattered it broadcast.

He turned at last, and lay with his head in his arms against the wall until the air should have time to clear, and meanwhile the sneezing had quickened his wits.

Here was possible tinder, and by means of those dried-up wrappings he might procure a light. If it lasted but five minutes it might enable him to solve the problem on which he had stumbled.

He groped again for the opened package, and found it on the dead man's face. The wrapper was of tarred cloth, almost perished with age, dry and friable. Shaking out the rest of the snuff at arm's length, he picked the stuff to pieces and shredded it into tinder. Then he felt about for half-a-dozen more packages, carefully slipped their cords and emptied out their contents, and getting out his flint and steel, flaked sparks into the tinder till it caught and flared, and the interior of the cavern leaped at him out of its darkness.

He rolled up one of the empty wrappers like a torch, and lit it, and looked about him.

His first hasty glance fell on the dead man, and he got another shock from the fact that his feet were lashed together with stout rope, and probably his hands also, for they were behind his back, and he lay face upward. His coat and short-clothes and buckled shoes spoke of long by-gone days, and the skin of his face was brown and shrivelled, so that the bones beneath showed grim and gaunt.

Beyond him was a great heap of the same small packages of tobacco, and alongside them a pile of small kegs. Gard lit another of his torches, and stepped gingerly over to them. He sounded one or two, but found them empty. Time had shrunk their stout timbers and tapped their contents.

Then he held up his flickering light and looked quickly round this prison-house which had turned into a tomb, and shivered, as a dim idea of what it all meant came over him.

It was a large, low, natural rock chamber, and all round the walls were black slits which might mean it passages leading on into the bowels of the island. To investigate them all would mean the work of many days.

The dead man, the perished packages, the empty kegs—there was nothing else, except his own boot lying in the mouth of the largest of the black slits, as though anxious on its own account to be gone.

The still air was already becoming heavy with the pungent smoke of his torches. He stepped cautiously across to the body again, and picked a couple of buttons from the coat. They came off in his hand, and when he touched the buckles on the shoes they did the same. Then he turned and made for his waiting shoe just as his last torch went out.

The smell of the fresh salt air, when he wriggled out into the well, was almost as good as a feast to him. He climbed hastily to the surface, and, as he crept out from under the topmost slab, took careful note of its position, and then scored with a piece of rock each stone which led up to it. For, if ever he should need an inner sanctuary, here was one to his hand, and evidently quite unknown to the present generation of Sark men.

He recovered his eggs, and crept round the shoulder of the rock. The gale pounced on him like a tiger on its half-escaped prey. It beat him flat, worried him, did its best to tear him off and fling him into the sea. But—Heavens!—how sweet it was after the musty quiet of the death-chamber below!

Inch by inch, he worked his way back in the teeth of it, and crawled spent into his bee-hive. Then, ravenous with his exertions, he broke one of his eggs into his tin dipper, and forthwith emptied it outside, and the gale swept away the awful smell of it.

The next was as bad, and his hopes sank to nothing.

The third, however, was all right. He mixed it with some cognac and whipped it up with a stick, and the growlers inside fought over it contentedly.

He was almost afraid to try another. However, he could get more to-morrow. So he broke the fourth, and found it also good, so whipped it up with more cognac, and felt happier than he had done since he nibbled his rabbit-bones.

As he lay that night, and the gale howled about him more furiously than ever, his thoughts ran constantly on the dead man lying in the silent darkness down below.

It was very quiet down there, and dry; but this roaring turmoil, with its thunderous crashings and hurtling spray, was infinitely more to his taste, wet though he was to the bone, and almost deafened with the ceaseless uproar. For this, terrible though it was in its majestic fury, was life, and that black stillness below was death.

To the tune of the tumult without, he worked out the dead man's story in his mind.

It was long ago in the old smuggling days. Some bold free-trader of Sark or Guernsey had lighted on that cave and used it as a storehouse. Some too energetic revenue officer had disappeared one day and never been heard of again. He had been surprised—by the free-traders—perhaps in the very act of surprising them—brought over to L'Etat in a boat, been dragged through the tunnel, or made to crawl through, perhaps, with vicious knife-digs in the rear, and had been left bound in the darkness till he should be otherwise disposed of. His captors had been captured in turn, or maybe killed, and he had lain there alone and in the dark, waiting, waiting for them to return, shouting now and again into the muffling darkness, struggling with his bonds, growing weaker and weaker, faint with hunger, mad with thirst, until at last he died.

It was horrible to think of, and desperate as his own state was, he thanked God heartily that he was not as that other.

Morning brought no slackening of the gale. It seemed to him, if anything, to be waxing still more furious.

He had only two eggs left, and they might both be bad ones, but he would not have ventured round the headland that day for all the eggs in existence.

He broke one presently, in answer to a clamour inside him that would brook no denial, and found it good, and lived on it that day, and mused between times on the strange fact that a man could feel so mightily grateful for the difference between a bad egg and a good one.

His sixth egg turned out a good one also, and the next day there came another hopeful lull, which permitted him to harry the puffins once more, and gave him a dozen chances against contingencies.

On the eighth day the storm blew itself out, and he looked hopefully across at the lonely and weather-beaten cliffs of Sark for the relief which he was certain they had been aching to send him.

The waves, however, still ran high, and, though he did not know it till later, there was not a boat left afloat round the whole Island. The forethoughtful and weather-wise had run them round to the Creux and carried them through the tunnel into the roadway behind. All the rest had been smashed and sunk and swallowed by the storm.

CHAPTER XXVI

HOW HE HELD THE ROCK

The sun blazed hot next day, and he spread himself out in it to warm, and all his soaked things in it to dry, and blessed it for its wholesome vigour.

Nance or Bernel would be sure to come as soon as the tide served at night, and he would net be sorry for a change of diet; meanwhile, he could get along all right with the unwilling assistance of the puffins.

The birds had all crept out of their hiding-places, and were wheeling and diving and making up for lost time and busily discussing late events at the tops of their voices whenever their bills were not otherwise occupied. Where they had all hidden themselves during the storm, he could not imagine, but there seemed to be as many of them as ever, and they were all quite happy and quarrelsome, except the cormorants, who were so ravenous that they could not spare a moment from their diving and gobbling, even to quarrel with their neighbours.

He levied on the puffins again, and, after a meal, prowled curiously about his rock to see what damage the storm had done, but to his surprise found almost none.

It seemed incredible that all should be the same after the deadly onslaught of the gale. But it was only in the valley of rocks that he found any consequences.

There the huge boulders had been hurled about like marbles: some had been tossed overboard, and some, in their fantastic up-piling, spoke eloquently of all they had suffered.

But one grim—though to him wholly gracious—deed the storm had wrought there. For, out of the pool where the devil-fish dwelt, its monstrous limbs streamed up and lay over the sloping rocks, and he dared not venture near. But, in the afternoon when he came again to look at it, and found it still in the same attitude, something about it struck him as odd and unusual.

The great tentacles had never moved, so far as he could see, and there was surely something wrong with a devil-fish that did not move.

He hurled a stone, picked out of the landslip at the corner, and hit a tentacle full and fair with a dull thud like leather. But the beast never moved.

He was suspicious of the wily one, however. The devil, he knew, was sometimes busiest when he made least show of business. And it was not till next morning, when he found the monster still as before, that he ventured down to the pool and looked into it, and saw what had happened.

The waves had hurled a huge boulder into it—and there you may see it to this day—and it had fallen on the devil-fish and ground him flat, and purged the rock of a horror.

Gard examined the hideous tentacles with the curiosity of intensest repulsion; yet could not but stand amazed at the wonderful delicacy and finish displayed in the tiny powerful suckers with which each limb was furnished on the under side, and the flexible muscularity of the monstrous limbs themselves, thick as his biceps where they came out of the pool, and tapering to a worm-like point, capable, it seemed to him, of picking up a pin.

He was mightily glad the beast was dead, however. It had been a blot on Nature's handiwork, and the very thought of it a horror.

The strenuous interlude of the storm, which, to the lonely one exposed to its fullest fury, had seemed interminable—every shivering day the length of many, and the black howling nights longer still—had had the effect of relaxing somewhat his own oversight over himself and his precautions against being seen.

L'Etat in a furious sou'-wester is a sight worth seeing. Possibly some telescope had been brought to bear on the foam-swept rock when he, secure in the general bouleversement and cramped with hunger, had turned the forbidden corner with no thought in his mind but eggs.

Possibly again, it was sheer carelessness on his part, born once more of the security of the storm and the recent non-necessity for concealment.

However it came about, what happened was that, as he stood in the valley of rocks examining his dead monster, he became suddenly aware that a fishing-boat had crept round the open end of the valley, and that it seemed to him much closer in than he had ever seen one before.

He dropped prone among the boulders at once, but whether he had been seen he could not tell—could only vituperate his own carelessness, and hope that nothing worse might come of it.

He lay there a very long time, and when at last he ventured to crawl to the rocks at the seaward opening, the boat was away on the usual fishing-grounds busy with its own concerns, and he persuaded himself that its somewhat unusual course had been accidental. The incident, however, braced him to his former caution, and he went no more abroad without first carefully inspecting the surrounding waters from the ridge.

They would be certain to come that night, he felt sure, either Nance or Bernel, perhaps both. Yes, he thought most likely they would both come. They would, without doubt, be wondering how he had fared during the storm, and would be making provision for him.

Perhaps Nance was cooking for him at that very moment, and thinking of him as he was of her.

In the certain expectation of their coming, he decided he would not go to sleep at all that night, but would crawl down to the landing-place to welcome them.

He wondered if that mad woman Julie had given up watching them, and, if not, if they would be able to circumvent her again. In any case, he hoped that if only one of them came it might be Nance. He fairly ached for the sight and sound of her—and the feel of her little hand, and a warm frank kiss from the lips that knew no guile.

The sufferings of the storm became as nothing to him in this large hope and expectation of her coming.

The intervening hours dragged slowly. It would be half-ebb soon after dark, he thought; and he crept up to the ridge and gazed anxiously over at the Race between him and Brenière, to see if it showed any unusual symptoms after the storm.

It ran furiously enough, but, he said to himself, it would slacken on the ebb, and they were so familiar with it that it would take more than that to stop them coming.

Before dark the great seas were rolling past, a little quicker than usual, he thought, but in long, smooth undulations, which slipped, unbroken and soundless, even along the black ledges of his rock. And when the stars came out—brighter than ever with the burnishing of the gale—the long black backs of the waves, and the darker hollows between, were sown so thick with trailing gleams that he could not be certain whether it was only star-shine or phosphorescence.

It was all very peaceful and beautiful, however, and very welcome to eyes that had not looked upon sun, moon, or star for eight whole nights and days, and whose ears had grown hardened to the ceaseless clamour of the gale. Nature, indeed, seemed preternaturally quiet, as though exhausted with her previous violence or desirous of wiping out the remembrance of it; just as small humanity after an outbreak endeavours at times to purge the memory of its offence by display of unusual amiability and sweetness.

Eager to welcome his confidently expected visitors, Gard crept along the ridge as soon as it was dark, and posted himself on the point which, in the daylight, commanded the passage from Brenière.

And he sat there so long—so long after his hopes and wishes had flown over to Sark and hurried Bernel and Nance into a boat and landed them on L'Etat—that the night seemed running out, and he began to fear they were not coming, after all.

In the troubled darkness of the Race, he caught gleams at times which might be oar-blades or might be only the upfling from the perils below. The tide was ebbing, and soon the black fangs with which it was strewn would be showing.

At times he convinced himself that the brief gleams moved; but when, to ease his eyes of the intolerable strain, he looked up at the stars, it seemed to him that they moved also, and so he could not be sure.

But surely there was a gleam that seemed to move and come fitfully towards him—or was it only star-shine dancing on the waves of the Race which always ran against the tide?

He stood to watch, then lost the gleam, and crouched again disappointed.

The boat must come round Quette d'Amont, the great pile of rock that lay off the eastern corner, and the first glimpse he could hope to get of it in the darkness would be there.

Then, suddenly, in that curious way in which one sometimes sees more out of the tail of one's eye than out of the front of it, he got an impression—and with it a start—of something moving noiselessly among the tumbled rocks below on his left.

It was a dark night, but the glory of the stars lifted it out of the ebony-ruler category. It was a wide, thin, lofty darkness, but still black enough along the sides of his rock, and down there it seemed to him that something moved, something dim and shadowy and silent.

He thought of the dead man in his chamber down below. Could he be in the habit of walking of a night? He thought of ghosts, of which, if popular belief was anything to go by, Sark was full; and there was nothing to hinder them coming across to L'Etat for their Sabbat. And he thought of monster devil-fish climbing, loathsome and soundless, about the dark rocks.

He longed for a pair of Sark eyes, and shrank down into a hollow under the ridge to watch this thing, with something of a creepy chill between his shoulder-blades.

There was certainly something lighter than the surrounding darkness down below, and it moved. It turned the corner and flitted along the slope, slowly but surely, in the direction of his shelter. Its mode of progression, from the little he could make out in the darkness, was just such as he would have looked for in a huge octopus hauling itself along by its tentacles over the out-cropping rock-bones.

He could not rest there. He must see. He crawled along the ridge as quietly as he could manage it, and would have felt happier, whatever it was, spirit or monster, if he had had his gun. Now and again it stopped, and when it stopped he lay flat to the ground and held his breath, lest it should discover him. When it went on, he went on.

When he came to the end of the ridge he saw that the nebulous something had apparently stopped just where his house must be.

And then, every sense on the strain, he heard his own name called softly, and he laughed to himself for very joy of it, and lay still to hear it again, and laughed once more to think that in her simplicity she still thought of him as "Mr. Gard." He would teach her to call him "Steen," as his mother used to do.

Then he got up quickly and cried, as softly as herself, but with joy and laughter in his voice—

"Why, Nance! My dear, I was not sure whether you were a ghost or a devil-fish;" and he sprang down towards her.

And then, to his amazement, he saw that she was clad only in the clinging white garment in which he had seen her swim.

Her next words confounded him.

"Is Bernel here?"

"Bernel, Nance? No, dear, he is not here. Why—"

"Did he not get here last night?" she jerked sharply.

"No. No one. I was hoping—"

But she had sunk down against the great stones of the shelter, with her hands before her face.

"Mon Gyu, mon Gyu! Then he is dead! Oh, my poor one! My dear one!"

"Nance! Nance! What is it all, dearest? Did Bernel try to come across last night—"

"Yes, yes! He would come. He said you must be starving. We were all anxious about you—"

"And he tried to swim across?"

"Yes, yes! And he is drowned! Oh, my poor, poor boy!"

She was shaking with the sudden chill of dreadful loss. He stooped, and felt inside the shelter with a long arm for the old woollen cloak and wrapped her carefully in it. He raked out the blanket and made her sit with it tucked about her feet. And she was passive in his hands, with thought as yet for nothing but her loss.

She was shaken with broken sobs, and in the face of grief such as this he could find no words. What could he say? All the words in the world could not bring back the dead.

And it was through him this great sorrow had come upon her. He seemed fated to bring misfortune on their house.

He wondered if she would hate him for it, though she must know he had had no more to do with the matter than with Tom's death.

He put a protecting arm round the old cloak, tentatively, and in some fear lest she might resent it, but knew no other way to convey to her what was in his heart.

But she did not resent it, and nothing was further from her mind than imputing any share in this loss to him.

Some women's hearts are so wonderfully constituted that the greater the demands upon them the more they are prepared to give. At times they give and give beyond the bounds of reason, and yet amazingly retain their faith and hope in the recipients of their gifts.

But that has nothing to do with our story. Except this—that these various demands on Nance's fortitude, incurred by her love for Stephen Gard, far from weakening her love only made it the stronger. As that love came more and more between her and her old surroundings, and exacted from her sacrifice after sacrifice, the more she clung to it, and looked to it, and let the past go. The partial ostracism brought upon her by Gard's outspoken declaration of their mutual feeling—even this final offering of her dearly-loved brother—these only bound her heart to him the tighter.

"Nance dear!" he said at last, when she had got control of herself again. "Is it not possible to hope? He was so good a swimmer. Maybe he found the Race too strong and was carried away by it. He may have been picked up, and will come back as soon as he is able."

"No," she said, with gloomy decision. "He is dead. I feared for him, for I had been to look at the Race just before sundown, and it looked terribly strong. But he would go—"

"Why didn't he get a boat?"

"Ah, mon Gyu!" and she started up wildly. "I was forgetting. I was thinking only of myself and Bernel. There isn't a boat left alive outside the Creux, and he couldn't get one there without them knowing. But"—in quick excitement now, to make up for lost time—"they have seen you here, and they may come to-night—Achochre that I am! They may be here! Come quickly! Your gun!" and she was all on the quiver to be gone.

Gard stooped and pulled out the gun from its hiding-place inside the shelter.

"Is it loaded?" she asked sharply.

"Yes. I cleaned it to-day."

"Take your charges with you, and do you hasten back to the place we landed the first night. You know?"

"I know. And you?"

"I will go to the other landing-place. But they are not likely to come there."

"And if they do?"

"I will manage them," and she slipped into the darkness with the big cloak about her.

Gard crept along the slope, and found a roost above the landing-place.

His brain was in a whirl. Bernel had tried to cross to him and was drowned. Nance had swum across. Brave girl! Wonderful girl! For him!—and for news of Bernel. It was terrible to think of Bernel, dead on his account—terrible! It would not be surprising if Nance hated him. Yet, what had he done?—what could he do? He had done nothing. He could do nothing; and his teeth ground savagely at the craziness of these wild Sark men who had brought it all about, and at his own utter impotence.

But Nance did not hate him. And she had swum that dreadful Race to warn him. Brave girl! Wonderful girl!

And then—surely the grinding of an oar, as it wrought upon the gunwale against an ill-fitted thole-pin—out there by the Quette d'Amont!

His eyes and ears strained into the darkness till they felt like cracking.

And the muffled growl of voices!

His heart thumped so, they might have heard it.

He must wait till he was sure they meant to come in. But they must not come too close.

It was an ill landing in the dark, and there were various opinions on it. But there was no doubt as to their intentions. They were coming in.

"Sheer off there!" cried Gard.

Dead silence below. They had come in some doubt, but their doubts were solved now, and there was no longer need for curbed tongues, though, indeed, his hollow voice made some of them wonder if it was not a spirit that spoke to them.

"It's him!" "The man himself!" "We have him!" "In now and get him!"—was the burden of their growls, as they hung on their oars.

"See here, men!" said Gard, invisible even to Sark eyes, against the solid darkness of the slope. "There has been trouble and loss enough over this matter already, and none of it my making. Do you hear? I say again—none of it my making. If you attempt to come ashore there will be more trouble, and this time it will be of my making. Keep back!"—as an impulsive one gave a tug at his oar. "If you force me to fire, your blood be on your own heads. I give you fair warning."

Growls from the boat carried up to him an impression of mixed doubt and discomfort—ultimate disbelief in his possession of arms, an energetic oath or two, and another creak of the oar.

"Very well! Here's to show you I am armed." The report of his gun made Nance jump, at the other side of the island, and set all the birds on L'Etat—except the puffins, deep in their holes—circling and screaming.

The small shot tore up the water within a couple of yards of the boat, which backed off hastily—much to his satisfaction, for he had feared they might rush him before he had time to reload.

He had dropped flat after firing and recharged his gun as he lay. He was sure they must have come armed, and feared a volley as soon as his own discharge indicated his whereabouts.

As a matter of fact, they had come divided as to the truth of the report that there was a man on L'Etat—even then as to him being the man they sought. In any case, they had expected to take him unawares, and never dreamt of his being armed and on the watch for them.

Thanks to Nance, he had turned the tables on them. It was they who were taken unawares.

But if he spoke again, he said to himself, they would be ready for him, and their answers would probably take the rude form of bullets. So he lay still and waited.

There was a growling disputation in the boat. Then one spoke—

"See then, you, Gard! We will haff you yet, now we know where you are. If it takes effery man and effery boat in Sark, we will haff you, now we know where you are. You do not kill a Sark man like that and go free. Noh—pardie!"

"I have killed no man—" A gun rang out in the boat, and the shot spatted on the rocks not a yard from him.

Coming in, they knew, meant certain death for one among them, and, keen as they were to lay hands on him, no man had any wish to be that one.

The oars creaked away into the darkness, and he climbed to the ridge to make sure they made no attempt on the other side.

But discretion had prevailed. One man could not hold L'Etat from invasion at half-a-dozen points at once. They could bide their time, and take him by force of numbers.

He heard them go creaking off towards the Creux, and turned and went back along the ridge to find Nance.

CHAPTER XXVII

HOW ONE CAME TO HIM LIKE AN ANGEL FROM HEAVEN

Nance was standing by the shelter, and even in the darkness he could tell that she was shaking, in spite of her previous vigorous incitement to defence.

"You—you didn't kill any of them?" she asked anxiously.

"No, dear. I warned them off and fired into the water to show them I was armed."

"I was afraid. But, there were two shots."

"One of them fired back the next time I spoke, but I was expecting it."

"They are wicked, wicked men, and cruel."

"They are mistaken, that's all. But it comes to much the same thing, and I don't see," he said despondently, "how we are ever to prove it to them."

"They will come again."

"Yes, they are to come back with every man and every boat in the Island. I shall have my hands full. Are there more than these two places where they can land?"

"Not good places, and these only when the sea is right. But angry men—and ready to shoot you—oh, it is wicked—"

"We must hope the sea will keep them off, and that something may turn up to throw some light on the other matter," he said, trying to comfort her, though, in truth, the outlook was not hopeful, and he feared himself that his time might be short.

"I will stop here and help you," she said, with sudden vehemence. "They shall not have you. They shall not! They are wicked, crazy men," and the little cloaked figure shook again with the spirit that was in it.

"Dear!" he said, putting his arm round her, and drawing her close. "You must not stop. They must not know you have been here. I do not know what the end will be. We are in God's hands, and we have done no wrong. But if ... if the worst comes, you will remember all your life, dear, that to one man you were as an angel from heaven. Nance! Nance! Oh, my dear, how can I tell you all you are to me!"—and as he pressed her to him, the bare white arms stole out of the cloak and clasped him tightly round the neck.

"But how are you going to get back, little one? You cannot possibly swim that Race again?" he asked presently, holding her still in his arms and looking down at her anxiously.

"Yes, I can swim," she said valiantly. "I knew it would be worse than usual, and I brought these"—and she slipped from his arms and groped on the ground, and presently held up what felt to him in the darkness like a pair of inflated bladders with a broad band between them. "And here is a little bread and meat, all I could carry tied on to my head. We feared you would be starving."

"You should not have burdened yourself, dear. It might have drowned you. And I have eggs—puffins'—"

"Ach!"

"They are better than nothing, and I beat them up with cognac. But are you safe in the Race, Nance dear, even with those things?"

"You cannot sink. If Bernel had only taken them! But he laughed at them, and now—"

He kissed her sobs away, but was full of anxiety at thought of her in the rushing darkness of the Race.

"I will go with you," he said eagerly, "and you will lend me your bladders to get back with."

"You would never get back to L'Etat in the dark"—and he knew that that was true. "We of Sark can see, but you others—"

"I shall be in misery till I know you are all right," he said anxiously.

"I will run home. My things are in the gorse above Brenière. And I will get a lantern and come down by Brenière and wave it to you."

"Will you do that? It will be like a signal from heaven," he said eagerly, "a signal from heaven waved by an angel from heaven."

"And to-morrow I will go to the Vicar, and the Sénéchal, and the Seigneur, if he has come home, and I will make them stop these wicked men from coming here again."

"Can they?"

"They shall. They must. They are the law and it is not right."

"It is worth trying, at any rate," he said cheerfully, as they reached the eastern corner and struck down across his puffin-warren to the point immediately opposite Brenière. But he had not much hope that the Vicar and the Sénéchal and the Seigneur all combined would avail him, for the men of Sark are a law unto themselves.

"But I've found another hiding-place, Nance, where they could never find me."

"Here?—on L'Etat?"

"Yes—inside. I'll show you some time, perhaps, if—"

"Is this where you came ashore?" he asked, as she came to a stand on a rough black shelf up which the waves hissed white and venomous.

"We—we always landed here when we swam across," she said, with a little break in her voice, as it came home to her again that Bernel would swim the Race no more.

"Nance dear, don't give up hope. He may come back yet."

"I have only you left, and they want to kill you," she said sadly.

"I wish I could come with you," as the dark waters swirled below them. "It feels terrible to let you go into that all alone."

"It is nothing. The tide is dead slack, and I have these"—swinging the bladders in her hand—"if I get tired. Oh, if Bern had only taken them—"

"I will kneel on the ridge and pray for your safety till I see your light. Dear, God keep you, and bless you for all your goodness and courage!"

He strained her to him again, as if he could not let her go to that colder embrace that awaited her below.

"I could kiss the very rocks you have stood on," he said passionately.

She kissed him back and dropped the cloak, waited a second till a wave had swirled by, then launched into the slack of it, and was gone.

He stood long, peering and listening into the darkness, but heard only the welter of the water under the black ledges below, and its scornful hiss as it seethed through the fringing sea-weeds.

Then at last he turned and climbed, slowly and heavily, up to the ridge; for now he felt the strain of these last full hours, coming on top of the longer strain of the storm; and this, and the lack of proper feeding, made him feel weak and empty and weary. He knelt down there in the darkness, with his face towards the Race where Nance was battling with the hungry black waters, and he prayed for her safety as he had never prayed for anything in his life before.

" God keep her! God keep her! God keep her—and bring her safe to land! O God, keep her, keep her, keep her, and bring her safe to land! "

It was a monotonous little prayer, but all his heart was in it, and that is all that makes a prayer avail. And when at last, from sheer weariness, he sank down on to his heels in science, gazing earnestly out into the blackness of the night, his heart prayed on though his lips no longer moved.

Could anything have happened to her? Could the black waters have swallowed her?

Anything might have happened to her. The waters might have swallowed her, as they had Bernel.

The thoughts would surge up behind his prayer, but he prayed them down—again and again—and clung to his prayer and his hope.

It seemed hours since they parted, since his last glimpse of her as the black waters swallowed the slim white figure, and seemed to laugh scornfully at its smallness and weakness.

" Oh, Nance! Nance! God keep you! God keep you! God keep you! Dear one, God keep you! God keep you! God keep you, and bring you safe to land !"

He was numb with kneeling. If one had come behind him and cut off his feet above the ankles, he would have felt no pain. He felt no bodily sensation whatever. His body was there on the rock, but his heart was out upon the black waters alongside Nance, struggling with her through the belching coils, nerving her through the treacherous swirls. And his soul—all that was most really and truly him—was agonizing in prayer for her before the God to whom he had prayed at his mother's knee, and whom she had taught him to look to as a friend and helper in all times of need.

He did not even stop—as he well might have done—to think that the friend sought only in time of need might have reasonable ground for complaint of neglect at other times.

He thought of nothing but that Nance was out there battling with the black waters—that he could not lift a finger to help her—that all he could do was to pray for her safety with all his heart and soul.

Then, after an age of this numb agony of waiting, a tiny bead of light flickered on the outer darkness, as though Hope with a golden pin-point had pricked the black curtain of despair, and let a gleam of her glory peep through. It swung to and fro, and he fell forward with his face in his ice-cold hands and sobbed, "Thank God! Thank God! She is safe! She is safe!"

When he tried to get up, his legs gave way under him, and he had to sit and wait till they recovered. And when at last he got under way along the ridge, he stumbled like a drunken man.

He tangled his feet in the blanket and fell in a heap. He wondered dimly where the cloak was— remembered Nance had worn it till she took to the sea—and stumbled off through the dark again to find it. Nance had worn it. To him it was sacred.

When he got back with it, he wrapped it round him and crept into his shelter and slept like a dog.

CHAPTER XXVIII

HOW THE OTHERS CAME TO MAKE AN END

He woke next morning with a start. The sun was high, by the shadow of his doorway; and by that same token the tide would be at half-ebb, if not lower, and the gates of his fortress at his enemy's mercy.

He picked up his gun, listened anxiously for sound of him, and then crept cautiously out, with a quick glance along each slope.

Nothing!—nothing but the cheerful sun and the cloudless sky, and the empty blue plain of the sea, and the birds circling and diving and squabbling as usual—and Nance's little parcel lying where she had dropped it. He had had other things to think about last night.

The composure of the birds reassured him somewhat. Still, they might have landed on the other side of the rock and be lying in wait for him.

He picked up Nance's parcel with a feeling of reverence. It might have cost her her life, in spite of her bladders. Then he climbed cautiously to the ridge and peered over.

Sark lay basking in the sunshine, peaceful and placid, as if no son of hers had ever had an ill thought of his neighbour, much less sought his blood.

Not a boat was in sight, and the birds on the north slope seemed as undisturbed as their fellows on the south.

The invasion in force needed time perhaps to prepare and would be all the more conclusive when completed.

Meanwhile, he would eat and watch at the same time, for he felt as empty as a drum, and an empty man is not in the pinkest of condition for a fight.

Never in his life had he tasted bread so sweet!—and the strips of boiled bacon in between came surely from a most unusual pig—a porker of sorts, without a doubt, and of most extraordinary attainment in the nice balancing of lean and fat, and the induing of both with vital juices of the utmost strength and sweetness. Truly, a most celestial pig!—and he was very hungry.

Had he been a pagan he would most likely have offered a portion of his slim rations as thank-offering to his gods, for they had come to him at risk of a girl's life. As it was, he ate them very thoughtfully to the very last crumb, and was grateful.

They had been wrapped in a piece of white linen, and then tied tightly in oiled cloth, and were hardly damped with sea-water. The piece of linen and the oiled cloth and the bits of cord he folded up carefully and put inside his coat.

They spoke of Nance. If they had drowned her she would have gone with them tied on to her head. He took them out again, and kissed them, and put them back.

Thank God, she had got through safely! Thank God! Thank God!

He shivered in the blaze of the sun as his eyes rested on the waves of the Race, bristling up against the run of the tide as usual, and he thought of what it might have meant to him this morning.

It had swallowed Bernel. In spite of his hopeful words to Nance, he feared the brave lad was gone. And it might have swallowed Nance. And if it had—it might as well have him, too. For it was only thought of Nance that made life bearable to him.

The sun wheeled his silvery dance along the waters; the day wore on;—and still no sign of the invaders. Sark looked as utterly deserted as it must have done in the lone days after the monks left it, when, for two hundred years, it was given over to the birds, till de Carteret and his merry men came across from Jersey and woke it up to life again.

And then, of a sudden, his heart kicked within him as if it would climb into his throat and choke him; for, round the distant point of the Lâches, a boat had stolen out, and, as he watched it anxiously, there came another, and another, and another. They were coming!

Four boat-loads! That ought to be enough to make full sure of him. He wondered why they had not come sooner, for the tide was on the rise, and the landing-places did not look tempting.

His gun was under his hand, and his powder-flask and his little bag of shot. He had no more preparations to make, and he had no wish to fight.

No wish? The thought of it was hateful to him, and yet it was not in human nature to give in without a struggle.

But it should be all their doing. All he wanted was to be left in peace. Every man has the right to defend his own life.

But then, again—there could be only one end to it, he knew. So why fight?

They were coming to make an end of him. What good was it to make an end of any of them?

Even if he should succeed in keeping them off this time, the end would come all the same, only it would be longer of coming. Why prolong it?

The boats came bounding on like hounds at sight of the quarry. They were well filled, four or five men in each boat, besides the oarsmen. Enough, surely, to make an end of one lone man.

Would they attempt to land in different places and rush him, he wondered. Or would they content themselves with lying off and attempting to shoot him down from a distance? The last would be the safest all round, both for them and for him—for, landing, they would, for the moment, be more or less at his mercy; and, snapping at him from a distance, he would have certain chances of cover in his favour.

The top of the ridge was flattened in places, there were even depressions here and there, very slight, but quite enough to shelter any one lying prone in them from bombardment from sea-level. He chose the deepest he could find, and crawled into it, and lay, with his chin in his hands, watching the oncoming boats.

If he could have managed it, he would have slipped down to the rock wall and crept into his burrow, but it was on that side the boats were coming, and the sharp eyes on board would inevitably see him, and so get on the track of his hiding-place.

If the chance offered—if they left that end of the rock unspied upon for three minutes—he would try it.

They parted at the Quette d'Amont, two going along the south side and two along the north. He could hear their voices, their rough jests and brief laughter, as they crept past.

It was an odd sensation, this, of lying there like a hunted hare, knowing that it was him they were after.

He pressed still closer to the rock, and did not dare to raise his head for a look. The voices and the sound of the oars died away, came again, died again, as the boats slowly circled the rock, every keen eye on board, he knew, searching every nook and cranny for sign of him.

Then a shot rang out, over there towards the south-west, and another, and another. Tired of inaction, they were peppering his bee-hive to stir him up in case he was fast asleep inside.

The other boats rowed swiftly round to the firing, and he could imagine them clustered there in a bunch, watching hopefully for him to come out; and his blood boiled and chilled again at thought of what might have been if he had been caught napping.

And then, seizing his chance, he crawled to the opposite side of his hollow, peeped over, and saw the way clear. If only they would go on peppering the bee-hive for another minute or two, he would have time to slip down the Sark side of his rock and get to the great wall, and so down into his new hiding-place.

If they tried to land, he could perhaps kill or wound two, three, half-a-dozen, at risk of his own life. But the end would be the same. With a dozen good shots coolly potting at him, he must go down in time, and he had no desire either to kill or to be killed.

He wormed himself over the edge of his hollow and hurried along to the tumbled rocks, carrying his gun and powder-flask—not that he wanted them, but wanted still less to leave them behind. He scrambled over, found his marked rocks, and slipped safely under the overhanging slab. There he could peep out without danger of being seen; and he was barely under cover when the first boat came slowly round again, every bearded face intent on the rock, every eye searching for sign of him.

The other boats passed, and as each one came it seemed to him that every eye on board looked straight up into his own, and he involuntarily shrank down into the shadow of the slab. They could not possibly see him, he was certain; and yet a thrill ran through him each time their searching glances crossed his own.

The rough jests and laughter of the boats had given way now to angry growls at his invisibility. He could hear them cursing him as they passed, and even casting doubts on the veracity of his visitors of the previous night. And these latter upheld their statements with such torrents of red-hot patois that, if they had come to grips and fought the matter out, he would not have been in the least surprised.

Then there came a long interval, when no boats came round. They had probably taken their courage in their hands and landed, and were searching the island. He dropped noiselessly into his well and clambered up into the tunnel, and lay there with only his head out.

And, sure enough, before long he heard the sound of big sea-boots climbing heavily over the rock wall, and the voices of their owners as they passed.

What would they do next, he wondered. Would they imagine him flown, as the result of their last night's visit? Or would they believe him still on the island and bound to come out of his hiding-place sooner or later? Would they give it up and go home? Or would they leave a guard to trap him when hunger and thirst brought him out?

He lay patiently in the mouth of his tunnel till long after the last glimmer of light had faded from under the big slabs that covered in his well. More than once he heard voices, and once they came so close that he was sure they had come upon his tracks, and he crept some distance down his tunnel to be out of sight. But the alarm proved a false one, and the time passed very slowly.

As he lay, he thought of the dead man with the bound hands and feet in the silent chamber behind him, bound by the forebears of these men, who, in turn, were seeking him, and would treat him as ruthlessly if they found him.

He took the lesson to heart, and braced himself to patient endurance, though, indeed, he began to ask himself gloomily what was the use of it all. In the end, their venomous persistence must make an end of him. One man could not fight for ever against a whole community.

And at that he chided himself. Not a whole community! For was not Nance on his side—hoping and praying and working for him with all her might and main? And her mother, and Grannie, and the Vicar, and the Doctor, and the Sénéchal? He was sure they all knew him far too well to doubt him. And all these and the Truth must surely prevail.

But the long strain had been sore on him, and in spite of his anxieties he fell asleep in his hole, and dreamed that the dead man came crawling down the tunnel, and dragged him back into the chamber, and tied his hands and feet, and went away, and left him to die there all alone. And so strong was the impression upon him that, when he woke, he lay wondering who had loosed his bonds, and could not make out how he had got back into the mouth of the tunnel.

It was still quite dark. He was stiff with lying in that cramped place. He was strongly tempted to climb out and see how matters lay. For he might be able to find out in the dark, whereas daylight would make him prisoner again.

He wanted eggs, too. Nance's provision had served him well all day, but if he had to spend another day there something more would be welcome.

But then it struck him that if he went up in the dark he might never be able to find his way back again. The cleft under the slab was difficult to hit upon even in daylight. There were scores of just similar ragged black holes among the tumbled rocks of the great wall.

As he lay pondering it all, the grim idea came into his head of dragging the dead man through the tunnel, and hoisting him up outside, and leaving him propped up among the boulders where they would be sure to find him.

He knew how arrantly superstitious they were, most of them. They had been brought up on ghosts and witches and evil spirits, and, fearless as they might be of things mortal and natural, all that bordered on the unknown and uncanny held for them unimaginable terrors. The dead man might serve a useful purpose after all; and the grim idea grew.

He could decide nothing, however, till he learned if he had the rock to himself; and he determined to take the risk of finding this out.

He cautiously climbed the well, and by the look of the stars he judged it still very early morning. A brooding grey darkness covered the sea; the sky was dark even in the east.

He slipped off his coat and left it hanging out of the cleft as a landmark, and lowered himself silently from rock to rock, till he stood among the rank grasses below.

Food first—so, after patient listening for smallest sound or sign of a watch, he crept down to the slope where the puffins' nests were, and, wrapping his hand in Nance's napkin, managed to get out a dozen eggs from as many different holes, in spite of the fierce objections of their legitimate owners.

He tied these up carefully in the blood-spotted cloth, and carried them up to his cleft. Then he stole away like a shadow, to find out, if he could, if there was any one else on the rock besides himself and the dead man.

There had been hot disputes on that head in the boats. Those who were there for the first time had even gone the length of casting strongest possible doubts as to whether those who were there the night before had seen or heard anything whatever, and did not hesitate to state their belief that they were all on a fool's errand. The others replied in kind, and when the further question was mooted as to keeping watch all night, the scoffers told the others to keep watch if they chose; for themselves, they were going home to their beds.

"Frightened of ghosts, I s'pose," growled one.

"No more than yourself, John Drillot. But we've wasted a day on this same fooling, and the man's not here; and for me, I doubt if he's ever been here."

"And what of the things we found in the shelter?" said Drillot. "Think they came there of themselves?"

"I don't care how they came there. It's not old cloaks and blankets we came after. Maybe he has been here. I don't know. But he's not here now, and I've had enough of it."

"B'en! I'm not afraid to stop all night—if anyone'll stop with me"—and if no one had offered he would have been just as well pleased. "Don't know as I'd care to stop all alone."

"Frightened of ghosts, maybe," scoffed the other.

"You stop with me, Tom Guille, and we'll see which is frightenedest of ghosts, you or me."

But Tom Guille believed in ghosts as devoutly as any old woman in Sark, and he was bound for home, no matter what the rest chose to do.

"There's not a foot of the rock we haven't searched," said he, "and the man's not here; so what's the use of waiting all night?"

"Because if he's in hiding it's at night he'll come out."

"Come out of where?"

"Wherever he's got to."

"That's Guernsey, most likely. His friends have arranged to lift him off here first chance that came; and it came before we did, and you'll not see him in these parts again, I warrant you."

"I'll wait with you, John, if you're set on it, though I doubt Tom's right, and the man's gone," said Peter Vaudin of La Ville. And John Drillot found himself bound to the adventure.

"Do we keep the boat?" asked Vaudin.

"No ... for then one of us must sit in her all night, or she will bump herself to pieces. You will come back for us in the morning, Philip."

"I'll come," said Philip Guille, and presently they stood watching the boats pulling lustily homewards, and devoutly wishing they were in them.

Every foot of the rock, as they knew it, had already been carefully raked over. The possible hiding-places were few. But no one knows better than a Sark man what rocks can do in the way of slits and tunnels and caves, and it was just this possibility that had set John Drillot to his unwonted, and none too welcome, task. The murderer—as he deemed Gard—might have found some place unknown to any of them, and might be lying quietly waiting for them to go. If that was so, he must come out sooner or later, and the chances were that he would steal out in the night.

So the two watchers prowled desultorily about the rock, poking again into every place that suggested possible concealment for anything larger than a puffin. There might be openings in the rifted basement rocks which only the full ebb would discover, and these might lead up into chambers where a man could lie high and dry till the tide allowed him out again. And so they hung precariously over the waves and poked and peered, and found nothing.

They had clambered over the great wall more than once before Vaudin said: "G'zamin, John, I wonder if there's any holes here big enough to take a man?"

"He'd have to be a little one, and this Gard's not that," and they stood looking at the wall. "'Sides, them rocks lie on the rock itself, and there's no depth to them."

But Vaudin was not sure that there might not be room for a man to lie flat under some of the big slabs, and began to poke about among them.

"Some one's been up here," he said, pointing to one of Gard's own scorings.

"Bin up there four times myself," said Drillot, "an' so have all the rest. There's no room to hide a man there, Peter. If he's hid anywhere, he'll come out in the night. Maybe Philip Guille's right, and he's safe in Guernsey by this. Come along to that shelter and let's have a drink."

They had their bottle out of the boat, and they had also come upon Gard's bottle of cognac, of which quite half remained. It was a finer cordial than their own, so they sat drinking them turn about, and watching the sun set, and chatting spasmodically, till it grew too dark to do more than sit still with safety.

They were by no means drunk, but the spirits had made them heavy, and when John Drillot solemnly suggested that they should keep watch about, Peter Vaudin as solemnly agreed, and offered to take first duty.

So John curled his length inside the bee-hive, and made himself comfortable with Gard's cloak and blanket, and was presently snoring like a whole pig-sty. And that had a soporific effect on Peter. He had only stopped behind to oblige John, and personally had little expectation of anything coming of it. Moreover, the night air was chilly. If he could get that cloak from John now! He crawled in to try, but big John was rolled up like a caterpillar. It was warmer inside there than out, anyway. And he could keep watch there just as well as outside; so he propped himself up alongside John, and braced his mind to sentry duty.

CHAPTER XXIX

HOW HE CAME INTO AN UNKNOWN PLACE

Having lodged his eggs in a ledge under the big slab, Gard stole away to learn, if he could, if he had the rock all to himself.

He wanted water, and he wanted his bottle of cognac and the tin dipper; for puffins' eggs, while not unpalatable beaten up with cognac, are of a flavour calculated to exercise the strongest stomach when eaten raw.

He feared the men would have made away with all his small possessions, but he could only try. So he stole like a shadow round the crown of the ridge and along towards the shelter, standing at times motionless for whole minutes till the rush of the waves below should pass and give him chance of hearing.

But on L'Etat the sound of many waters never ceases night or day, and the night wind hummed among the stones of the shelter, and, as it happened, John Drillot had just lurched over in avoidance of a lump of rock which was intruding on his comfort, and in so doing had lodged his heavy boot in Peter Vaudin's ribs, and so their sonorous duet was stilled, and neither of them was very sound asleep, when Gard, after listening anxiously and hearing nothing, dropped on his hands and knees and felt cautiously inside.

Peter felt the blind hand groping in the dark, and was wide awake in an instant. He hurled himself at the intruder, as well as a man could who had been lying back against the wall half asleep a moment before; and Gard turned and sped away along the side of the ridge, with Peter at his heels and John Drillot thundering ponderously in the rear.

"What is't, Peter boy?" shouted John.

"It's him. This way!" yelled Peter, out of the dimness in front, as he stumbled and staggered along the ragged inadequacies of the ridge.

If Gard had had time for consideration, he would have led them a chase elsewhere first, but, in the sudden upsetting of lighting on what he had persuaded himself was not there, he lost his head and made straight for cover.

Peter Vaudin was at the base of the rock wall as he wriggled silently under the big slab, and it was only by a violent jerk that he got his foot clear of Peter's grip. And Peter, strung to the occasion, kept his hand on the spot where the foot had disappeared, and waited a moment for John Drillot to come up before he followed it.

"Gone in here," he jerked, as he climbed cautiously up.

"Can't have gone far, then," panted John. "Sure it was him?"

"Had him by the foot, but he got loose. Here we are," as he poked about, and came at last on the hole below the slab. "Come on, John ... can't be far away.... Big hole"—as he kicked about down below—"no bottom, far as I can see."

"Best wait for daylight, to see where we're getting."

"Oui gia! Man doux, it's not me's going down here till I know what's below."

So they sat and kicked their heels and waited for the day, certain in their own minds that their quarry was run to earth and as good as caught.

Gard had swept down both his coat and his cloth full of eggs in his sudden entrance. He stood at the bottom of the well to see if they would follow, while Peter's long legs kicked about for foothold. He heard them decide to wait for daylight, and then he noiselessly picked up his coat and his soppy bundle of broken eggs, pushed them into the tunnel, and crawled in after them.

He was trapped, indeed, but he doubted very much if any fisherman on Sark would venture down that tunnel. They were brawny men, used to leg and elbow room, and, as a rule, heartily detested anything in the shape of underground adventure. They might, of course, get over some miners to explore for them. Or they might content themselves with sitting down on top of his hole until he was starved out. In any case, his rope was nearly run; but yet he was not disposed to shorten it by so much as an inch.

As he wormed his way along the tunnel, the recollection of those other openings off the dead man's cave came back to him. He would try them. He pushed on with a spurt of hope.

The tunnel was not nearly so long now that he knew where he was going; in fact, now that nothing but it stood between him and capture, it seemed woefully inadequate.

When his head and elbows no longer grazed rock he dropped his coat and crawled into the chamber. He felt his way round to the dried packages, and cautiously emptied half-a-dozen and prepared them for his use.

This set him sneezing so violently that it seemed impossible that the watchers outside should not hear him. It also gave him an idea.

He struck a light and kindled one of his torches, and the dead man leaped out of the darkness at him as before. That gave him another idea.

Propping up his light on the floor, he emptied package after package of the powdered tobacco into the tunnel, and wafted it down towards the entrance with his jacket. Then with his knife he cut the lashings from the dead man's hands and feet, and carried him across—he was very light, for all his substance had long since withered out of him—and laid him in the tunnel as though he was making his way out.

If he knew anything of Sark men and miners, he felt fairly secure for some time to come, so he sat himself down, as far as possible from the snuff, and made such a meal as was possible off puffins' eggs, mixed good and bad and unredeemed by any palliating odour and flavour. They were not appetising, but they stayed his stomach for the time being.

It was only then that he remembered that he had left his gun and powder-flask behind him. He had placed them on a ledge just inside the mouth of the tunnel, and in his haste had forgotten to pick them up. He had no intention of using them, however, and he would not go back for them.

When his scanty meal was done, he cautiously emptied a number of the packages and rolled them into torches, and deliberated as to which of the black openings he should attempt first.

That one opposite, out of which the dead man's legs sprawled grotesquely, was the one by which he had entered. This one, then, near which he sat, must run on towards the centre of the island—if it ran on at all; and, since all were equally unknown and hopeful, he would try this first.

His tarred paper torches, though they burned with a clear flame, gave forth a somewhat pungent odour, so he kicked one of the small barrels to pieces, and with three of the staves and a piece of string made a holder which would carry the torch upright, and also permit him to lay it on the ground or push it in front of him, if need be.

The first tunnel ran in about thirty feet, and then the slant of the roof met the floor at so sharp an angle that further passage was impossible.

The second, third, and fourth the same; and he began to fear they were all blind alleys leading nowhere.

The openings near his own entrance tunnel he had left till the last, since they obviously led outwards.

Two of them shut down in the same way as all the others, and it was only the dogged determination to leave no chance untried that drove him, with a fresh supply of torches, down the last one of all, the one alongside that out of which the dead man's legs projected.

It took a turn to the left within a dozen feet of the entrance, and, like the rest, it presently narrowed down through a slope in the roof; but just at its narrowest, when he feared he had come to the end, there came a dip in the flooring corresponding to the slope up above, and he found he could wriggle through. Once through, the passage widened and continued to widen, and the going became very rough and broken, with piles of ragged rock and deep black pitfalls in between.

Then, of a sudden, he saw the walls and roof of his passage fall away, and his light flickered feebly in the darkness of a vast place, and he crouched on the rock up which he had climbed, and sat in wonder.

Somewhere below him he could hear the slow rise and fall of water, dull and heavy and without any splash, like the dumb breathing of a captive monster.

And every now and again there came, from somewhere beyond, a low dull thud, like the blow of a padded hammer, and a distant subdued rustle along the outside of the darkness. He knew it was not inside the place he was in, for he could hear the soft rise and fall of the water quite clearly, but these other sounds came to him from a distance, muted as though his ears had suddenly gone deaf.

"Those dull blows," he said to himself, "are the waves on the outside of L'Etat. That low rustling is the rush of them along the lower rocks. The water inside here probably comes in through some openings below tide-level. I am quite safe here, even if they get past the dead man's cave—quite safe until I starve. Unless there are fish to be had"—and he felt a spark of hope. "And maybe there are devil-fish"— and he shivered and glanced below and about him fearfully.

His homely torch did no more than faintly illumine the rock he sat on and those close at hand, and cast a gigantic uncouth shadow of himself on the rough wall behind. All beyond was solid darkness, blacker even than a black Sark night.

He sat wondering vaguely if any before him had penetrated to that strange place. It was odd and uncanny to feel that his eyes were the very first to look upon it. And then, away in front, and apparently at a great distance above him, he became aware of a difference in the solid darkness. It seemed almost as though it had thinned. His eye had seemed able for a moment to carry beyond the narrow circle of the torch, but when he peered into the void to see what this might mean, it all seemed solid as before.

As his straining eyes sought relief in something visible, their side-glance caught once more that same impression of movement in the darkness. And presently it came again and stronger—a strange greenish fluttering up in the roof—very faint, as though the roof were smoke on which a soft green light played for a moment and vanished.

But by degrees the light grew, though at no time did it become more than a wan ghost of a light, and from its curious fluttering he judged that it came through water.

Reasoning from the trend of the cavern, he came to the conclusion that somewhere on that further side there were openings into the deep water beyond, on which the sunlight played and struck at times into the cave, and he was keen to look more closely into it.

He lowered his torch to the side of his rock, and its feeble flicker fell on a chaos of rocks below. He looked long and cautiously for supple yellow arms or tiny whip-like threads which might coil suddenly round his legs and drag him to hideous death.

But he saw nothing of the kind. The rocks were dry and bare, not a limpet nor a sea-weed visible, and leaving his jacket for a landmark as before, he slowly let himself down from one huge boulder to another, till he found himself climbing another great pile in front.

When at last his head rose above this ridge, he almost rolled over at the sight of two huge green eyes blinking lazily at him out of the darkness in front—two great openings far below sea-level, through which filtered dimly the wavering green light whose refractions fluttered in the roof.

The vast trough below him heaved gently now and then, with a ponderous solemnity which filled him with awe. He felt himself an intruder. He felt like a fly creeping about a sleeping tiger. He hardly dared to breathe, lest the brooding spirit of the place should rise suddenly out of some dark corner and squash him on his rock as one does a crawling insect; and his anxious eyes swept to and fro for the smallest sign of danger.

But, plucking up courage from immunity, and dreading to be caught in the dark in that weird place, he crawled over the boulders towards the side wall of the cavern to get as near to those openings as possible. From the very slight movement of the water, which was ever on the boil round the outside of L'Etat, he judged them deep down among the roots of the island, far below the turmoil of the surface, but he must see and make sure.

With infinite toil and many a scrape and bruise, he got round at last, and could look right down into the dim green depths, and what he saw there filled him with sickening fear.

The water was crystal clear, and in through the nearer opening, as he looked, a huge octopus propelled itself in leisurely fashion, its great tentacles streaming out behind, its hideous protruding eyes searching eagerly for prey.

Just inside the opening it gathered itself together for a moment, and seemed to look so meaningly right up into his eyes that he found himself shrinking behind a rock lest it should see him. Then it clamped itself to the side of the opening and spread wide its arms for anything that might come its way.

He watched it, fascinated. He saw fishes large and small unconsciously touch the quivering tentacles, which on the instant twisted round them and dragged them in to the rending beak below the hideous eyes. And then he saw another similar monster come floating in on similar quest, and in a moment they were locked in deadly fight—such a writhing and coiling and straining and twisting of monstrous fleshy limbs, which swelled and thrilled, and loosed and gripped, with venom past believing—such a clamping to this rock and that—such tremendous efforts at dislodgment.

It was a nightmare. It sickened him. He turned and crawled feebly away, anxious only now to get out of this awful place without falling foul of any similar monsters among the rocks.

CHAPTER XXX

HOW NANCE WATCHED FROM AFAR

From the headland above Brenière, Nance had watched the boats go plunging across to L'Etat.

Very early that morning she had sped across the Coupée and up the long roads to the Seigneurie, but the Seigneur was away in Guernsey still, busied on the vital matter of raising still more money for the mines in which he was a firm believer, mortgaging his Seigneurie for the purpose, assured in his own mind that all would be well in the end.

Then to the Vicar and the Sénéchal, and these set off at once for the harbour, but found themselves powerless in the face of public opinion. Argument and remonstrance alike fell on deaf ears. The Vicar appealed to their sense of right; the Sénéchal forbade their going. But their minds were doggedly set on it, and they went.

"I shall hold you to account," stormed Philip Guille.

"B'en, M. le Sénéchal, we'll pay it all among us," and away they went; and back to her look-out by Brenière went Nance, and the Vicar with her for comfort in this dark hour.

They watched the boats circling the rock, round and round. They heard the firing, and Nance flung herself on the ground in an agony of weeping, sure that the end had come. For they could only be firing at Gard, and what could one man do against so many?

"They have killed him," she moaned.

And the Vicar could only tighten his pale lips, and smooth her hair with his thin white hand, as she writhed on the ground at his side. For he could but think she was right. They were good shots, the Sark men, and it needs but one bullet to kill a man.

If Nance had looked a moment longer she might have seen Gard slip down from the ridge to the wall, but the bombardment of the shelter, which gave him his chance, made an end of her hopes, and her face was hidden in the turf.

The Vicar's sight was not keen enough to see clearly what was passing. But when the men landed on the rock, and overran it in their search, he could not fail to see their figures on the ridge against the sky, and an exclamation of surprise roused Nance.

"What is it?" she jerked.

"They have landed over there. They seem to be searching the rock."

"Then—" and she sat up suddenly and gazed intently across at L'Etat, and then sprang to her feet, a new creature. "For, see you, Mr Cachemaille," she cried, "if they had killed him they would not be searching for him, nenni-gia!"

"That is true, child," said the Vicar hopefully, and then, less hopefully, "but where shall a man hide on L'Etat?"

"Ah now! I remember. Just as I was leaving him last night, he told me—"

"As you were leaving him—last night?" and the old man gazed at her as though he doubted his ears or her right senses.

"But yes," she cried impatiently. "I swam across there last night to see if Bernel was there and to take him some food. But you are not to tell that to any one. And he told me—"

"You swam across?—to L'Etat?"

"Yes, yes! We have done it many times, and, besides, I had the bladders—"

The Vicar shook his head helplessly. She forgot to explain so much that he did not understand. But he grasped at one thread.

"And Bernel?"

"Ah, my poor Bernel! He is drowned," she said, with a heave of the breast, but with her eyes intent on L'Etat. "I wanted him to take the bladders, but he would not; and it was the first night after the storm, you see, and the waves were big still, and he never got to L'Etat, and he never came back; so, you see—"

"Truly, you are being sorely tried, my child. But your brother was a better swimmer than most. May we not hope—"

But she shook her head, intent on the doings on the rock, and full, for the moment, of the hope she could draw from Gard's hint about a hiding-place of which she knew nothing. For if she and Bernel had never discovered it, how should these others? And obviously they were searching, for they prowled about the rock like ants, and poked here and there, and wandered on and came back. And if they still sought they had not yet found; and so there was a new spring of hope in her heart.

"Yes, truly, they are searching," she murmured, and forgot the Vicar and all else.

He tried to induce her to go back home with him, but she would not move. For the moment all her hope in life was in peril on the rock, and she must see all that went on; and finally he had to leave her there, and she hardly knew that he had gone. She wanted only to be left alone, to nurse her new-born hope and watch in fear and trembling for any symptom of its overthrow.

But she was not to be left in peace, for Madame Julie had heard the firing also, and had come round the headland by the miners' cottages, exulting in the fact that her enemy was run to earth at last and was meeting righteous punishment.

And as she prowled about there, chafing at the delay in the return of the boats, she came suddenly on Nance gazing out at L'Etat with a face—not, as Julie would have expected, downcast and woe-begone, but full of eager expectancy. And the sight of her, and in such case, stirred Julie to venom.

"Ah then—there you are, mademoiselle, listening to the end of your fancy gentleman! And the right end, too, ma foi! A man that goes knocking his neighbours on the head—it's right he should be shot like a rabbit—"

Nance's face quivered, but she did not even look round.

"You'll see them coming back presently, and they'll bring his body back with them in the boat, all full of holes. And then I'll feel that my Tom's paid for—"

"Do you hear?" she cried, planting herself in front of Nance, and jerking her hands up and down in her excitement and the exaspeiation of receiving no response. "Do you hear me—you? Or are you gone crazy for love of your murderer?"—and she made as though to lay wild hands on the girl.

"You are wicked! You are evil! You are a devil!" said Nance through her little white teeth, and looked so as though she might fly at her that Julie drew off.

"Aha—spitfire!—wildcat!—you would bite?"

Nance, all ashake with disgust, stooped suddenly and picked up a lump of rock.

"Go!" she said, in a voice of such concentrated fury that it was little more than a whisper. "Go!—before I do you ill;" and she looked so like it that Julie turned and fled, expecting the rock between her shoulders at every step.

But the rock was on the ground, and Nance was intent again on L'Etat.

She stood there watching, until she saw the boats put off, and then she turned and sped like a rabbit—across the waste lands—across the Coupée—over Clos Bourel fields into Dixcart—over Hog's Back to the Creux.

She ran through the tunnel just as the boats came up, and her eyes were wide with expectant fear, as they swept them hungrily.

"What have you done then, out there, Philip Vaudin?" she cried, as his boat's nose grated on the shingle.

"Pardi, ma garche, we have done nothing."

"But the shooting?"

"Some one shot at the shelter to see if he was inside, and the rest shot because they thought there must be something to shoot at."

"And you have not got him?" asked another disappointedly.

"Never even seen him."

"Ah ba!"

"Either he's gone or he's under cover, though, ma fé, I don't know where he'd find it on L'Etat," and Nance's heart beat hopefully. "However, John Drillot and Peter Vaudin are stopping the night in case he is still there and ventures out of his hole," and her heart sank again, and kicked rebelliously that a man should be hunted thus, like a rabbit.

She spent a night of misery, wondering what was happening on L'Etat, and was at her post above Brenière as soon as it was light.

She saw Philip Vaudin come round from the Creux in his boat and run across to the rock, and almost as soon as he had disappeared round Quette d'Amont, he came speeding back, alone, and not to the harbour, but straight to the fishermen's rough landing-place inside Brenière.

"What is it then, Philip?" she asked anxiously, as he hauled himself up the rocks on to the turf.

"I've come for two miners," he panted, for he had come quickly. "They've run him to earth in a hole, but they won't either of them go in after him, and they want some one who will."

"Ah, then!"

"Yes. He came out in the night, and they chased him, but he got into his hole, and they're sitting on it ever since," and he hurried away through the waste of gorse and bracken to the miners' cottages.

Volunteers were evidently not over plentiful. It was a considerable time before he came back with a Welshman, Evan Morgan, and a young Cornishman, John Trevna, and neither of them seemed over eager for the job.

"For, see you," had been Morgan's view, "coing in a hole after a man what hass a gun iss not a nice pissness, no inteet!" and the Cornishman agreed with him.

However, they put off, and Nance crouched in the bracken and watched all their doings.

She had long since caught sight of John Drillot and Peter Vaudin sitting on the rock wall, and wondered what kind of a hiding-place Gard could possibly have found therein. A poor one, she feared, and that the end would be quick.

The boat disappeared round the corner, and presently she saw the three men join the others at the wall, and they all clustered there and talked, and then one by one they disappeared into the wall itself, and she sat watching in fear and trembling.

CHAPTER XXXI

HOW TWO WENT IN AND THREE CAME OUT

"It iss better to sit here two, three days till he comse out than to go in and get yourself killt, yes inteet!" was the burden of Evan Morgan's answer to all their arguments for a speedy assault. And "Iss, sure!" was Trevna's curt, complete endorsement.

But when, at John Drillot's suggestion, they had squeezed under the slab to have a look at what lay below, and had peered down the slit that Gard tried first, and had then lighted on the tunnel, and had found the gun and powder-flask jammed in a crevice—that put a different face on the matter.

And, after prolonged discussion as to the proper method of procedure, especially in the matter of precedence, it was at last arranged that Evan Morgan should go first with his miner's lamp, and that John Trevna should follow close behind, carrying the gun.

"And iss it understood that I shoot him if I see him?" asked Trevna, to make sure of his ground and make his conscience easy.

"Pardi, yes, mon gars! Shoot straight, and the Island will thank you," asserted John Drillot.

"Ant for Heaven's sake, John Trevna, see you ton't shoot me behint by mistake," urged Evan Morgan; and they disappeared slowly into the tunnel, while the other two stood waiting expectantly in the well.

Accustomed as they were to narrow places, this long worm-hole of a tunnel, with the doubtful possibilities that lay beyond it, seemed as endless to the militant members of the expedition as it did to the waiters outside.

Occasionally a hollow sound came booming down the tunnel, when one or other grunted out a word of objurgation on the narrowness of things, but for the most part they wormed along in silence, Morgan shifting forward his lamp, foot by foot, and straining his eyes into the darkness ahead, Trevna close behind with his gun at full cock and ready for instant action.

"Gad'rabotin, but they take their time, those two!" said John Drillot, impatiently, outside.

"It iss going right through to Wailee, I do think," growled Evan Morgan inside.

And it was just after that that there broke out in the depths of the tunnel a commotion so extraordinary that the listeners outside could make nothing at all of it, and could only lurch about in amazement and climb up and push their heads into the tunnel, and wonder what it all meant. Then, in the midst of the turmoil, there came the thunderous bellow of the gun, and after a time a trickle of thin blue smoke floated lazily out and hung about the well; and the men outside sniffed appreciatively, and said, "Ch'est b'en!" and waited hopefully.

Evan Morgan, shifting forward his light, got an impression of something in the narrow way in front, and suddenly he was taken with the biggest fit of sneezing he had ever had in his life. He banged down the lamp and threw up his head till it cracked against the roof, then banged his chin against the floor, and finally propped himself, like a sick dog, on his two front paws, and sneezed and sneezed and sneezed for dear life.

Then John Trevna began. He had the sense to lay down his gun, or Morgan might have got the charge in his back. And so they sneezed in concert, until their heads were clearer than they had been for many a day. And the sound of it all to those outside was like the sound of mortal combat.

Then Morgan, wiping his streaming eyes on the sleeve of his coat, in a state of extreme exhaustion, caught sight of that which lay just beyond him, and he saw that it was a man crawling down the tunnel to meet him.

"Shoot, John, shoot! He iss here," he yelled, and laid himself flat to give Trevna his chance.

And Trevna, between two sneezes, picked up his gun, though he could see nothing to shoot at, and ran the barrel forward above Morgan's head and fired, and the roar of it in that confined space came near to deafening them both.

The smoke hung thick and choked them, as they gasped it in in gulps while they sneezed, and the light had gone out with the concussion.

They lay for a time exhausted. Then the atmosphere cleared somewhat, and they lay in the thick darkness straining their ears for any sound, but heard nothing.

"What did you see, Evan Morgan?" whispered Trevna at last.

"It wass a man."

"Then I have killed him, for he does not move. Can you light the lamp?"

"I can not—in here. I am coing out. I haf hat enough of this."

"We must take him out, too."

"You can tek him, then, John Trevna. I haf hat enough of him and this hole."

"Don't be a fool, Evan Morgan. If it wass a man, and he got that load in him as close as that, he iss deader than Tom Hamon."

"Well, you can go an' see. I am coing out," and he began to wriggle backwards, and Trevna was fain to go too.

But presently they came to one of the somewhat wider places where the wall had fallen away, and Trevna squeezed himself tightly into this.

"You go on, then, Evan Morgan," he said, "if you can get past, and I will go back and bring him out."

"You are a fool, John Trevna, to meddle with him any more. Iff the man iss dead, he iss just as well left there."

"If he iss dead he cannot harm me, and I would like to see the man I have killed."

"Ugh!" grunted Morgan, and crawled on, legs first.

Trevna wormed along up the tunnel, groping cautiously in front of him at each forward lurch, and at last his hands fell on what he sought, and at the same moment he began sneezing again.

It would be no easy job dragging a dead man all down that tunnel, he thought. But when, after cautious feeling here and there, he got a grip of the man's coat collar, to his surprise it came away in his hand, but at the same time it seemed to him that the body was extraordinarily light.

He tried again with a fresh grip on the coat, but it tore like paper, and, after thinking it over, he unstrapped his leather belt and got it round the man below the armpits, and so was able to haul him slowly along.

When Evan Morgan's wriggling legs came slowly out of the tunnel, John Drillot and Peter Vaudin were almost dancing with excitement, and their first surprise was the sight of him when, by rights, John Trevna should have been the one to come out first.

"Well then? What have you done? And where is John Trevna?" cried John Drillot.

"Ach! He iss a fool. He hass shot the man and now he will pring him out when he woult pe much petter buried where he iss."

"He's quite right. What was all the noise about?"

"That wass the shooting."

"Before that. You all seemed to be howling at once."

"That wass the sneezing. It iss full of sneezing down there," and his red eyes still showed the effect of it.

It was a long time before they heard the laboured sounds of Trevna's coming. But at last his legs wriggled out, then his body, then with a lurch he hauled up to the mouth of the tunnel that which he had brought with him. And at sight of it they all started back against the sides of the well, with various cries but equal amazement.

"O mon Gyu!" cried Peter Vaudin.

"Thousand devils!" cried John Drillot.

"Heavens an' earth!" gasped Evan Morgan.

John Trevna gazed open-mouthed, for he had little breath left in him.

And from the black mouth of the tunnel the strange and terrible figure of the dead man looked quietly down at them and filled them with amazement.

Trevna's heavy charge had blown in the top of the skull. The shrunken yellow face wore the gaunt eager look of one who had died the slow death of starvation. It seemed to be trying to get at them to bite and rend them.

Peter Vaudin was the first to climb the wall behind him, but the rest were close at his heels, and hustled him up through the crack under the slab.

Peter struck down towards the landing-place the moment he had wriggled through.

"Stop then, Peter," called John Drillot, in a low insistent voice, lest that dreadful thing below should hear him.

"Not me! I've had enough, John Drillot. That is not what we came for ... and I had hold of its leg last night," and he shivered at the recollection, and the thought that it might have turned on him and gripped him with its grisly hands.

"I don't know what it is," began John Drillot, "but—"

"It's the man I shot inside there," said Trevna.

"That man hass peen det a hundert years," said Morgan.

"All the same, he was running about last night," said Peter, "and I had hold of his leg"—with another shiver.

"He's dead enough now, anyway," said Drillot.

"Eh b'en! leave him where he is, and let's get away. I've heard say there were ghosts on L'Etat, and now I know it. No good comes of meddling with these things."

"But we ought to take him with us."

"Take him with us!" almost shrieked Peter. "And let him loose on Sark! Why then?"

"Whatever he was last night, he's dead enough now.... Will you help me to get him up, John Trevna?"

"Iss, sure! He's got my belt."

"Not in my boat, John Drillot," cried Peter. "Not in my boat. I've had enough of him, pardi!" and he set off at speed for the boat.

"Don't be a fool, Peter. You, Evan Morgan, run down and stop him going. Come on, John Trevna," and after peering cautiously down to make sure the dead man had not moved, they dropped into the well again.

The shrivelled figure was very light, as Trevna had found. It was only their repugnance at handling it that made their task a heavy one. One above and one below, they managed at last to get it up above ground, and then John Trevna slipped his belt to its middle, and carried it with one hand down the slope to the boat.

There they found Evan Morgan holding the approach to the landing-place against Peter, with a lump of rock, while Philip, in the boat below, stood shouting at them to know what was the matter.

At sight of the others and their burden, however, he had no eyes for anything else.

"What have you got there, John Drillot?"

"A dead man."

"Aw, then! That's not Gard."

"It's the only man here, anyway. Pull close up, Philip—"

"Not in my boat, John Drillot!" from Peter.

"We must take this to the Sénéchal," said John angrily. "If you don't want to come you can wait here. If you don't make less noise, I will knock you on the head myself," and he jumped down into the boat, and took the dead man from Trevna, and laid him carefully in the bows. The others jumped in, and Peter, sooner than be knocked on the head or left behind, sulkily followed, and sat himself on the extreme edge of the stern as far away from the dead man as he could get.

CHAPTER XXXII

HOW JULIE MEDITATED EVIL

Nance had crouched all the morning, in the bracken above Brenière, on the knife-edge of expectancy. And behind her, at a safe distance, crouched Julie Hamon, watching Nance and L'Etat at the same time, as a cat in the shade watches a sparrow playing in the sunshine.

"What will be the end? What will be the end?" sighed Nance. They had all gone down out of sight, across there, and it was terrible to sit here waiting, waiting, waiting for what she feared.

If they had indeed run Gard to his hiding-place, as Philip Vaudin had said, there could be but one possible end to it; and she sat, sad-eyed and wistful, waiting for them to come up again.

It seemed as if they would never come, and she never took her eyes off the rock wall on L'Etat.

And then at last she sprang to her feet. One of them had come up again. She could not see which. Then the others appeared, and they seemed to stand talking. Then one went off round the slope and another ran after him, and the other two went back into the rock wall.

What could they be at? She stood gazing intently.

The two came up again, and—yes—they carried something, or one of them did, and they two went off round the corner also. And presently she saw the boat coming round, and saw by its head that it was for the Creux. She turned and sped across by the same way as yesterday, and Julie followed her at a safe distance. And it seemed to Nance, as she hurried through the familiar hedge-gaps and lanes and across the headlands, that the world had lost its brightness, and that life was desperately hard and trying.

On Derrible Head there might be a chance of seeing. She ran up to the highest point by the old cannon, just as the boat was coming in under La Conchée.

And—oh, mon Dieu! mon Dieu! yes—there, in the bows, lay the body of a man!—and the tears she had kept back all day broke out now in a fury of weeping. She could hardly see, but she ran on, falling at times and bruising herself, staggering to her feet again, stumbling blindly through a mist of tears.

The boat was drawn up by the time she got there, and a curious crowd surrounded it. She pushed through. She must see.

And then the weight fell off her heart, and it was all she could do to keep from screaming. For this poor thing, whatever it was, was not Stephen Gard and never had been.

She wanted to sing and dance and scream her joy aloud. They had not found him.

"What is this, John Drillot?" asked Julie, alongside her, black with anger, as she pointed to the body.

"Ma fé—a ghost, they say. John Trevna shot him, but he had been dead a long time before that, though he was alive last night, for Peter had hold of his leg as he ran."

"And where is the other—the one you went for?"

"He's not on L'Etat, anyway, ma fille," and they lifted the body on to a piece of sailcloth, and carried it off through the tunnel for the Sénéchal to look into.

So Stephen Gard's hiding-place had proved effective, and they had not found him. But, of a certainty, he must be starving, and so away home sped Nance, to prepare a parcel of food to take across to him. And Julie, her black brows pinched together and her face set in a frown of venomous intention, never once let her out of her sight.

It was after midnight when Nance stole across the fields, carrying her little parcel and her swimming-bladders, and made her way to Brenière point.

It was a still night, with a sky full of stars, and her heart was high for the moment, though when her thoughts ran on, in spite of her, it fell again. For things could not go on this way for ever, and she saw no way out.

She dropped her outer things by a bush, and let herself quietly down the rocks and into the water, and the black-faced woman who presently stood by that bush snarled curses after her and was filled with unholy exultation. For Nance could have only one reason for going across there, and on the morrow the men should hear of it, and she would give them no rest till Gard was made an end of.

What that thing was that they had brought home, she did not know, but they were fools to be satisfied with that when the man they had gone after was undoubtedly still on the rock.

So she sat down by Nance's gown and cloak, and revolved schemes for her discomfiture and the undoing of Stephen Gard.

CHAPTER XXXIII

HOW HOPE CAME ONCE AGAIN

Nance found the passage of the Race more trying then ever before. The strain of these latter days had been very great, and the thought of Bernel tended to unnerve her.

On the other hand, the knowledge that Gard had outwitted the whole strength of the Island cheered and braced her, and she struggled valiantly through the broken waters till at last she hung panting on the black ledge where she was in the habit of landing.

She scrambled up among the boulders and made straight for the great wall. She had decided in her own mind that he would probably be somewhere in there, possibly afraid to come out, as he would not know if the Sark men were still on the rock.

As nearly as she could, she climbed to the place she had seen the men go in, and then she cried softly, "Steve! Mr. Gard!" and went on calling, as she moved up and down along the base of the wall.

And at last her heart jumped wildly as she heard her name faintly from inside the wall, and presently Gard himself came crawling from under the big slab and jumped down to her side.

"Nance! You are a good angel to me," and he flung his arms round her and kissed her again and again.

"But oh, my dear, I would not have you risk your life for me like this."

"It is nothing. I am all right," said Nance, forgetting the weariness and dangers of the passage in her joy at finding him alive and well. "I have brought you food," and she pushed her little parcel into his hands.

"I hardly dare to eat it when I think what it has cost you."

"That would be foolish, and you must be starving."

"Truly, I am hungry—"

"Eat, then!" and she seized the package and began to tear it open. "It will make me still more glad to see you eat."

"Well, then—" and Nance was gladder than ever that she had come.

"Have they all gone back?" he asked anxiously, as he munched.

"They came back this morning, bringing a strange dead man."

"I know. I put him there—"

"Who is he?"

"I found him in a cave inside the rock. He had been left there very many years ago with his hands and feet tied. I think he must have been a Customs officer of long ago."

Nance shivered, and he felt it.

"You are cold, Nance dear, and I am thinking only of myself;" and he took off his jacket and put it over her slim wet shoulders, in spite of herself.

"If they have all gone back we could go to the shelter. They may have left some of the things there;" and they went along and found the cloak and blanket, and he wrapped them about her.

"I found a still larger cave out of the other one, and I was in there when they came after me. I had put the dead man in the tunnel, and when I came back he was gone; but I did not dare to come out, for I was afraid they might be on the watch still."

"The dead man frightened them. I do not think they will come back. They are afraid of ghosts."

"I hoped he would scare them. But what is to be the end of it all, Nance dear? Things cannot go on this way. Would it be possible to get me a boat and let me get over to Guernsey?"

"If you will wait a little time, that is what we must do, if the truth does not come out."

"And meanwhile you may be drowned in trying to keep me from starving."

"I shall not be drowned and you shall not starve," she said resolutely.

"I would sooner live on puffins' eggs than have you swim across that place. My heart goes right down into my feet when I think of it."

"There is no need. I am all right."

"The Sénéchal and the Seigneur could not stop them?"

"Mr. Le Pelley is in Guernsey still. The Sénéchal they would not listen to. But the truth will come out if only you will wait."

"If I get away, will you come to me, Nance? And all my life I will give to making you happy."

"Yes, I will come. But it will be sore leaving Sark. To a Sark-born there is no other place in the world like Sark."

"All my life I will give to making up for it."

"We will see. Now I must go, or it will be daylight before I get back."

"I shall be in misery till I know you are safe."

"It will be nearly light. I will wave to you from Brenière;" and they went slowly round to the ledges, and parted with kisses; and in the grey morning light he could, for a time, follow the little white figure as it slipped bravely through the bristling black waves of the Race.

But presently he could see her no more, and could but wait, full of anxiety and many prayers, for the signal that should tell of her safety.

But it did not come, and he grew desperate and full of fears.

CHAPTER XXXIV

HOW JULIE'S SCHEMES FELL FLAT

Nance found the return journey still more trying to her strength, but she struggled through, and was devoutly thankful when the slack water under Brenière was reached.

She waded ashore almost too weary to stand, and had to cling to the rough rocks till she recovered her breath. Then, slowly and heavily, she dragged herself up the lower ledges to the little plateau where her clothes were.

Julie had sat revolving grim schemes in that black head of hers.

She hated the girl. She hated Gard. She hated Sark and every one in it. Why had she ever come into these outer wilds? She would have done with it all and get away back to the life that was more to her taste.

But first—yes, mon Dieu, she would leave them something to remember her by.

She had not a doubt that Gard was still on L'Etat. Nothing else would take this girl across there. The shameless hussy!—to go swimming across to see her man with nothing but a white shift on!

She could wound Gard through Nance. She could wound Nance through Gard.

She could wait for the girl as she came up the side of the Head, and push her down again or crush her with a lump of rock.

But that might mean reprisals on the part of the Islanders. She had had experience of the way in which they resented any ill done to one of their number by an outsider. She had no wish to join Gard on his rock.

It would be better to hold the girl up to the scorn and contempt of the neighbours; that would punish her. And by setting the men on Gard's track again, that would punish him and her too.

And so she restrained the natural violence of her temper, which would have run to rocks and bodily injury, and waited in the bracken till Nance came stumbling along in the half-light. Then up she sprang, with an unexpectedness that for the moment took Nance's breath and set her heart pounding with dreadful certainties of ghosts.

"So this is how you go to visit your fancy monsieur on the rock, is it, little Nance? And with nothing on but that! Oh shame! What will the neighbours say when they hear how you swim across to him, and you will not dare deny it?"

But Nance, relieved in her mind on the score of ghosts, and regaining her composure with her breath, simply turned her back on her and proceeded as if she were not there.

"And he is there still!" screamed Julie, dancing round with rage to keep face to face with her. "I was sure of it, though those fools could not find him. I'll see that he's found or starved out, b'en sûr! Yes, if I have to go myself and see to it. As for you—shameless one!—it's the last time you'll swim across there, yes indeed!"—and she raved on and on, as only an angry woman with a grievance can.

Nance slipped her dress over her head and, under cover of it, dropped off her wet undergarment, coolly wrung it out, put on her cloak and walked away, Julie raging alongside with wild words that tumbled over one another in their haste.

Nance walked to the highest point behind Brenière, and waved her white garment a dozen times to let Gard know she was safe, and then turned and set off home through the waist-high bracken and the great cushions of gorse. And close alongside her went Julie, raging and raving the worse for her silence; for there is nothing so galling to an angry soul as to find its most venomous shafts fall harmless from the triple mail of quiet self-possession.

So they came through the other cottages to La Closerie, but the neighbours were all asleep, and those who woke at the sound of her violence, turned over and said, "It's only that mad Frenchwoman in one of her tantrums. Why, in Heaven's name, can't she go to sleep, like other folks?"

Nance went into her own house and quietly closed the door. Julie hammered on it with her fists, as she would dearly have liked to hammer on Nance's face, and then cursed herself off into her own place, slamming the door with such violence as to waken all the fowls and set all the pigs grunting in their sleep.

CHAPTER XXXV

HOW AN ANGEL CAME BRINGING THE TRUTH

Gard's eyes, straining into the dimness of the coming dawn through what seemed to him a most terrible long time, so packed was it with anxious fears, caught at last the white flicker of Nance's signal, and he dropped down just where he stood, among the rough stones of the ridge, with a grateful sigh.

The strain was telling on him. He felt physically weak and worn. Nance's devoted love and courage made his heart beat high, indeed, but his fears on her account strung his laxed cords to breaking point, and then left them looser than before.

He must get away somehow, if only to prevent this constant and terrible risking of her life on his behalf.

He hardly dared to hope that his strategy with the dead man would be of any permanent benefit to him, though there was no knowing. Examination of the body would show that it had been dead for very many years, but his knowledge of the Island superstitions made him doubt if any Sark man would willingly spend a night on L'Etat for a very long time to come.

On the other hand, if the result of their discussions confirmed them in the belief that he was still there, and if, as he constantly feared, they should learn of Nance's comings, and visit upon her the venom they harboured for him, they might so invest the rock that escape would be impossible.

Meagre living, starvation even, he would suffer rather than live more amply at risk of Nance's life, but if the hope of ultimate escape was taken from him then he might as well give in at once and have done with it.

So he lay there, in the broken rocks of the ridge, and looked grimly on life. And the sun rose in a red ball over France, and cleft a shining track across the grey face of the waters, and drew up the mists and thinned away the clouds, till the great plain of the sea and the great dome above were all deep flawless blue, and he saw a thin white curl of smoke rise from the miners' cottages on Sark.

He lay there listless, nerveless, careless of life almost, an Ishmael with every man's hand against him—worse off than Ishmael, he thought, since Ishmael had a desert in which to wander, and he was tied to this bare rock.

But there was Nance! There was always Nance. And at thought of her, his bruised soul found somewhat of comfort and courage once more.

He felt her quivering in his arms again as he pressed her close. He felt again the willing surrender of her sweet wet face. And the thought of it thrilled his cold blood and set it coursing through his veins like new life. Yes, truly, while there was Nance there was hope.

Perhaps the Sénéchal and the Vicar would prevail upon them. Perhaps they would give it up and leave him alone, and then Nance would find him a boat and they would get across to Guernsey. Perhaps, as she kept insisting, something would happen to discover the truth.

So he lay, while the sun mounted high and baked him on the bare stones, but he did not find it hot.

And then, of a sudden, he stiffened and lay watching anxiously. For there, from out the Creux had come a boat—and another, and another, and another—four boat-loads of them again!

So they were coming, after all, and his hopes died sudden death.

Well—let them come and take him and have their will. He was not the first who had paid the price for what he had not done, and human nature must fall to pieces if hung too long on tenterhooks.

He watched them listlessly. He could crawl into his innermost cavern, of course, and could hold it against them all till the end of time, which in this case would be but a trifling span, for a man must eat to live. But what was the use? As well die quick as slow, since there could be but one end to it. And then, to his very great surprise, the boats crept slowly out of sight round the corner of Coupée Bay, and he lay wondering.

What could be the meaning of that? Why had they put in there? Why couldn't they come on and finish the matter?

The sea was all deserted again. If he had not just happened to catch sight of them stealing across there, he would have felt sure they were not coming to-day.

Perhaps they were going to wait there till night, though why on earth they should wait there instead of at the Creux, was past his comprehension.

And then, after a time, to his amazement, he saw them all go crawling back the way they had come. One, two, three, four—yes, they were all there, and they crept slowly round Lâches point and disappeared, and left him gaping.

It was past believing. It was altogether beyond him. He lay, with his eyes glued to the point round which they had gone, stupid with the wonder of it.

They had actually given it up—for to-day, at least, and gone back! He cudgelled his brains for the meaning of it all, till they grew dull and weary with futile thinking.

Perhaps Nance and the Vicar and the Sénéchal had prevailed after all! Perhaps something had turned up at last to prove to the Sark men their misjudgment! Perhaps—well, any way, it was good to be left alone.

He lay there, laxed with the over-strain of all this upsetting, but rejoicing placidly in this one more day of life.

He felt like one granted a day's respite as he stands on the scaffold with the rope round his neck.

Never had the sun shone so brightly. Never had the silver sea danced so merrily. It might be the last he would see of them.

And the sun wheeled on towards Guernsey, and made his deliberate preparations for a setting beyond the ordinary; for the sun, you must know, takes a very special pride in showing the great cliffs of Sark what he can do in the way of transformation scenes and most transcendent colouring.

And Stephen Gard lay there under the ridge on L'Etat, with the wonder and beauty of it all in his face and in his heart, and said to himself that it was probably the last sunset he would ever see, and he was glad to have seen it at its best.

He had a vague idea that heaven would be something like that—tenderly soft and beautiful, and glowing with radiances of unearthly splendour, which whispered to weary hearts of the peace and joy that lay beyond, and gently called them home to rest.

His theology was, without doubt, of the most elemental and objective, and would not have carried him any great lengths in these days; but, for the time being, at all events, it lifted its possessor to a plane of thought above his usual, and tended to quietness and peace of mind.

The sky right away into the east was glowing softly with the wonders of the sunset, and there the delicate tones changed almost momentarily. As his eye followed the tender grace of their transformations, with a delight which he could neither have expressed nor explained, it once more lighted suddenly upon that which he had been looking for so anxiously all day long, and brought him to earth like a broken bird.

Once more a boat had come round the point of Les Lâches, and this time it was speeding towards him as fast as a sail that was as flat almost as a board, and looked to him no more than a thin white cone, could bring it.

So they were coming, after all, and this wonderful sunset might be his last indeed;—and all the tender beauty of the fleecy clouds thinned and paled, and the glory faded as though it had all been but a glorious bubble, and that sharp point of white, speeding across the darkening sea, had pricked it.

But why on earth were they coming now? They had missed the ebb, and it was hours yet to next half-ebb, and they could not hope to land. The white waves were boiling all along the ledges, and the sea for twenty feet out was a surging dapple of foam laced with seething white bubbles. It would be more than any man's life was worth to try and get ashore on L'Etat for many an hour yet.

And there was only one boat! What had become of all the others—of the threatened invasion in force? He sat and watched it in gloomy wonder.

The boat came racing on. As she cleared Brenière her white sail turned to red gold, and the sea below grew purple. There was something white in her bows. He got up heavily, doggedly, forced to it against his will, and walked along the ridge to the eastern point which commanded the landing-place on that side.

There was, without doubt, something white in the bows of the boat, and as he stood gazing at it, it took, to his dazed imagination, the strange form of Nance waving joyful hands to him.

He drew his hands across his eyes. The storm had been sore on them.

The bristling waves of the Race burst in sheets of spray under the glancing bows, but the white spray and the white figure and the pointed white sail were all ablaze in the last rays of the sun, and they all swam before him as if his head was going round.

She came round Quette d'Amont with a fine sweep, like one bound on business of which she had no reason to be ashamed, and dropped her sail and lay in the shelter of the rock.

And the white figure in the bows was truly Nance, and she was standing and waving and calling to him. And the grey-headed man aft was surely Philip Guille, the Sénéchal, and the faces of the rest were all friendly.

He stumbled hastily down to the lower ledges, but the rush and the roar there drowned their voices.

What were they trying to tell him? What could they want of him?

The Sénéchal was standing, hands to mouth, waiting his chance. The restless waters below drew back for a moment to gather for a leap, and the big voice came booming across the tumult—

"Jump! We'll pick you up! All is well!"

And Gard, without a moment's hesitation, sprang out into the marbled foam, and struck out for the boat.

They were all friendly hands that gripped him and hauled him over the side, and patted him on the back to get the water out of him—all friendly faces that were turned to him; and the dearest face of all, lighted with a heavenly gladness, was to him as the face of an angel.

"Tell me!" he gasped, still all astream, wits and clothes alike. And it was the Sénéchal who told him.

"Peter Mauger was killed last night, at the same place as Tom Hamon, and in the same way. So these hot-blooded thickheads are convinced at last that it wasn't your work."

"Peter Mauger!" he said, gazing vaguely at them all. "But who—"

"We haven't found out yet. But even the thickest of the thickheads can't put it down to you"—and the thickheads present grinned in friendly fashion, and they ran up the sail with a will, and turned her nose, and went racing back to the Creux quicker than they had come.

And Gard sat still with his hand in Nance's two, feeling very weak and shaky, and looked vaguely back at L'Etat as it faded and dwindled into a dim black triangle of rock.

CHAPTER XXXVI

HOW HE CAME HOME FROM L'ETAT

This is what had happened.

Since Tom Hamon's death, his friend Peter and his widow Julie had, as we know, found themselves drawn together by a common detestation of Stephen Gard and a common desire for his extinction.

For Peter considered he had been supplanted in Nance's regards, though Nance had never regarded him as anything but a nuisance and a boor. And Julie considered herself scorned and slighted, though Gard had never considered her save as Tom Hamon's wife.

It was they who had stirred up the Sark men against Gard, and they missed no opportunity of keeping their ill brew on the boil.

Their offensive alliance brought them much together. Peter was often at La Closerie. He was like wax in the hands of the fiery Frenchwoman, and she moulded him to her will. The neighbours might have begun to talk, but that it was obvious to all that the only bond between them at present was their ill-will towards Gard, and in that feeling many shared and found nothing strange in Tom's wife and Tom's chief friend joining hands to make some one pay for his death.

In time, if it had gone on, the neighbours would doubtless have had plenty to say on the subject, for old wives' tongues rattled fast of a winter's evening, when they all gathered in this house or that, and sat on the sides of the green bed with their feet in the dry fern inside, and the oil crasset hanging down in the midst, and plied their needles and their tongues and wits all at once, and wrought scandalously good guernseys and stockings in spite of it all.

But these were summer evenings yet, and the veilles had not begun, and reputations were out at grass till the time came round for their inspection and judgment.

And so, when Peter Mauger never reached home the night before this day of which we are telling, his old housekeeper, whatever she thought about it at the time, only said afterwards that she supposed he had stopped somewhere and would turn up all right in the morning, though she admitted that he was not in the habit of staying out of a night. Anyway, she was an old woman and all alone, and she was not going out to look for him at that time of night.

The morning surprised her by his continued absence. Never in his life, so far as she knew, had he behaved like this before. Vituperation of him gave place to anxiety about him.

She questioned the neighbours. All they knew was that he had been seen going down to Little Sark soon after sunset.

"That black Frenchwoman of Tom Hamon's twists him round her finger," said one.

"You tie him up, Mrs. Guille," chuckled another, "or sure as beans she'll steal him from you and leave you in the cold."

And then, who should they see coming striding along the road but Madame Julie herself, and evidently in a hurry;—in a state of red-hot excitement, too, as she drew near. And they waited, hands on hips, to hear what she was up to now.

"Where's Peter?" she demanded, a long way in advance. "Tell him I want him. That man Gard is still on L'Etat, though those fools who went across for him couldn't find him. Cré nom! What are you all staring at, then?"

"Where's our Peter?" demanded Mrs. Guille shrilly, with the strident note of fear in her voice, as she becked and bobbed towards the Frenchwoman like an aged cormorant.

"Peter? I'm asking you. I want him. Where is he?"

"He went to Little Sark last night, and he's never come home."

"Never come home? Why, what's taken him? If he'd been with me last night he'd have seen something! That Nance Hamon swam across to the rock with nothing on but her shift to take food to Gard, and I caught her at it—the shameless hussy!"

"Maybe Peter's heard of it an' gone across with 'em again," suggested one. "He was terrible hot against Gard."

"And reason he had to be hot against him," cried Julie. "Who'll find out for me where he's got to, and when they're going out after Gard? I would go too and see the end of him."

A couple of burly husbands came rolling round the corner towards their breakfasts and caught her words.

"Doubt you'll have to go alone, mistress," said one, phlegmatically. "There's ghosts on L'Etat, they do say, though sure the one John Drillot brought across was dead enough."

"If he's there," said the other, plumbing Julie's feelings, "he's safe as a pig in a pen."

"Where's our Peter?" demanded Mrs. Guille.

"Peter? I d'n know. What's come of him?" and they stared blankly at her.

"He went to Little Sark last night to see her"—with a beck of distaste towards Julie—"and he's never come home."

The men looked from the speaker to Julie, as though the next word necessarily lay with her.

"I never set eyes on him. I was out after that girl. I came here to tell him about Gard. Has he been to the harbour?"

"No, he hasn't. We are from there now."

"He's maybe with some of them arranging about going to L'Etat," said Julie. "I'll go and find out;" and she set off along the road past the windmill.

The morning passed in fruitless enquiries. She asked this one and that, every one she could think of, if they had seen Peter, and was met everywhere with meaning grins and point-blank denials. Apparently no one had set eyes on Peter, and every one seemed to imply that she ought io know more about him than any one else.

It was past mid-day before she was back at Vauroque, but Mrs. Guilie was still standing in the doorway of Peter's empty house as if she had been looking out for news of him ever since.

"Eh b'en? Have you found him?" she cried.

"Not a finger of him!" snapped Julie savagely, tired out with her fruitless labours.

"Then he's come to some ill, bà sú. And if he has—ma fé, it's you!—it's you!" The old lady's scream of denunciation choked itself with its own excess, and the neighbours came running out to learn the news.

Stolid minds travel in grooves, and old Mrs. Guille's had been groping along possibilities of all kinds, clinging at the same time to the hope that Peter would still turn up all right.

Now that her hope was shattered her mind dropped naturally into a grim groove, along which it had taken a tentative trip during the morning and had recoiled from with a shudder.

The last time Mrs. Tom Hamon had come seeking a man who was missing, that man had been found under the Coupée, and so old Mrs. Guille set oft for the Coupée as fast as her old legs and her want of breath and general agitation would let her.

"Nom de Dieu! What—?" began Julie, with twisted black brows, and then drifted on with the rest in Mrs. Guille's wake—all except one or two housewives whose men were due for dinner, and knew they must be fed whatever had come to Peter Mauger.

"Gaderabotin!" said one of these as he came up, and stood scratching his head and gazing down the road after them. "What's taken them all?"

"Think because they found Tom Hamon there, they'll find Peter too," guffawed another, and they rolled on into their homes, chuckling at the simplicity of women and children.

Arrived at the Coupée, the little mob of sensation-seekers peered fearfully about. One small boy, cleverer or more groovy-minded than the rest, struck off along the headland to the left. It was from there Charles Guille had seen Tom Hamon. Perhaps from there he would see something, too.

And no sooner was he there, where he could see to the foot of the cliffs in Coupée Bay, than he commenced to dance and wave his arms like a mad thing, because the words he wanted to shout choked him tight so that he could hardly breathe.

They streamed out along the cliff and huddled there, struck chill with fright in spite of the blazing sun.

For there, under the cliff, in the same spot as they found Tom Hamon, lay another dark, huddled figure, and they knew it must be Peter.

The finding of Tom had filled them with anger against Gard. The finding of Peter filled them with fear.

Gard had sufficed as explanation and scapegoat for Tom's death, and as vent for their feelings. But what of Peter's?

It had not been Gard, then? And if not Gard, who?

For, whoever it was, he was still at large, and any of them might be the next.

There were new terrors in the eyes that gazed so wildly on the narrow white path and the towering pinnacles of the Coupée. They had been familiar with it all, all their lives, but suddenly it had become strange to them.

If grisly Death, all bones and scythe, had come stalking along it before their eyes at that moment, they would have shrieked, no doubt, and fallen flat, but he would have no more than answered to their feelings and fulfilled their expectations.

As it was, when the Seigneur's big white stallion stuck his head over the green dyke behind them, and gave a shrill neigh at the unexpected sight of so many people in a field which was usually occupied only by Charles Guille's two mild-eyed cows and their calves, the women screamed and the children lied.

"Man doux! but I thought it was the devil himself," said old Mrs. Guille. "Oui-gia!" and shook an angry fist at him.

But the discoverer of the body was already away along the road to Vauroque, covering the ground like a little incarnation of ill-news.

The exertion of running cleared away the choking, if it took his breath. He shouted as he drew near the houses.

"Ah, bah!" growled one of the diners inside. "What's to do now, then?"

"He's there ... Peter ... under Coupée ... Where Tom Hamon...." panted the news-bearer as he tore past to his own home. And the rest of Vauroque emptied itself into the road and stood looking along it, as the stragglers came up, white-faced and wild-eyed.

"He's there," confirmed one woman, twisting up her loosened hair. "And just same place where Tom Hamon lay."

"'Tweren't Gard killed him , then," said one of the diners, chewing over that thought with his last mouthful.

"Nor Tom neither, then, maybe," said another.

"We've bin on wrong tack, then;" and they went off round the corner at a speed their build would hardly have credited them with.

One to the Sénéchal and one to the Doctor, and then to the Creux, both telling the news as they went. So that when the officials came hurrying through the tunnel the greater part of the Island was waiting for them on the shingle, except those who preferred the wider view from the cliff above.

Some of the men had been for pulling across at once, but they were overborne.

"Doctor said he'd like to have seen him afore he was moved last time," said old John de Carteret weightily, and would not let a boat go out till the Doctor and the Sénéchal came.

It was all waiting for them the moment they arrived, however, and they stepped in and swung away round Les Lâches, and three other boats followed them so closely that it looked almost like a gruesome race who should get there first.

There was little talking in any of the boats, but there was some solid hard thinking, in a mazed kind of way.

Until they knew more of the facts, indeed, they scarce knew what to think yet. But more than one of them remembered disturbedly how they had gone in force two days before to fetch Gard off his lonely rock, or to make an end of him there; and here they were going in force on a very different errand—an errand which, they could not help seeing, would bring him off his rock in a very different way, if this present matter was what it looked as if it might be.

And the Doctor was not long in giving them the facts, when they had run up on to the shingle, and then crunched through it to the place where Peter's body lay under the steep black cliff—in the exact spot where Tom Hamon's had lain just eighteen days before.

But that it was undoubtedly Peter's face and body, those who had come after Tom the last time might have thought they were going through their previous experience over again. It was all so like.

They all stood round in a dark, silent group while the Doctor carefully examined the body, and the Sénéchal looked on with stern and troubled face.

"It is most extraordinary," said the Doctor, straightening up from his task at last, and his face, too, was knitted with perplexity, but had something else in it besides. "This man has been done to death in exactly the same way as Hamon"—a rustle of surprise shook the group of silent onlookers. "The head has been beaten in just as Hamon's was—with some blunt rounded tool, I should say. These other wounds and contusions are the results of his fall down the cliff. He has been dead at least eight hours. Lift him carefully, men. We can do nothing more here—unless by chance the one who did it flung his weapon after him, and we could find it."

They scattered, and searched the whole dark bay minutely, but found nothing. Then with rough gentleness they bore the body to the boat and laid it under the thwarts.

"Men!" said the Sénéchal weightily, as they were just about to climb back into their boats. "This matter brings another matter home to all our hearts. You have been persecuting another man under the belief that he killed Tom Hamon. From what some of us knew of Mr. Gard, we were certain he could have had no hand in it. This, I take it, proves it?" He looked at the Doctor.

"Undoubtedly!" nodded the Doctor. "The man who killed this one killed the other, and that man could not be Stephen Gard, for he is on L'Etat."

"It's God's mercy that you haven't Mr. Gard's blood on your heads. Some of you, I know, have done your best that way. Suppose you had killed him that other night—what would you have felt as you stood here to-day? Take that thought home with you, and may God keep you from like misjudgment in the future!"

And they had not a word to say for themselves, but crawled silently aboard, and in silence pulled back to Creux Harbour.

Once only old John de Carteret spoke to the Sénéchal, soon after they had started.

"One of them"—nodding over at the boats behind—"could go to the rock and bring him off," he suggested.

"I thought of that, but there's one I want to go with me. She'll be down at the Creux, I expect, and we'll go as soon as we've disposed of this."

There was a very different feeling visible in the silent crowd that awaited them at the harbour this time from that manifested on the last occasion, Then, it was a sympathetic anger that united them all in a common feeling against the perpetrator of the deed. Now—even before the whisper had run round that Peter Mauger had been done to death in the same way as Tom Hamon—fear was among them, and doubt. Fear of they knew not exactly what, and doubt of they knew not whom.

But here were two men done to death in their midst, and the man on whom all their suspicions had settled in the first case could not possibly have had anything to do with the second, and so had most likely had nothing to do with either—in which case the man who had was still at large among them, and no man's life was safe, much less any woman's or child's.

Their thoughts did not run, perhaps, quite so clearly as that, but that was the result of it all, and their faces showed it. Furthermore, every man and woman there began at once to cast about in his and her mind for the possible murderer, and men looked at the neighbours whom they had known all their lives, with lurking suspicions in their eyes and the consideration of strange possibilities in their minds.

Tom Hamon's death had bound them closer together; Peter Mauger's set them all apart. The strange dead man up in the school-house added to their discomfort.

It was not until the hastily-constructed litter with its gruesome burden had been sent off to the Boys' School, in charge of the constables and the Doctor, that the Sénéchal caught sight of Nance's eager white face and anxious eyes, in the crowd that lingered still in answer to another whisper that had flown round.

If they were at once pig-headed and hot-blooded and suspicious, they were also warm-hearted and willing to atone for a mistake—once they were sure of it.

No crowd followed Peter on his last journey but one, though the whole Island had swarmed after Tom Hamon.

They wanted to see the man who would have been killed for killing Tom, though he didn't do it, but for—circumstances, and his own pluck and endurance.

And when the Sénéchal beckoned to one of the circumstances, and put his hand on her slim shoulder, and said—

"We are going for him. I thought you would like to come too," her face went rosy with gratitude, and the brave little hands clasped up on to her breast, as she murmured—

"Oh, M. le Sénéchal!" and choked at anything more.

Those nearest gave her rough words of encouragement.

"Cheer up, Nance! You'll soon have him back!"

"That's a brave garche! Don't cry about it now!"

"We'll make it up to him, lass. We'll all come and dance at the wedding"—and so on.

But the Sénéchal patted her on the shoulder and asked—

"And where is your brother? He should come, too. I hear you have both been in this matter."

"Ah, monsieur!" she said, with brimming eyes and a pathetic little lift and fall of the hand, which expressed far more than she could put into words. "We fear ... we fear he is drowned. He swam out to the rock taking food, and ... and ... we have not seen him since;" and her hand was over her face and the tears streaming through.

"Mon Dieu! Another!" said the Sénéchal, aghast. "When, child? When was this?"

"The night after the storm, monsieur."

"Perhaps he is there, on the rock."

"No, monsieur. I was over there myself last night. He never got there, and we fear he must be drowned."

"You were over there, child? Why, how did you get across?"

"I swam, monsieur;" and he stared at her in amazement.

"Mon Dieu! Mon Dieu! You make up for some of the others," he said bluntly. "Come then, and we will make sure of this one, anyhow;" and he led the way to John de Carteret's boat, and all the people gave them a cheer as they pulled out of the harbour to catch the breeze off the Lâches.

Then the crowd waited for their return, and talked by snatches of all these strange happenings, and discussed and discounted the chances of Bernel's being still alive.

"For, see you, the Race! And that was the first night after the storm, and it would be running like the deuce, bidemme!" "It's best not to know how to swim if it leads you to do things like that, oui-gia!" "When a man's time comes, he cuts his cleft in the water, whether he can swim or not, crais b'en!" "And that slip of a Nance had been over there last night—par madé, some folks have the courage!" "All the same, it was madness—"

But behind all the broken chatter, in every mind was the grim question, "Who is it, then, that is doing these things amongst us?" And there was a feeling of mighty discomfort abroad.

All the same, they cheered vigorously as the boat came speeding back, and they saw Gard sitting between Nance and the Sénéchal, and crowded round as it ran up the shingle, and would have lifted him out and carried him shoulder-high through the tunnel and up the road, if he would have had it.

They saw how his imprisonment on the rock—"Ma fé, think of it!—all through that storm, too!"—had told upon him. His cheeks were hollow, and his eyes sunken, and he looked very weary—"and, man doux, no wonder, after eighteen days on L'Etat!"—though their friendly shouts had put a touch of colour in his face and a spark in his eyes for the moment.

"Now, away home, all of you!" ordered the Sénéchal. "We've all had enough to think about for one day. To-morrow we will see what is to be done."

"Too much!" croaked one old crone, who had something of a reputation among her neighbours. "What I want to know is—who killed Peter Mauger?"

And that was the question that occupied most minds in Sark that night.

CHAPTER XXXVII

The Doctor insisted on taking care of Gard. He took him into his own house at Dixcart, and began at once a course of treatment based on common-sense and the then most scientific attainment, and calculated to repair the waste of the Rock and build him up anew in the shortest time compatible with an efficient and permanent cure.

Even when Gard felt quite himself again and would have returned to his work, the genial autocrat would not hear of it.

"Just you stop here, my boy," he ordered. "An experience such as you have had needs some getting over. You can stand a good rest and some fattening up, and those — mines must wait."

Meanwhile, the Island was in a smoulder of suspicion and superstition.

No one had yet ventured openly to point the finger at any reasonably possible doer of deeds so dark. Behind carefully closed doors of a night, indeed, here and there a whisper suggested that the Frenchwoman might be at the bottom of it all. But the mistake that had already been made, and the consequences that came so terribly near to completing it beyond repair, made them all cautious of open speech or action.

Gard's story explained the mystery of the dead stranger and relieved the public mind to that extent.

The Sénéchal was disposed to agree with his views on the matter.

"I never heard of those caves on L'Etat," he said musingly, as they sat over their pipes one night; "and I'm sure no one else knew of them. But there was much free-trading round here in the old times, and I've no doubt many a Customs man disappeared and was never heard of again, just like this one. All the Islands felt very sore about the new regulations, and our people stick at nothing when their blood is up."

"They do not," said Gard feelingly.

"I'd like to get into that inner cave," said the Doctor longingly.

"You couldn't," said Gard, looking at his size and girth. "It's a mighty tight squeeze under the slab, and that tunnel would beat you. Unless you've been brought up to that kind of thing, you couldn't stand it. It would give you nightmares for the rest of your life."

"That's a rare lass, that little Nance," said the Sénéchal. "There's some good in Sark after all, Mr. Gard."

"She was an angel to me," said Gard with feeling. "If it had not been for her, I could never have held out. Not for what she brought me, but the fact that she came. But it was terrible to me to think of her coming through that Race. I begged her not to, but she would have her way. Three times she risked her life for me—"

"Three times!" said the Sénéchal. "Ma fé, but she's a garche to be proud of!"

"Ay, and to be more than proud of," said Gard. "She has given me my life, and I will give it all to making her happy."

"I wouldn't swim across to L'Etat for any woman in the world," said the Doctor. "Because, in the first place, I couldn't. She must have nerves of steel, to say nothing of muscles. In the dark, too! And you wouldn't think it to look at her."

"It needed more than nerves or muscles," said Gard quietly.

Not a man among the Islanders—much less a woman—would go anywhere near the Coupée after dark. Even Nance confessed to a preference for daylight passages. And Gard, when he went down into Little Sark for a walk, as part of his cure, could not repress a cold shiver whenever he passed the fatal spot where two men had gone over to their deaths.

All the old wives' tales were dug up and passed along, growing as they went. Little eyes and mouths grew permanently rounded with horrors, and the ground was thoroughly well spaded and planted with sturdy shoots warranted to yield a noisome harvest of superstition for generations to come.

The occupants of Clos Bourel and Plaisance carefully locked their doors of a night now.

Old Mrs. Carré at Plaisance vowed she had heard the White Horses go past, on the nights before Tom Hamon and Peter were found. And every one knew that when the ghostly horses were heard, some one was going to die. But as she had said nothing about it before, her contribution to the general uneasiness was received with respect before her face but with open doubt behind her back.

Old Nikki Never-mind-his-name—lest his descendants, if he had any, take umbrage at the matter— swore that he had not only seen the ghostly steed pass Vauroque in the dead of night, but that it bore a rider whose head was carried carefully in his right hand. Unfortunately, the headless one passed so quickly that Nikki said he could not distinguish his features—having looked for them first in the wrong place—and so he could not say for certain who the next to die would be; but from the knowing wag of his head the neighbours were of opinion that he knew more than he chose to tell, and he gained quite a reputation thereby.

But, even here again, doubts were cast upon the matter by some, especially those who were acquainted with the old gentleman's proclivities towards raw spirits of the material kind that paid the lightest of duties in Guernsey.

All these and very many similar matters were discussed by the Doctor—who disturbed their minds with horrific accounts of homicidal mania taking possession of apparently innocent souls—and the Sénéchal and the Vicar and Stephen Gard, as they sat over their pipes of an evening in the Doctor's house. But chiefly the great and troublesome question of "Who?"

They were all of one mind that the matter must be looked into. The feeling that a danger was loose in the Island, and might at any moment fall upon any man, woman, or child, was past endurance. The suspicion that It might be any one of those they met every day was insufferable.

The only difficulty was to decide how to look into it—what to do, and how.

Each day they feared to hear of some new outrage. But until the perpetrator was discovered they could do nothing towards his suppression. And, on the other hand, it looked as though they could do nothing towards his discovery until he perpetrated some new outrage.

It was Gard who suggested they should watch the Coupée every night, armed, and unknown to any but themselves.

And, after much discussion, following out his idea, he and the Sénéchal and the Doctor, who could bowl over a rabbit as well as any of them, lay in the heather, on the common above the cutting on the Little Sark side, for many nights, guns in hand, and eyes and ears on the strain, but saw and heard nothing.

One night, indeed, when there was a high wind, the Doctor's marrow crawled in his backbone at the sound of groanings and moanings and most dolorous cries for help, coming up out of black Coupée Bay, where they had picked up Tom Hamon's and Peter Mauger's dead bodies.

He sweated cold terrors, for he was on the east headland right above the bay, till the Sénéchal crawled over to him and whispered—

"Hear 'em?"

"Y-y-yes. What the d-d-deuce and all—"

"Knew you'd wonder what it was—"

"W-w-wonder?" chittered the Doctor.

"It's only the wind in the cave at the corner below here—"

"Ah! Thought it must be something of that kind," said the Doctor through his teeth, clenched hard to keep them in order. "Don't wonder folks fight shy of the Coupée. Sounded uncommonly like spirits. Might give some folks the jumps."

On another dark and windy night it was the Sénéchal's turn to get something of a fright.

As he lay in the heather, gun in hand, and well wrapped up in his big cloak, with all his faculties concentrated on the wavering pathway below, it seemed to him that he heard slow heavy footsteps approaching.

His nerves were strung tight. He craned his head to look down into the cutting, when suddenly there came a wild snuffle at the back of his neck, and as he jumped up with a startled yelp, one part anger and nine parts fright, a horse that had grazed down upon him in the darkness, leaped back with a snort and a squeal and disappeared into the night.

"Ga'rabotin! but I thought it was the devil himself," said the Sénéchal, as the others came hurrying up. "Why the deuce can't people tie up their horses as they do their cows? I'll bring it up at the next Chef Plaids"—which consideration restored his shaken equanimity somewhat, and made him feel himself again.

Nothing more came of all their watching, and over a jorum of something hot one night, after they had returned to the Doctor's house, it was himself who said—

"After all, it stands to reason. Some evil-possessed soul seeks victims, and has fixed on the Coupée as the place best fitted for his work. No one now goes near the Coupée at night—ergo, no victims; ergo, no—er—no manifestations."

"H'm! Very clever!" said the Sénéchal, through his pipe. "Where does that leave us, then?"

"We must have a decoy, of course."

"H'm! You'll not get any Sark man to act as decoy to the devil. Besides, they would talk, and that would upset the whole thing."

"What about one of your men, Gard?"

"It's a dangerous game for any man to play, Doctor.... I don't quite see how one could ask it of them,"—and after a pause of concentrated thought and many slow smoke-puffs—"What would you say to me?" and all their eyes settled on him—the Doctor's professionally.

"Surely you have suffered enough in this matter, Mr. Gard," suggested the Vicar.

"I would give a good deal, and do a good deal, to get to the bottom of it all. Things will never settle down properly till this matter is disposed of."

That, of course, was obvious to them all, but all had the same feeling that he had already suffered enough in the matter.

But consideration of the Doctor's suggestion in all its aspects only served to convince them that, if any such scheme was to be carried out, it could only be done among themselves, and its dangers were obvious.

It was not a matter to be lightly undertaken by any man. For whoever undertook the rôle of decoy, undoubtedly took his life in his hands; and they spent many evenings over it.

The Vicar was absolutely against the idea, but had no alternative to suggest.

"It is simply playing with death," said he, "and no man has a right to do that."

"It means a good deal for the Island if we can clear it up," said the Sénéchal.

But, by degrees, they got to discussion of how it might be done, and from that to the actual doing was only a heroic step.

The decoy's head must be well padded, of course, for the heads of both victims had been the points of attack.

He must be well armed also, and being forewarned and more, he ought to be able to give a certain account of himself.

And then the Doctor and the Sénéchal would be close at hand and on the keen look-out for emergencies.

The Doctor undertook to pad his head with something in the nature of a turban under his hat, which, he vowed, would resist the impact of iron blows better than metal itself.

"Leave my ears loose, anyway," said Gard. "I'd like at all events to be able to hear it coming."

The Sénéchal had a weapon, part pistol and the rest blunderbuss, which had belonged to his father, who had always referred to it affectionately as his "dunderbush." It had seen strange doings in its time, but had been so long retired from the active list, that he undertook to load and fire it himself before he said any more about it.

And he did it next day, with a full charge, in his meadow, with the assistance of a gate-post and a long cord, and reported it at night as in excellent order, and calculated to blow into smithereens anything blowable that stood up before it within the short limit of its range.

At this stage in its proceedings the Vicar reluctantly retired from the Committee of Public Safety. He acknowledged the sore need of ending the suspicious and superstitious fears which were beginning to affect the life of the community in various ways. But he could not see his way to any participation in means so dangerous to the life of one of their number as those suggested.

He did his best to dissuade Gard from it. He even reminded him of the duty he owed to Nance. She had undoubtedly saved his life, and she had a premier claim upon his consideration—and so on.

To all of which Gard fully assented.

"But," he said gravely, "we are at a deadlock in this other matter, and it is just barely possible that this plan may clear it all up. I can't say I'm very sanguine that it will. On the other hand, I really don't see that any great harm can come to me. The others probably suffered because they were taken unawares. I shall go in the hope of meeting it, and shall be ready for it. Unless, Vicar, you really think it is the devil or something of that sort?"

"I don't know what to think," said the Vicar solemnly. "I cannot bring myself to believe any of our Sark men would do such dreadful things. I look at each man I meet and say to myself, 'Now, can it be possible it is you?—or you?—or you?'—and it does not seem possible; and yet—"

"And yet some one did it, Vicar," said the Doctor, brusquely, "and that's just the trouble. Until we find out who did it, any man may have done it, and we all look at everybody else, just as you do, and say to ourselves, 'Is it you?—or you?—or you?' Though I'm bound to say I've not got the length yet of doubting either you or the Sénéchal, or Gard, and I don't think it's myself. It might quite conceivably be any one of us, however, prowling about in our sleep and utterly unconscious afterwards of evil-doing."

"A most awful possibility," said the Vicar. "God grant it may turn out differently from that."

"You never know what this inexplicable machine may do," said the Doctor, tapping his head. "However, we'll hope for the best, and I think the Sénéchal and I ought to be able to see Gard through without any very disastrous results. If we succeed, he will deserve better of this Island than any man I know—and a sight more than this Island deserves of him. I quite understand," he said, as Gard looked quickly up. "And it does you credit, my boy; but there are not very many men would do it."

"Well, I'm afraid I must leave you to it," said the Vicar, and did so.

CHAPTER XXXVIII

HOW THEY LAID THE DEVIL BY THE HEELS

When it began to be noised abroad that Gard was going to and fro across the Coupée, even by night, as if nothing had ever happened there, the Sark men shrugged their shoulders and said, "Pardie!—sooner him than me—oui-gia!"

It was obviously necessary, however, that this should be known. Even the cormorant does not fish where fish are never found.

But when he went to and fro by night, he went mailed—according to the Doctor's ideas—and armed—according to the Sénéchal's; and each night the Doctor and the Sénéchal went quietly down, some time in advance, and lay hidden on the headlands with their guns, and never took their eyes off him and all his surroundings, while he was in sight.

And Gard, in nearing the Little Sark cutting, always kept carefully to the right-hand side of the path, though it was somewhat crumbly there and had fallen away down the slope towards Grande Grève. For he had gone cautiously over the ground beforehand, and decided that if there was any possibility of being knocked overboard unawares, he would prefer to go over the much gentler slope on the right, where one might even at a pinch find lodgment among the rubble and bushes, than over the sheer fall into Coupée Bay, where you could drop a stone almost to the shingle below.

Nance knew nothing whatever of the matter, or she would undoubtedly and most reasonably have had something to say about it. But knowledge of it could only upset her, and so perhaps himself, and he had carefully kept it from her. Little Sark, moreover, was more isolated than ever by reason of the Coupée mystery, and word of his goings and comings—save such as had La Closerie for their object in the day-time—never reached her.

They were in grievous sorrow down there over Bernel. Gard still preached hope, but each day's delay in its realisation seemed to them to make it the more unlikely, and their hearts were very sore.

Julie had gone about her work for days after Gard's return like a bereft tigress. Then one morning she locked the door of her house, put the key in her pocket, and took the cutter for Guernsey; and none regretted her going.

And, as it turned out, though that had not been her intention at the time, it was the last Sark was to see of her. Rumours reached them later of her marriage to a fellow-countryman, with whom she had gone to France. The one thing they knew for certain was that she never came back to La Closerie, and after due interval, and consequent on other matters, they broke open the door and resumed possession of the house.

Night after night Gard slowly crossed the Coupée, lingered in its shadows, went on into Little Sark, and came lingering back.

And night after night the Doctor and the Sénéchal lay in the heather of the headlands, guns in hand, waiting for something that never came, and then going stiffly home to one or other of their houses, to lubricate their joints and console their disappointment with hot punch and much tobacco.

"I'm afraid it's no go," was the Doctor's grudging verdict at last, on the fourteenth blank night.

"Let's keep on," said Gard. "Things generally happen just when you don't expect them."

"That's so," grunted the Sénéchal. And they decided to keep on.

Fortunately, the nights were warm and mostly fine. When neither moon nor stars afforded him light enough for a safe crossing, he took a lantern, so that no one who desired to knock him on the head need miss the chance for lack of seeing him.

And when, after their lonely waiting, the watchers in the heather saw the lantern come joggling down the steep cutting from Sark, they braced themselves for eventualities, and hefted their guns, and pricked up their ears and made ready.

And when it had wavered slowly along the path between the great pits of darkness on either hand, and had gone joggling on into Little Sark, they sank back into their formes with each his own particular exclamation, and lay waiting till the light came back.

Times of tension and endurance which told upon them all, but bore most heavily on Gard, since the onslaught, when it came, must fall upon him, and the absolute ignorance as to how and when and whence it might come, kept every nerve within him strung like a fiddle-string.

It was the eeriest experience he had ever had, that nightly trip across the Coupée;—bad enough when moon or stars afforded him vague and distorted glimpses of his ghostly surroundings:—ten times worse when the flicker of his lantern barely kept him to the path, and the broken gleams ran over the rugged edges and tumbled into the black gulfs at the sides;—when every starting shadow might be a murderer leaping out upon him, every foot of the walling darkness the murderer's cover, and every step he took a step towards death.

A trip, I assure you, that not many men would have been capable of. For it did not by any means end with the Coupée. When he got to bed of a night, and fell asleep at last, he was still crossing the Coupée with his joggling lantern all night long, and suffered things in dreams compared with which even his actual experiences were but holiday jaunts.

And at times these grisly imaginings came back upon him as he actually walked the narrow path next night, and it was all he could do to keep his head and not fling the lantern into the depths of the pit and follow it.

They were all getting exceedingly weary of the whole business; indeed, it was getting on all their nerves in a way which threatened consequences, when, mercifully, the end came—suddenly, not at all as they had looked for it, quite outside all their expectation.

It was one of the shrouded nights. The Doctor and the Sénéchal, flat in the heather, saw the lantern issue from the Sark cutting and come joggling towards them. They heard a snort of surprise behind them, but gave it no special heed. The Sénéchal grinned briefly at remembrance of his fright when the beast snuffled down his neck that other night.

Then, this is what happened.

Gard—his lantern in his left hand, and the Sénéchal's father's "dunderbush" in his right—his eyes pinching spooks out of every inch of the black wall about him, and every string at its tightest—had reached the crumbly bit of path near the Little Sark side, when, like a clap of thunder out of a blue sky, the black silence of the cutting vomited uproar—the wild clang and beat of what sounded, in that hollow space, like the trampling of a thousand dancing hoofs—shrill neighings and whinnyings and screamings, all blended into an indescribable and blood-curdling clamour that gashed the night like an outrage.

And then, before even he had time to wonder, the great white stallion was upon him—dancing on its hind legs on that narrow path like an acrobat, towering above him to twice his own height, striking savagely down at him with its great front feet, screaming like a fiend.

He had no time to think. His left arm and the lantern went up with the natural instinct of defence. Just one glimpse he got—and never forgot it—of vicious white eyes and teeth, flapping red nostrils, wild-flying hair, and huge pawing feet descending on him, with the dirty white hair splaying out all round them as they came down. Then his right hand went up also, and he fired full into all these things. The lantern and the blunderbuss went spinning into the gulf, the great feet beat him to the ground, and rose and jabbed down at him with all the vicious might that lay behind them—the savage white muzzle shrilling its blood-curdling screams of triumph all the while—and all this in the space of a second. "Good God!" cried the Doctor, craning over the eastern bank of the cutting, but fearful of firing into the turmoil lest he should hit Gard, so dropped himself bodily over on to the path.

Then the Sénéchal's Sark eyes saw the great white head, with its flying veil of hair, as it towered up for another vicious jab at the fallen man, and he emptied both barrels of his gun into it.

A wild scream that shrilled along the night and woke Plaisance and Clos Bourel and Vauroque, and the great white devil reared to his fullest with wildly beating forefeet, toppled over backwards, and disappeared with one hideous thud and a final crash on the shingle of Coupée Bay.

It was worse than they had ever dreamed—as bad almost as some of Gard's own nightmares.

"Good God! Good God! Good God!" babbled the Doctor, as he groped in the dark for what might be left of their unfortunate decoy.

"Mon Dieu! Mon Dieu! Mon Dieu!" gasped the Sénéchal, with catching breath and shaking legs, as he ran round to join him in the search.

But there was no sign of Gard.

"Run, man!—Plaisance—a light!" jerked the Sénéchal.

"I can't see," groaned the Doctor.

"I'll go!" and he set off at the best pace his years and his shaking legs could compass.

Plaisance was standing at its doors, trembling still at that fearsome cry, and wondering if it was, perchance, the last trump.

At sight of the panting figure coming up from the Coupée, it scuttled and banged the doors tight. "Open! Open, you fools!" cried the Sénéchal, and flung himself against the first door, while those inside, under the sure belief that they were keeping out the devil, heaped themselves against it to prevent him.

"Dolts! Idiots! Fools!" he cried. "It's me—the Sénéchal. I want your help!" and at that a man peeped out from the next door to make sure this was not just another wile of the devil.

"A lantern! Quick!" ordered the Sénéchal. "And a blanket and a rope—and get ready a bed for a wounded man. Come you with me and help!"

"Mais, mon Gyu—!" began the man.

"We've killed the devil, and the Doctor's down there with him—"

"But we don't want him here, M. le Sénéchal," quavered a woman's voice, in terror.

"Fools! It's Mr. Gard that is hurt. The devil's down in Coupée Bay, and we've killed him for you."

"Ah then, Gyu marchi! Here's a blanket—and the lantern—rope's in barn. You get a bed ready," to the woman, and they went off towards the Coupée.

And mighty glad the Doctor was to see them coming. He had begun to fear the Sénéchal had lost his head and made a bolt for home.

He had been sitting under the bank of the cutting as the surest way of keeping out of one or other of the black gulfs. But the interval had given him time to recover himself, and he jumped up at once, all ready for business, and hailed them.

"Down this side, I think," he said, and they swung the lantern over the Grande Grève slope below the bit of crumbly pathway.

"Le velas!" said Thomas Carré, and handed the lantern to the Sénéchal, and let himself heavily over the side, and groped his way down to the motionless form among the bramble bushes.

"Pardie, he is dead, I do think!" as he bent over it.

"Let's see!" said the Doctor's quick voice at his elbow. "Hand down the light;" and the Sénéchal waited above in grievous anxiety.

"Not dead," said the Doctor at last. "Stunned and badly knocked about. He'll come round. Now, how are we to get him up?"

"Here's a blanket—and a rope."

"Good! The blanket!... So!... Now—gently, my man!... Got it, Sénéchal? Right! Ease him down on to the path. That's right! Give me a hand, will you? My legs aren't as limber as they used to be. Now we'll get him on to a bed and see what the damage is;" and they set off slowly for Plaisance.

"My God, Sénéchal! That passed belief! To think of our never thinking of that infernal brute!" said the Doctor, as they stumbled slowly along in the joggling light.

"He was possessed of the devil, without a doubt. That last scream of his when he got my two bullets—"

"'T woke us," said Carré. "And we wondered what was up. What was it, then, monsieur?"

"That devil of a white stallion of Le Pelley's. It was him killed Tom Hamon and Peter Mauger, and he tried to kill Mr. Gard. We've been on this job for weeks past, while you were all sleeping in your beds."

"Mon Gyu! and we none of us knew anything about it till we heard yon scream! And he's dead—"

"He's dead—unless he's the devil," said the Sénéchal sententiously.

CHAPTER XXXIX

HOW THEY THANKED GOD FOR HIS MERCIES

Vast was the wonder of the Sark folk when they heard next day of that night's doings, and learned who the murderer of the Coupée was, and how and by whom he had been laid by the heels.

The whole Island breathed freely once more, and was outspokenly grateful to the courage and pertinacity which had lifted from it the cloud and the reproach.

Some of them even had the grace to be not a little ashamed of their previous doings, but ascribed the greater part of the blame to Tom's widow and Peter Mauger.

But it was days before Stephen Gard took any interest in the matter, past or present, or in anything whatsoever.

The Doctor's pad undoubtedly saved his life, but no amount of padding could avert entirely the fiendish malignity of those merciless iron flails.

He lay unconscious for eight-and-forty hours; and the Doctor—though he never breathed a word of it, and prophesied complete recovery with the utmost cheerfulness and apparent sincerity—had his own grim fears as to what the effect of the whole hideous event might be on one who had already suffered such undue strain of mind and body.

Fortunately, his fears proved groundless. On the third day, Gard quietly opened his eyes on Nance, who had barely left his bedside since the Sénéchal went down to La Closerie himself and brought her back with him to Plaisance.

"I've been asleep," he said drowsily. "Anything wrong, Nance dear?" and he tried to sit up, but found his head heavy with cold water bandages, and a pain about his neck and left shoulder, and his left arm in splints, and all the rest of him one great aching bruise.

"Why—" he murmured, in vast surprise.

"You're to lie quite still," said Nance dictatorially, with lifted finger. "And you're not to talk or think till the Doctor comes."

"Give me a kiss, then!"—good prima facie evidence, this, that his brain had suffered no permanent injury.

"Well, he didn't say anything about that," and she bent over him and kissed him with a brimming flood of gratitude in her blue eyes, and he lay quiet for a time.

"Is it dead?" he asked suddenly, with a reminiscent shudder which set all his bruises aching.

"The white horse? Yes, Dieu merci, it's dead! But you're not to talk or think."

"Give me another kiss, then!"—from which it was apparent that he knew very well what kind of medicine was best adapted to his ailments.

The Doctor came down to see him the very first thing every morning, and now he came quietly in, just as Nance had been administering her latest dose.

"Ah—ha, nurse! What are you doing to my patient!"

"I'm only keeping him quiet, sir, as you told me to," said Nance, with a rosy face.

"It's the doctor you ought to pay, not the patient. Well, my boy, how are we this morning? Head aching yet?"

"It does feel a bit queer. Tell me all about last night, Doctor!"

"Ah—ha, yes—last night! Well, you caught the murderer with a vengeance, my boy—or he caught you,"—and then, seeing the puzzlement in the tired eyes, he briefly explained the whole matter.

"And do you mean it was that awful beast killed the others?"

"Without a doubt—and would have killed you in exactly the same way, and exactly the same place, but for my pads and the Sénéchal's bullets. Queer thing—they found the brute lying all in a heap in Coupée Bay on the very spot where Tom Hamon and Peter Mauger were found."

"Ay-y-y-y-y!" breathed Gard, with a long sigh of relief and a shiver. "I shall never forget him."

"Oh yes, you will—in time. Think of little Nance here. She's a sight better worth thinking of. And now, Miss Nancy, how much good news can you stand all at once, if you try your very hardest?" he asked, with a sparkle in his eyes that somehow seemed to set hers sparkling too.

"Oh madé, Doctor!" and the little hands clasped up on her breast, as was her way when greatly moved. "Not—?"

She dared not hope for so much—the wish of her heart—just an inch or so behind the desire for Gard's recovery.

"The cutter this morning brought over one we had feared was lost—"

"Not—not Bernel?"

"Yes, my child, Bernel, by God's good mercy! He was picked up by a Granville trawler, and lay there ill for some days, and could only get back by Jersey and Guernsey. He was to come along with the Sénéchal in a quarter of an hour—"

But Nance had fallen on her knees and buried her face in the bed-clothes, lest any but God should see it in the rapture of its breaking.

"Dieu merci! Dieu merci! Dieu merci!" she was crying, though none of them heard it.

And "Thank God!" said Stephen Gard with fervour—for Bernel, and for himself, but most of all for Nance.

John Oxenham – A Concise Bibliography

God's Prisoner (1898)
A Princess of Vascovy (1899)
Under the Iron Flail (1902)
Barbe of Grand Bayou (1903)
Bondman Free (1903)
Hearts in Exile (1904)
John of Gerisau (1904)
A Weaver of Webs (1904)
White Fire (1905)
Giant Circumstance (1906)
Profit and Loss (1906)
The Long Road (1907)
Carette of Sark (1907)
In Christ There Is No East or West (1908)
Pearl of Pearl Island (1908)
The Song of Hyacinth (1908)
My Lady of Shadows (1909)
Great Heart Gillian (1909)

A Maid of the Silver Sea (1910)
The Coil of Carne (1911)
The Quest of the Golden Rose (1912)
The Gate of the Desert (1912)
Bees in Amber (1913)
Broken Shackles (1914)
The King's High-Way (1916)
All's Well (1916)
The Fiery Cross (1917)
The Vision Splendid (1917)
High Altars (1918)
Hearts Courageous (1919)
The Wonder of Lourdes: what it is and what it means (1924)
The Hidden Years' (1927)
Gentlemen - the King! (1928)
God's Candle (1929)
Hearts in Exile (1930)
The Splendour of the Dawn (1930)
The Man Who Would Save the World (1930)
The Pageant of the King's Children (1930) (with his son Roderick Dunkerley)
Cross-Roads: The Story of Four Meetings (1931)
A Saint in the Making (1931)
Christ and the Third Wise Man (1934)

www.ingramcontent.com/pod-product-compliance
Lightning Source LLC
Chambersburg PA
CBHW072151170626
46813CB00004BA/1760